DREAMTIME DAMSELS & FATAL FEMMES

A Dreamtime Fantasy Tales Anthology

DREAMTIME DAMSELS & FATAL FEMMES

By Dreamtime Fantasy Tales authors
October 2019

ISBN Paperback: 978-1-9162342-2-2
ISBN Kindle: 978-1-9162342-3-9

A CBS Green Man Publication
Cider Brandy Scribblers
Brighton, Sussex
England

Cover design by Guy Donovan.
Image licensing:
Paperback: ID 124947140 © Denis Prokofev - Dreamstime.com
Kindle: ID 124946590 © Denis Prokofev- Dreamstime.com

Text copyright@
What They do not Tell You @A.M. Young
Better the Thorn @Guy Donovan
Falling out of the Sky: A Beginner's Guide @Nimue Brown
Mulo @Penny Blake
The Wizard's Quandary @Jaq D. Hawkins
Count Vlasko's Curse @Paul Michael
Red, the Wolf (Part 1) @Leslie Conzatti
Red, the Wolf (Part 2) @Leslie Conzatti
Miss Hattie and the Hoppers @Mary R. Woldering
Mobius @Thomas Woldering
Lyana Rikmon, Warrior of Donothor @Benjamin Towe & Nils Visser
Nicole Falling: A Southwest Horror Story @Greg Alldredge
Sacrificed to the Dragon @Johan Klein Haneveld
Sleeping Dragon @Marc vun Kannon
Dangerous @Morgan Smith
Muliebral the Bald (or Bold) @Nav Logan

This anthology is dedicated to female authors who have paved the way for more girl-power in fantasy and sci-fi fiction. To name but a few:

Ursula LeGuin

Octavia Butler

Mary Shelley

Daphne Du Maurier

Angela Carter

Anne McCaffrey

Anne Rice

Mary Stewart

C.M. Moore

Andre Norton

Margaret Cavendish

Margaret Weis

Tamora Pierce

Evangeline Walton

CONTENTS

WARNING: Contributing authors hail from Canada, the USA, the UK, Ireland, and the Netherlands. Some authors have used US English spelling, others GB English spelling, and don't even get us started on the Irishman. I.e. spelling may differ from story to story.

ALL PROCEEDS OF THIS ANTHOLOGY HAVE BEEN
PLEDGED TO THE ABINGTON FERRET REFUGE

www.abingtonferretrefuge.com

What They do not Tell You

A.M. Young

My name is not Galatea. That is the first thing you should know about me.

The second is that my life began with pain. Before I was I, there was nothing but scraping and scratching and cutting away. I did not understand what was happening, I had no awareness beyond sensation, but I knew that I did not want it. The hurt was overwhelming, obliterating, and I tried to recede deeper away from it. There is a choice made in becoming, and I know now that I made the wrong one.

So what drew me forth? Warmth, simple and comforting as the sun. There were moments when the chiseling would stop, the sharp edges were withdrawn, and I would feel a slow, seeping, delicious warmth. Cupping my hip. Cradling my calf. More than anything, more than the taste of soft cheese on warm bread or the smell of hyacinths or the sight of my darling chasing butterflies, I miss the feeling of being touched. Skin to skin. Or skin to stone, as it was and as it is again. Those moments of warmth would reawaken me, beckon me forward from my retreat. And gods pity me, I decided that the loveliness, the pleasure of that contact was enough reason to accept becoming. I decided that surely the pain must be worth it if there was that kind of pleasure on the other side. I stopped retreating.

Of course, this was before I knew what kind of man he was. *Such an amazing artist*, the people said. *But so lonely. So haughty.* What they meant but were too nice to say was, *Such a prick.* That's the part that irks me the most in the myths, the stories they tell about him, where I do not appear until the end, beautiful and passive. Really, who would think that a guy who had never had an actual relationship in his entire life could suddenly be the perfect husband? Even Psyche got a better deal.

You know what else they forget to tell you? He *agonized* over my face. My body was something familiar to him, came as easily as he did when we first slept together. But he left my face blank, rough, undone for days, too scared to touch me. I wanted to scream. I had already endured so much pain for him as he planed my stomach, whittled at my waist. My right foot was in a perpetual pointed position, and it ached from the marble's weight. And he had the audacity to leave me, alone and unfinished, in his studio while he hid in a wine jug and tried to drown his fears of inadequacy (which I knew because he came crawling back, weeping at my feet the next day). By that point I was aware, I knew that there was I and there was him. And at the time, I wanted nothing more than to truly *be* and perhaps to be with him.

When a man spends hours upon hours making you what you are, you assume that he must love you. You assume that you must love him too.

Those of you born whole and shrieking into the world will not know what it is like to exist without a face. I could feel, already had possession of the most intimate of my senses. But I could not see, could not hear, could not smell. And worst, I had no way of knowing just who I was. I felt incomplete. Lacking. So close to being whole and absolute and real but denied by the one who created me. I had waited so long, suffered in silence. It was torture to be ignored and avoided. I began to wonder if I wanted it too much, if he could somehow feel the desire and resentment pulsing through the veins in the marble. Had I driven him away? Was he distracted by another project I could not see? Carving my sister? My usurper?

Relief and gratitude coursed through me when he came back to me, when he began to form my face.

As he made my ears, my nose, my eyes, I began to hear. To smell. To see.

It was awful.

This is why babes are born dumb. This is why they cry, why the real fall from innocence happens when they leave the womb. Suddenly, I heard the pained brays of a beaten donkey, the susurrations of the wind in the grass, competing birdsongs, off-key drunken singing, the wails of a child. I smelled donkey shit and cow shit and human shit on the same air as incense and flowers and linen and old wood. I was overcome by how much there was, the never-ending sounds and smells. It was too much to comprehend, and I reeled internally. I had never imagined how much there was.

Then he gave me my eyes. And I saw him, brown and hairy, his brow creased in concentration as he molded my cheekbones. He had long, curly black hair that fell over a broad forehead. His face was squat, his nose looking as if it had been squished down in his childhood. Squared shoulders, thick arms, and strong hands that befitted a sculptor. Now that I have seen many more people, I know that he was no Adonis. But then, I did not care. He was beautiful, so careful and tender and thoughtful as he shaped me. I loved him in that moment, intensely, with all the shallow understanding I had. I focused on him and the rest fell away.

He paused to take a simple meal, eating at a small table to my right. He spoke to me. Told me that I was lovely, perfect. Told me how much better I was than other women, like his mother who died after giving birth to a stillborn, or his father's second wife whom his father found fucking another man, so he chased her naked into the street and beat her. Or the hetaira he went to when he felt it was time for him to become a man, those sluts who laughed at how he could not stay hard. Women are treacherous, he said, and you hear stories from all over about how they betray the men who care for them. How they leave. But you would never leave me, he said as he stood and approached me. He embraced me, a hand on my back, the other at my breast, and he nestled his head upon my shoulder. You are perfect, he whispered, and I know you would love me as I deserve to be loved.

If you've read the stories they tell about us now, then you know that he enjoyed the shape of me long before I was flesh. I will tell you that only in bars and brothels do they ever get all the details right.

He finished my face that night. I was complete.

He began to bring me gifts the next day. Wooing me, trying to buy my affections. Naively, I thought him sweet, and I wished I could tell him that he did not need to bother. That I already loved him. Looking back, I can see his actions for what they truly were: a charade. He had made himself a plaything so that he could parody a courtship without any of the complications a real woman would bring. Without challenge. Such a coward.

When the festival approached, he told me of his plans. I had no knowledge of gods or rituals or sacrifices, but I grew excited. Every day I wished that I could embrace him, that I could respond to his kisses. I felt I owed it to him to be everything he wanted me to be. I could not light incense or bring gifts, but I prayed. With the fervent focus of one who could do nothing else, I prayed for hours that I be allowed to breathe, to move. To live as he did.

While he was away, as he knelt in the temple, I heard a voice. She simply asked, *Is this what you want?*

The gods are cruel, petty creatures.

You know what happens next, and I won't waste your time telling it to you again. But I will say that the first time, in his bed so full of joy and wonder, both of us feeling infinitely blessed to be there… That night was one of the best of my short life.

I understood that pain was necessary for pleasure, but childishly, I thought that pain would always lead to pleasure. That the two would naturally balance out, with neither ever overshadowing the other. How quickly I learned the truth.

He was a horrible husband. They never mention that. Convinced that I would leave him, that I looked at other men with seductive eyes, he forbade me to leave our house without him. When we went to the market, he refused to let go of my arm. Squeezed until I bruised if another man came to talk to me. For a long time, I thought pain like that was just part of our relationship. It hurt when he made me and it hurt to live with him. That was how things were meant to be. And, to be fair, he apologized often. Told me that it was just because he loved me so much, couldn't bear the thought of losing me, that he was just so scared. The apologies would always come before taking me to bed, where he would softly kiss the bruises he made. As time went on though, I believed his apologies less and less. I began to doubt myself and the choice I had made. I had been given life, but I was not allowed to live.

The truth was that I did not allow myself to live. That I cowered beneath his hand and even when I did not believe his appeals for forgiveness, I told myself that this was all I had. That I had no choice but to live here. What would I, a woman alone and without name, be able to do by myself? If I left, where would I go? I trapped myself just as much as he trapped me.

Until she came. My darling.

Being pregnant was like becoming for a third time. Senses and feelings I did not know I had awoke and became prominent. I realized that again I had a choice to make. I was unsure of how he, my husband and artificer, would react to a baby. Would he take joy in it, softened by its vulnerability and dependence? Or would the child be seen as an invader, something that would usurp my attentions away from him? We had both been convinced that I was barren, which did not seem unreasonable given my making. When I realized I was with child, I wept for all that I had gained and all I might lose.

I remained there for the pregnancy, but I resolved, as soon as I was able, to take the babe and escape. I did not trust my husband to be a loving father, and I refused to subject my child to him. Though ignorant, I had chosen my lot. My child had made no such choice, and I would not let my darling live a life of punishment.

The pain of giving birth was familiar and oddly comforting for me. Afterwards, I held my little girl, stunned by the dark beauty I had created. And for a little while, my doubts were forgotten.

Three weeks later, in the darkness of the early morning, I took my child and left my sleeping creator. We went to a city on the northern coast. I wanted to put as much distance between him and us as I could, and I would have sailed away entirely if I had been able to afford passage.

Five years. I had five sweet years of freedom with my daughter. I watched her grow strong and pretty. As she learned of the world around her and of her own body, I saw a reflection of myself, the strange experiences I had gone through to be there with her. In those years, I regretted nothing, convinced once more that pain was simply the payment for pleasure and joy.

During my darling's fifth summer, I heard a rumor that a great artist in the south was dying. They said he wasted away for love of a woman. They said he was beaten by a patron, angry that the artist refused to sculpt anymore, and was beyond saving. One woman told me that he was cursed by the gods for abusing the gifts they had given him. But whatever the circumstances, one part of the stories remained the same: he was dying, alone.

I was crushed by guilt. Though he had caused me so much pain, so much suffering, he was still my creator. My lover. The father of my beautiful child, whom he had barely met. I knew I could not save him, nor did I want to, but I felt that I should be there as he died. Let him meet his daughter and make sure he was not alone when he left this world. My debt to him would be paid, and I would continue to raise our daughter on my own.

Although it was summer and travel was easy, we were almost too late. I wonder about that sometimes, how things might have been different if I had still been on the road when he died.

As it was, I nearly did not recognize him when we came to the house. Gone was the strength in his hands and arms. Gone was the passion, the brightness of his eyes. The man that lay in bed before me was frail and sad and dim. Still, he smiled when he saw me. He held my little girl's hand, dryly kissed the top of her head. He did not ask me why I had left nor why I returned. He only said that he was so happy to see me, that I was beautiful as ever.

He was dead the next day.

I gave a small, silent prayer for him after his final exhalation. Then, I rose from the bedside, intending to call my darling to me, but my throat felt cold and heavy. I made no sound. As I turned, I felt a terrible familiar coldness rushing up my legs, felt myself grow heavy and hard. Just as quickly and easily as his last breath had come, I was again transformed to my original form. A perfect statue at my would-be lover's side.

The gods are cruel, but not heartless. It takes feeling to know how to so exquisitely torture someone.

My poor little girl! She came looking for me after a little while, and when she saw me, she cried. Ran up to my legs, hugged me, saying *Mama, mama,* over and over again. I raged inside, weeping and cursing and pleading. My daughter needed me, and I was helpless to do anything. Eventually, she tried to get help from the man in the bed, but when he was still and cold to her touch, she ran away. She returned soon after, followed by an old woman who lived nearby. The woman surveyed the room, the artist dead and me again marble, and seemed to understand what had happened. She hugged my girl and wiped her tears. Told her to say goodbye to me, that the gods had taken her mama away. *I'm right here,* I wanted to beg. I felt the warmth of my daughter's arms for the last time.

They pledged her to the temple of Aphrodite, where I was brought a few days later. My beauty was a tribute to the goddess, they said. The goddess had guided his hands when he sculpted me, and it was only fitting that I be brought to her house now. I saw my little girl often, but because I was said to be a form of Aphrodite herself, no one was ever allowed to touch me.

It was so cold.

That was many, many, many years ago. These days I mainly sleep, mostly forgotten by the world around me. I have been moved to various places through time, but still I am denied touch. *An act of preservation,* they say. Everlasting torture, I reply.

My girl is long dead. But sometimes I catch a glimpse of her in the crowd. A young woman throws her head back in laughter, a mother cradles and kisses her baby, a toddler looks up at me with awe… In all of them I see my darling. The comfort is short and piercing, and loneliness always returns to swallow me. *But,* I tell myself in the abyss of my existence, *I am the mother of a multitude.*

Some days it is almost enough.

THE END

Better the Thorn

Guy Donovan

As explosions went, Lash thought it was the prettiest one yet. It was certainly the largest. She squinted against the brilliant glare and heat, her coarse goblin lashes whisking together. Even so, she glimpsed several tumbling and flailing fae warriors silhouetted against the blast's colorful flames. Yellow shifted through orange and red before fading to an oily black. The seemingly living way in which the flames roiled and writhed never ceased to fascinate her.

Plasma, she thought, shielded from the effects of her handiwork by a thick tree trunk. *The humans call it plasma, I think. Or was that something to do with their blood?*

Whatever the humans called it did not matter, she decided. Only the staggering variety of their deadly weapons did. She stole all she could from them to use against her enemies in the world of Faerie. She was, after all, a goblin, and killing fae was what she did. She had just returned from her latest trip to Earth when the fae patrol had stumbled into her on the way back to her fortress home. In order to escape them, she'd had to sacrifice the wagon loaded with corroded steel drums of kerosene, but she had many other caches of deadly weapons squirrelled away in that wood.

The shrieks of the dying punctuated the survivors' moans as she scrambled higher up the tree, her claws sending shredded bits of bark flying through the air. Near the top, she leaped for the next tree over, using her momentum to bend it toward yet another. Snagging a branch, she spiraled her way back down into thick, autumn foliage that concealed her from even the sharpest-sighted Fae on the ground.

At the bottom, Lash spied her enemies through a gorse bush's prickles. While the roughly two dozen survivors tended to the dead or injured, a pair of tall and stately fae conferred. Of all the golden-hairs, those two most concerned her. One was clearly male, and she knew him to be an adept by the Rowan staff he carried. The other's elaborate, shining armor, feminine by its shape, identified her as the captain of the patrol that had found her there in the Goblin Wood. When the captain removed her gleaming, winged helmet, Lash's black heart skipped a beat.

Is it? she thought. Then, *No…it can't be!*

The fae captain and the adept both looked like all the others of their hated race. The same even, angular features. The same golden hair. But their ears…those were the true means of identifying individual fae. The captain's ears were familiar to her.

Lash spun about and tore through the underbrush, putting the confusing, maddening sight far behind her. Like any goblin, she was as savagely efficient at running on all fours across the forest floor as she was leaping and flying through its dry-leafed canopy. Turf, grass, and bits of arboreal debris dragged out behind her like a tail as she scurried deeper and deeper into the wood. Doubt assailed her tiny, blackened, and hateful heart for the first time in many years.

I am goblinkind…goblinkind…goblinkind… she chanted to herself, galloping headlong through brush, hedges, and deadfalls, uncaring for the injuries she sustained in her flight.

She finally stopped, panting more from agitation than exhaustion. Goblins felt neither fatigue nor remorse. They felt only a burning desire to destroy their enemy—their distant and haughty, golden-haired kith and kin.

I am black, Lash told herself. *Born to the light, but turned to the dark. Darkness was my gift and my refuge from the light!*

Her skeletal, greenish-black fingers stroked at the jagged and double-pointed tip of her left ear, which matched so perfectly those of the fae captain. Goblin that she was, she could not deny the implication of what she had seen. Deep within her, a pinprick of painful light burned where before there had only been cold, comforting dark. The feeble light illuminated a youthful memory long since suppressed.

I was not always Lash, she acknowledged. *I was once…*

She could not allow herself to think it, let alone say it aloud. Whoever, *whatever* she had once been, she was now Lash. She was a goblin. More, she too was an adept, like the fae she had just seen with her—

No! My true sisters and brothers are goblinkind, she thought. *I made that decision long ago, when my false family refused even to seek me out.*

The light died, extinguished by her belief that goblins had not stolen her as a child, but rather rescued her from the fae. Had they not done so, it might be she out there now, living the same haughty and meaningless life of resistance to change that those arrogant nobles who pursued her did.

The sounds of renewed pursuit shocked her back to the present. Reassurance came at a quick look about though. There in that dark forest where hazel and elder dominated the rowan, oak, and yew, the means to defeat her family-turned-pursuers lay strewn about in carefully laid traps.

The kerosene made for pretty effect, Lash told herself, *but the fae will fall in greater numbers yet.*

She removed from her tattered black shift's pocket a twig of hazel that helped to focus her magic. While far smaller than the fae's rowan staff, its power was great nonetheless. She inscribed an arcane symbol in the air with it before leaping into the lower branches of an elder. Scrambling upward, she paused near the top and then cackled out a challenge toward the approaching fae.

"Come and get one in the yarbles! If ya *have* any yarbles, that is!"

On one of her many trips to the human world, she'd heard a young, spotty faced brute shout that to another, earning a great howl of laughter from his companions and defiant snarls from his enemies. Lash had no idea of its meaning, but in the semi-permanent twilight of the faerie world, she saw it had a similar effect upon her own enemy. The fae charged the base of the tree while a handful of others stood off with bows, nocking arrows to their strings. With quick, practiced movements, Lash removed three metallic canisters from a leather belt about her shift, and lobbed them toward her enemies.

The running fae stopped when the unfamiliar objects landed among them. They laughed up at her, taunting her failed attempt to hit them. Lash laughed too, flicking her twig at each canister in turn.

The fae's laughter ceased as a dense yellow smoke belched forth from the three canisters and enveloped them in a thick, oily cloud. Their coughing became a hacking that drove them to their knees and prompted the archers to back away. When those first victims began retching up blood and pus, the panic-stricken archers fled.

Regretting that she could not stay to watch the glorious effects of the mustard gas, Lash descended nearly halfway back to the ground before leaping from trunk to trunk again. All the while, she loudly croaked and warbled a filthy goblin ditty to goad the surviving fae into following her. If any were stupid enough to charge through the remaining gas that pooled in the forest's hollows, well that was fine with her.

She dropped to the ground several times, giving her enemy enough of a trail to follow her. Up against a thick tree trunk, she propped a heavy and pointed metal cylinder. Next, she scattered a series of roughhewn boards all about the tall grass beneath the tree, each sporting rusty nails pounded up through them. She had only just settled into another tree a suitable distance away when her pursuers reached the trap.

Parting around the thick trunk, the unsuspecting fae continued until the nails penetrated their boots' leather soles. Their shrieks only drew more that way who would otherwise have gone wider around the tree. Soon, nearly a dozen warriors were on their backs, wailing and grabbing at their hobbled feet. That was when Lash flicked her twig at the cylinder propped up against the trunk.

The exploding artillery shell sent the huge tree crashing down on top of the wounded fae, killing the luckiest of them instantly.

Lash looked down through the smoke and debris from high above, relishing her success. It pleased her that the tree had been one of the old and rotten oaks rather than a type more cherished by goblins. As for the few surviving fae, they would either die of their injuries soon, or else were too badly maimed to continue the pursuit. She heard others, however, rushing that way from farther off in the wood. Of either the adept or the winged-helmeted captain, she saw nothing.

Then the branches about her disintegrated with a nearly silent blast of fae magic that launched her out of that tree and into another, a conifer that time. But for a few scratches, her armor-like hide and quick reflexes spared her from any serious injury as she clambered upward through the sap-sticky branches in a shower of needles. Camouflaged by the pine boughs, she spotted the adept on the ground, his staff still aimed at where she had been. She grinned to see that he now bore an angry red gash across his forehead, blood matting his long, blonde hair and smeared over his no longer gleaming chest plate.

Lash gave one of her own wounds a quick lick with her warty tongue before announcing, "That crimson goes as well with gold as it does silver, you poncy mudpout!" His senses augmented by magic, he locked his crystalline eyes on her almost immediately. "Oh ho! Such sharp eyes for such a dull wit," she crowed. "Keep following me, you keckberrish, and see what else I've got to maybe put 'em out!"

Just then, the captain revealed herself, wiping blood from her sword.

"And *you*!" Lash howled. "Did you just finish putting some dear fae out of his misery for breaking a nail?"

The captain only offered her a stoic look while the rest of the warriors entered the blasted clearing. Each carried a sword or spear that showed signs of neither wear nor age. While Lash had come to appreciate the rust-prone steel of the humans, the fae's impervium was the bane of all goblindom—more hated even than the fae who worked and wielded it. For a goblin, even its lightest touch caused agony beyond compare. In the eyes of those fae, she saw an intense desire to skewer her with their shiny weapons and then laugh as she writhed and howled.

Shaking the pine branches, she wagged her long, copper-green tongue at them. "Follow me, you pompous golden gits, and I'll show you what happens to shiny little shits!"

Then she clawed her way around the tree's far side in a spray of needles, branches, and pinecones before she leaped through the air. Landing in the high crotch of an aspen, she shredded its bark too, leaving it to flutter like paper to the forest floor after she leaped again. She did that several more times on her way directly toward the next trap.

"No!" she heard the captain commanding the men behind her. "It will only lead you to further death. Spread out to the sides and pinch it between you."

Perfect.

When she was certain the fae were going the way she wanted them to, she hugged tight to a trunk and watched them pass by on the ground, their faces up to the branches and their heads turning left and right. She crept silently down and padded across the bed of fallen leaves composting on the forest floor. Keeping an eye out for the adept and the captain, she waited for the right moment before springing back into furious action.

Racing on all fours through a knot of three warriors, she taunted them with a brief, rude noise before angling sharply to one side, aiming for the other half of the pursuing force. Predictably enough, the three followed. When the other party spotted her, she pivoted away and dashed through a patch of brambles between two broad trunks. Certain that both halves were now coming together behind her, she sprang up onto a mossy outcropping of boulders and assumed a fighting stance.

"Come on then! Have at you!" Lash snarled, beckoning with one hand for them to advance.

The fae paused, weapons raised to strike. Uncertainty showed on their perfect, angular features. Then the two leaders smiled at each other before guiding their teams to either side of the two trees and the thorny brush between them.

"No!" Lash cried, pretending to be disappointed. "From the front! Come at me from the front, you pretty little poufs!"

Grinning, the fae advanced from the sides…straight into Lash's real trap. The first at either side stumbled through a line strung low through the grass. That, in turn, popped open the bottoms of two dark green tubes tied to either trunk. From inside those tubes, half a dozen round objects rolled out and bounced into the opening while parts of them spun away through the air with a metallic pinging. Lash waved goodbye to her enemies before hopping backward into the safe space behind the boulder.

"Not very loud," she murmured, making a face at the hand grenades' disappointingly small explosions. She peered cautiously over the boulder's top. "Very effective though."

She grinned at the fae lying dead where they had meant to kill her. The grenades' shrapnel could not penetrate their impervium breastplates and helmets, but had done an admirable job of reducing their exposed arms, legs, and perfect faces to bloody tatters. At a bright flash from between the two trees, Lash ducked back behind the boulder just before it shattered into several large pieces. Flying bits of rock threatened to do to her what the grenades had done to the fae.

"Foul fiend!" she heard the adept shout through the ringing of her ears.

Raising her hazel twig over the top of the boulder remnant, she let loose a green blast of goblin fire his way. She knew the adept would counter it, understanding her own magic better than he did the human weapons, but she only needed a few seconds. As expected, the revoltingly sweet scent of fae magic filled the air when he turned her flame into a cloud of harmless butterflies. She vaulted back into the trees before he could cast another spell.

Lash passed up a cache of something called "nerve gas" in her focused flight toward the safety of her home. She did not need it anyway. After suffering such losses, the fae would pursue her to the last one of them rather than allow her to get away. Springing flea-like from tree to tree, she soon glimpsed her fortress home ahead. Where the broad valley pinched into a mountain pass, a barrier both natural and unnatural blocked the way. It had taken her years to build, and many, many trips to the human world to acquire the materials, but it was essentially complete now.

Heavily rusted steel from a place called Ford's Island composed most of it. At either end, two twisted hulks of framework towers with multifaceted, armored tops rose up nearly sixty feet into the cream-and-amber sky, with the bulk of the wall between them made from scrap left over from a long-ended human war. Thick, thorny vines held it all together through a goblin enchantment. Even through the rust and thorns, the faded numbers and letters "BB-39" remained legible in one place.

Well ahead of the fae, Lash reached the forest's edge and slowed her pace toward her home. Proud as she was of it, the most important part lay behind it. There, she had persuaded, threatened, or bribed her fellow goblins into helping her dig a pit so deep its bottom could not be seen from the surface. They had completed it just a few weeks before. Now she anticipated needing only one more return to the human world to acquire the thing she meant to put into that pit.

And with it, we goblins will finally overcome the arrogant, noble fae.

She looked up to the top of her fortress home, misty eyed at the sight of the enormous human guns bristling there. Some of them, she knew, could fire explosive shells miles through the air. Then, only a few dozens of feet from the wall she had built to resist even the strongest fae magic, the armored troops emerged from the forest behind her.

"Well crap," she muttered, borrowing a human phrase.

The quickly advancing fae held their weapons at the ready while their captain led the way. The adept followed just behind her. Lash whipped her hazel twig up, hoping to get off one final blast of green fire that might give her time to escape. Before she could, the very air about her seemed to thicken, compressing inward and making it hard to breathe. She lifted off the ground, her clawed toes dangling barely above the dry and weedy grass. She struggled to maintain her grip on the twig, but the adept sent it flying away from her with a twitch of his staff.

Lash fought the enchantment, but finally forced herself to relax so she could breathe. All the while, the fae soldiers formed a semicircle about her, the ends of which reached the base of the thorn-and-rusted-steel wall. Lash floated while the captain and adept drew up close.

"So you finally came for me?" Lash croaked against the enchantment's constriction.

"You thought me too weak or cowardly to pursue you?" the captain asked, her perfect lips curled in a snarl below her helmet's nose guard. "You thought wrong, you horrible creature."

Lash could only gurgle and choke in response. At a subtle gesture from the captain, the adept lessened the force of his hold. Lash drew in ragged breaths of air for a moment before surprising the fae with laughter rather than the curses she knew they had expected.

"Am I horrible?" she asked, unable to wipe the drool from her cracked lips. From behind the curtain of her filthy and matted, black hair, she flicked a glance left and right to the warriors standing guard.

The captain spoke in cold, hard tones of hatred. "You are a goblin."

Lash laughed again. "I *am* a goblin! But I was not always…was I, Amnestria?"

The captain jerked back, her eyes flashing wide in surprise. At the same time, the adept's resolve wavered slightly. It was just enough for Lash to palm a hard, plastic object from within the sleeve of her threadbare goblin shift. The captain, whose name was indeed Amnestria, cocked her head while Lash did the same, her coarse hair falling away from her left ear.

Amnestria's fine, pale fingers went to her own left ear, tracing the twin points of it that matched Lash's perfectly. "Breesha?" she gasped.

"My name is *Lash*!" She struggled anew at the adept's enchantment. "The fae you knew as Breesha died when none of you could bother yourselves with looking for her!"

Amnestria lowered her sword and turned a sad look to the adept. "Let her down, Halueth."

"But—"

"Do it!"

The adept obeyed, reluctantly.

On the ground again, Lash pressed a button on the plastic box in her hand. A series of pops sounded out as two dozen cylindrical objects sprang up from the ground inside the semicircle of fae warriors. They detonated at waist height. All the remaining fae warriors fell, shredded by the thousands of shiny, steel balls sprayed by the leaping mines. Only a quick reaction from the adept Halueth spared himself, Amnestria, and Lash when he used his staff to create a domelike, invisible shield over them. Upon touching the shield, the lethal projectiles turned to roses and piled harmlessly on the ground in a circle about them.

"*Why?*" a distraught Amnestria shouted as she pulled Lash in close by her shift, the sword again hovering close to the goblin's neck. "Why are you so full of hate for us, Breesha?"

Rather than laugh that time, Lash tightened like wire in Amnestria's grip. "*Never* call me that!" she spat. Then, going limp, she growled, "Hate is all I have left for you. Any of you."

Amnestria wept openly. "I thought you dead, sister!"

"It is no longer our kin, captain." Halueth lay a hand on her shoulder. "It is goblinkind now, and it has killed many of our brethren this day. You know the price it must pay."

Amnestria shrugged his hand away and knelt before Lash. "I *did* look for you, sister. I did."

Lash snatched herself away from the fae's touch. "I am not your sister. I am your enemy."

"Will you do as the law commands, captain?" Halueth asked, brandishing his Rowan staff like a weapon again. "The *law*…"

"I know the law!" Amnestria snarled, whipping her sword about toward Halueth in more of a warning than a threat. "But *I* am this patrol's captain, and *I* will administer the justice as *I* see fit."

Turning back to Lash, Amnestria took in the imposing sight of the human technology married with goblin magic. She surveyed the destruction and the bodies of her soldiers. Then she turned a look of pity mixed with a cold sadness on the goblin.

"Whether Lash or Breesha, you *are* my sister. But you are also, through no fault of your own, become goblin." She gestured about the carnage. "I cannot bring myself to kill you, so I sentence you instead to be part of that world you clearly prefer over the one into which you were born. There, you will wield magic no more." Her look gone soft again, she murmured, "I am sorry, but it must be so."

Lash issued a harsh, guttural laugh. Her capture by the fae would not be the end of her plan, but rather the key to her eventual victory over them. The irony of it tickled her more than anything else ever had, whether fae child or goblin adult.

To Halueth, Amnestria snapped, "You know what to do, cousin."

She backed away, and the adept stepped up to Lash. In contrast to the captain's heartbreak, Lash saw in his eyes only a hate she knew mirrored her own. Then he smiled, intensifying that hatred rather than diminishing it as the butt of his rowan staff wavered above Lash's withered, heaving chest.

"Here among the roses, I withdraw your goblin magic from you like a thorn from a wound, and banish you from this world to the other."

At the first touch of his staff against her chest, she felt it begin to suck her power away. Shuddering, she matched his cold gaze, grinned, and said, "Better the thorn than the rose!"

Lash fell back onto the ground as soil and roots closed over her. The last thing she saw of the world of Faerie were two perfect faces looking down on her, their sharp features framed by pale golden hair. One wept while the other cackled with maniacal glee. Finally, everything went a dark, reddish-black like a scab over her eyes.

She felt herself growing heavier, denser, and infinitely weaker in that darkness. Her heart, so sluggish in its beats before, slowed further until it finally seemed to stop. Then, after a time she could not account for, a sharp pain seared through her very center even as a tiny ball of golden-white light sparked into existence. Both the pain within and the light from without grew until she curled up on herself and cried out. As she cowered, she heard a distant, familiar sound. The humans called it "radio."

Squinting, she peered out from behind a curtain of fine, black hair to see a dirty and pale animal's hide covering her skinny forearms in place of her goblin's chitinous carapace. The abhorrently bright sun of the humans' Earth had burned her like acid on her previous forays there, but now it only felt uncomfortably warm. A few yards away, two men approached from a thick stand of trees. They wore clothing meant to mimic the look of woodland, and carried black weapons of steel and plastic. One carried his slung over a shoulder while the other pointed his at her with shaking hands.

She recognized the place. Her stolen maps referred to it Mag Group 25, and it was part of something called Naval Weapons Station, Yorktown, Virginia. She knew the men too, or at least their type. They called themselves marines and the weapons they carried were M16A1 rifles. She had stolen many such rifles and stored them somewhere she knew she might never return to now.

"It's a single female, Punch Mike One-Five," the marine with the slung rifle said into his radio. "She appears to be in distress." After the garbled squawking of a voice on the radio, he replied, "No, we didn't challenge her…it's operational hours!" Looking at her, and then the other marine, he said, "Don't be a numbnuts, Jimmy. Lower your weapon." Then, into the radio again, "Punch Mike One-Five, Punch Mike Two-One, call the OD out and send an ambulance to our location."

The last thing Lash heard before a noisy vehicle with flashing lights arrived was the man called Jimmy saying to the other, "Y'know, Elmer…she ain't bad lookin' under all those scabs an' dirt. Kinda hot, even."

Epilogue

Stockholm's summer of 1991 was warmer than usual, reaching well into the eighties Fahrenheit. Like the rest of Europe, the Swedes used the admittedly more sensible Centigrade measurement, but her time in America had conditioned her to use the older method. When Lash strolled out the door of her agent's high-rise office building at Sveavägen 9J to await her driver, she fished about in her purse for a pair of big, dark sunglasses. In addition to protecting her eyes from the harsh sun to which she had never adapted well, she knew it would help to keep any of the passersby from recognizing her. She sometimes regretted the career she had chosen after being banished from the world of Faerie, particularly the swarming mobs of photographers that dogged her every move. She had to admit though, that the money she earned for nothing but posing for pictures in her silly human underwear had been vital to her success.

"Ms. Ashcroft!" someone called from the revolving door behind her.

Turning, she told the lean, sandy brown-haired young man, "Just call me Lilly, dear. The world has seen too much of me to stand on formality, I think."

"Of course," he said, coloring visibly. He held out a scrap of paper. "I have the reservation number for the hotel in Rota that you asked for."

Lash's brows arched, legitimately impressed with the young Swede's efficiency. "My, that *was* fast, Björn," she remarked in her signature, smoky tone.

"If you don't mind me asking, umm, Lilly," he said, his eyes flicking up and down from her to the sidewalk and then back again, "what in the world would interest you about an American naval base in Spain?"

She trilled a delicate laugh. "I know someone there. Someone I met when I first arrived in America. He says he's acquired something for me that I've wanted for a long time."

As she took the slip from him, a number of men appeared, shouting for her attention in Swedish, German, Italian, and English, all the while clicking away with their cameras.

Hating the paparazzi no less than did any other celebrity, many of whom were also banished goblins, Lash put on a false smile and granted their request. She even gave them all a friendly wave. Bathed in the strobing flashes, she then hooked an arm around the young Swede's waist and rose onto her toes to give him a big, wet kiss as she tucked the paper into a pocket of her silk blouse. Inspired by the ever-annoying photographers' wolf whistles, she flipped them her middle finger before leaving the astonished young man in a daze on the sidewalk.

"Thanks again, Björn," she said over her shoulder, strutting over to a car that had just pulled up to the curb. "You'll be famous on two continents by tonight. Enjoy it."

The driver opened her door and she plopped into the back seat of the big, dark sedan. Looking out the window before he got back in and drove away, she grinned at the dumb look on young Björn's face, his fingers tracing over his lips and a glazed-but-happy look on his face. Then, the pleasantly naughty moment forgotten, she retrieved the paper from her pocket.

"Where to next?" the driver asked, already pulling away from the crowd.

"The airport." She regarded the paper a moment longer before adding, "I'm off to Spain."

The driver made a "whew" sound. "It'll be even hotter there than it is here."

Lash chuckled. "You've no idea, Benny."

Later that evening, her chartered jet on final approach to Aeropuerto Jerez in Spain, Lash reflected on the chain of events leading to the end of her mission she had started so long ago and in another world entirely. She had to assume that her Earthly beauty had been a sort of tongue-in-cheek gift from her onetime sister, Amnestria. It seemed fittingly evil that such a "gift" would prove the means of ending the stranglehold with which the fae held all of Faerie. Without Amnestria's sentimentality, granting her that which the humans valued so highly, Lash might never have been able to amass the wealth necessary to acquire the single, deadly item she now planned to import back to Faerie through her contacts in Hollywood.

Thanks to James G. Wilcox, a lowly private first class upon her arrival in his world but now a platoon sergeant at the marine barracks in Rota, Spain, she would have the key to not only her own revenge upon the fae, but for all goblinkind. Rota had many such keys in its rows of concrete bunkers, but she would only need the one.

Her seatbelt buckled securely and the tray table returned to its upright position, Lash grinned when another thought flitted bat-like into her mind. She hoped that she might get her magic back once her agents in Faerie used the Tomahawk missile to bring the fae to their knees. She knew though, that she might not. That wiped the smile from her pretty face. Then another thought sent her full, sensuous lips curling upward again.

Her detestable beauty would eventually fade, as it did for all humans. In order to continue providing wealth after that so she might at least live in comfort if she were to be stuck there forever, she needed a new plan. Since humans valued beauty and fame so much, it seemed sensible to sell them something else once she could no longer sell them herself.

A perfume, she decided. *I think I'll call it 'Thorn.'*

THE END

Falling out of the Sky: A Beginner's Guide
Nimue Brown

(Being a short story set on the island of Hopeless Maine, at a point in time of uncertain nature)

Something slapped the back of her neck, damply. Hair, or tentacles, most likely. She couldn't afford to lose focus right now, but, too late already.

"Owen," she said, her voice loaded with growl.

"Sorry."

Salamandra took a long, deep breath and tried to refocus her mind on matters of magic, spatial awareness, tentacle prediction and rope finding. She ducked, twisted, blasted and swore a couple of times, to little effect. There were rather too many things to concentrate on all at once, and the minor botheration of her friend's flapping hair somehow took all of her attention again.

"I could tie it up for you," Salamandra said.

"It's fine." Owen sounded muffled now, as though he had a mouthful of something. No more than he deserved.

She could feel him, back to back with her, stumbling, bumping into her sometimes, not really helping at all. But at least each bump meant he hadn't been crushed to death, strangled by ropes or become too intimate with the other living being in this hazardous quartet.

"How about plaits?" She pictured twin pigtails and snickered to herself. Something rubbed across her shoulder but she couldn't see what it was for the sagging body pressed against that side of her face. Something leaned into her that felt like skin against her skin. Too much sensation. The living skin, or the dead skin? Too much information. Focus. Focus harder.

Owen quickly scuppered that, exclaiming a loud "No!" He'd probably pictured the same thing. Then he made an ominous gurgling noise.

"You're bloody useless and you can't see what you're doing," she said, worried about him, but not wanting to say so.

"I'm fine," he replied, sounding as though he'd got a throat full of tentacle now. Which seemed likely, with all the mouth opening he'd been doing.

She knew he wasn't fine. His default state was perilously close to disaster.

Another line of rope became visible and she lashed out at it with a quick, concentrated burst of energy, cutting it before any other tentacles could swarm across her field of vision.

"This is insane," Owen sounded muffled but had probably yelled.

She quietly agreed. Owen's wet hair slapped the back of her neck again. She spotted another entangled rope, and went for it, parting the living from the unliving. She supposed forward planning might have helped, but it wasn't her strong point.

§ § §

They'd gone to the balloon launch because life on Hopeless, Maine could get a bit samey and you had to make the best of whatever turned up. The balloon itself was an ugly thing, made out of stitched together hides. It looked like a badly assembled, re-animated corpse. A larger scale version of the kinds of things her father made out of mice on long winter evenings.

Beneath the corpse bag were a large bucket of unknown provenance, and a fire dish. The single occupant – Mr Jeremiah Fuzzlepump – had been on the island precisely as long as it had taken him to build this large abomination. He spent the launch laughing too loudly and trying not to set himself alight. There wasn't really room in the bucket for both the man and the fire. No doubt a significant contributor to his later falling out.

By lunchtime of launch day, the bucket had lifted only twelve feet or so, and bored boys were throwing stones at it. Everyone else had given up except for Sal and Owen. She had stayed because the scene reminded her of her grandfather, and nostalgia was an unfamiliar emotion. Owen stayed because, despite the lack of drama, he apparently thought it was really neat.

Once the balloon finally cleared the rooftops, the wind caught it. For a good ten minutes it looked like Mr Fuzzlepump might escape from the island after all. That was when the tentacles came from the sky. It was a satisfying moment for the on-looking boys. Proof that being clever wouldn't get you out of here either.

Owen – always one for a rescue attempt – ran off after the flailing mass of tentacles and balloon as it headed groundwards. Salamandra – never inclined to let Owen kill himself for a good cause – trotted along behind. Mostly to save him from himself. But also curious.

Mr Fuzzlepump's scream as he fell out of the bucket was slow; an elongated sound, trailing on longer than it should have done.

When the rest of this tangled nightmare hit the ground it became an almost incomprehensible mingling of sky beast and balloon. Sal felt inclined to let nature take its course, but Owen was doing the supposed-to-be-heroic Owen thing, so she followed him into the chaos. She wondered, briefly, why she never felt like letting nature take its course with him.

Here they now stood, back to back and as usual, she had no idea why they were doing any of this.

"We should get out of here," she shouted as a tentacle wrapped around her wrist.

"We'll never get another chance like this!" Owen yelled into her ear, which she did not appreciate, although it meant he no longer had anything awful in his mouth and she supposed that was a good thing.

"We can die any time, Owen. It doesn't have to be today."

"But this is a giant, oceanic gnii!"

"And?"

"They were supposed to be all gone. All dead. This one's alive. That's amazing. Aren't you excited?"

Sal thought about the abandoned gnii refinery, and the loss of the industry that had one made the island wealthy, and shrugged.

"We've got to rescue it, set it free," Owen said. Against all the odds, he'd managed to wrestle some of the balloon corpse down, now, as it deflated into more of a sad dead bag than a dangerously sad dead balloon.

Fighting a furious creature who does not show signs of wanting to be saved from the remains of a hot air balloon, is no easy task. Quite what the many limbed gnii thought it was doing with the balloon, Sal had no idea. Did it see the balloon as a rival, or a mate? Was it bored? Angry? How could you tell? Did it just want something to hide behind? The smaller, regular island gnii had an uncanny knack for gathering most of themselves behind small objects so as to hide from viewers.

Once untangled, the vast monster from the sky skittered along the ground and tucked itself behind the balloon so they couldn't see most of it. By this time, Frampton Jones had found them, juggling camera, notebooks and pencils as he approached, clearly in a state of excitement.

"It's a giant oceanic gnii, isn't it?" Owen asked him.

"Undoubtedly." The island's only journalist beamed. As a man not prone to beaming, it looked as though he was both delighted, and straining some muscles that weren't used to the exertion.

Salamandra paid little attention to the excited conversation that followed. She watched the tentacles creep round to explore the balloon, and then pull away. A small bang lit a flame somewhere on the body of the beast. A second, rather lovely balloon appeared behind the first and hideous one – flimsy and delicate and rising skyward at speed. The new balloon lifted. The bucket lifted, gripped by tentacles as the gnii disappeared behind this modest object. The corpse balloon- untethered now - remained limp and lifeless on the ground.

Evidently that filmy, shimmering second balloon belonged to the giant oceanic gnii. Salamandra watched as the whole, improbable array rose above her. It looked as though the creature was trying to hide itself behind the bucket, or was clutching it affectionately. She couldn't quite tell.

"My guess," said Frampton Jones, "Is that it mistook the hot air balloon for a fellow gnii. Saw it as a potential mate or a rival, no doubt."

Salamandra wondered if it had been about the bucket all along.

"Amazing," said Owen. He swung round enthusiastically and his wet hair slapped her in the face this time.

"Tie it up," she said. "Or I swear I will turn it pink."

Owen sighed, and tucked the soggy mess into the back of his coat.

"It's funny how hard it can be to distinguish between fighting and courting," Frampton said, scribbling furiously.

Sal thought about kicking Owen and said nothing.

THE END

Mulo

Penny Blake

Aleksa

In the city, where the fog curls just above the cobble stones, there are many lights; the flickering gas lamps breathing milky pools against the evening's cool, dark breast; the tinder sparks from flaring pipes; the window-stars like cold diamonds or bright catalysts of life.

Move out beyond the streets, out into the woods, follow that lonely ribbon of road away through the marsh, and the lights out there do not cast the same impression on our minds.

Lights, we understand, mean there is someone and who, we ask ourselves, *who* could be out there in the dark and the mist? Who on a night like *this*?

The word for the carriers of the marsh lanterns is *Mulo* and Baba always told me that this word means demon. After Mammy and Daddy and little Dragan were gone, and all that was left was Baba and me, she taught me to light the tallows in their little glass bottles and set them all around the farm each night, to keep the demons away.

She knew a lot of things my Baba, how to keep us safe through the long dark nights in Indigo. But she didn't know how to make the water safe, and in the end it was only me, and I didn't know either.

Ndrita

"Pffth", Ndrita spat the grey-blue sludge out of her mouth and hurled her empty water flask into the coils of grey-green mist. The leather straps were carefully tattooing agony into the raw meat of her shoulder muscles, but even as she wiped the stinging sweat and grime from her eyes she heard Sihana give the order to move on.

"Ak, she always says the same thing!" Beside her, Little Kejda braced her own harness against her back and began to haul. "'Move on now, move on,' she says, 'where to, Boss Lady?' is what I'm gonna ask her if she deigns to step down here and get her brow wet for a bit."

Ndrita managed a weary grin and, as each of the twenty prisoners slowly took the strain, the metal beast behind began to creep forwards through the rancid mire of the Indigo Marsh.

"Anywhere that isn't here is fine by me, Kiji," Ndrita's voice was little more than a grunt now as the weight of the machine threatened to drag her face down into the muck. "The scouts didn't come back again last night,"

"How do you..."

"I pay attention. So should you. That's the fourth night in a row and Sihana's said nothing."

"You think something got em?"

"Like what? Seems like there's nothing but empty marsh for miles."

"Oh there's something," Kejda gritted her teeth as her foot struggled to keep purchase on the sliding mud, "and don't tell me it's just the marsh gasses or fox fire neither! I saw it last night, and the night before – lights, out there, tiny flickerings, far off, sure, but moving about..."

"There's no need to fish about for ghost stories Kiji, if we don't find drinkable water soon we'll all be ghosts ourselves."

"You're jokin' me gal! We're cartin' a year's supply of water in them tanks up there, and all the while droppin' like flies of thirst! And where we takin' it, eh? Who's it for?"

Ndrita grimaced, "As guests of the crown Kiji, I don't think we're entitled to ask that. My bet's on some secret military unit they've got hidden out here in the sticks," she let out a laugh like a whip crack, "Now there's an explanation for your night-lights eh?"

"Nah, they…"

"SPLITTERRRRRRS!"

The high pitched screams of energy pistols pierced the thick curtain of mist. At once the line broke as the workers all hit the dirt, not wanting to be mistaken for those who were running away.

Ndrita raised her head a little from her arms and caught sight of the three figures vanishing into the mist, "Idiots, they won't get anywhere on their own."

"They won't get anywhere at all now."

They watched in silence as Sihana's Elite Guard swiftly put an end to the lives of the three would-be-escapists, reducing them to pitiful piles of smouldering ash that melted swiftly into the toxic mire beneath their feet.

Anika

We tried not to think about them but every night since our caravan rolled into this cursed marsh they are there, sometimes on the edge of the horizon, sometimes nearer but never near enough to discern a form behind the glow. *Mulo*, the souls of the dead, waiting.

"It's the water."

Ma wrapped her shawl around her tighter and hugged her tin mug in work-gnarled hands, "T'aint the water, child. How can it be the water eh?"

"What else is it gonna be?"

She squinted her old eyes out into the gloom, *"Mulo"*

I rolled my eyes but not so she could see.

"You see them out there? Eh? They've put a curse on this ground we should never 'ave come."

"Didn't have a choice did we? They've banned caravans from passing along the city road, we don't need another run in with the law, not with Kizzy about to drop twins at any minute."

Ma's eyes flickered to the van where fever threatened to take her second child before morning. "Don't tell her Sully's gone yet, will yer? Wait an' see if she makes it through the night."

"I'M NOT WAITIN' ANY LONGER!" Fear and frustration turned to rage at the thought of dumbly sitting by and watching my loved ones slowly poisoning themselves one by one.

"Sit down, gal!"

"No. I'm gonna find us some clean water, Ma, there's gotta be a farm or a settlement around here somewhere or… something… we can't go on like this, we'll never make it across this marsh alive."

"And what y'going to pay for it with, eh? Our coins aren't worth nothin' anymore, they all wants that new crest stampin' on 'em…"

I marched over to the van and took down Pa's old energy-rifle he used for keeping the wolves away, "I'll ask nicely, won't I?"

Aleksa

How is it often the way that the soul becomes enchanted with the source of its own demise? What fascinates the rabbit in the weasel's sarabande? What fascinated me about those soft glowing death lights? I don't know, but every night I watched them.

There was one large, soft, flickering glow, red and orange, that danced and wavered through the dark, always stationary but each night in a different place, sometimes just on the horizon, sometimes a little closer but never close enough that I could see exactly what it was.

Then there was the group of bobbing bouncing little orbs, which shone pale green and yellow through the mist. They were always moving along a straight path, every night a little nearer it seemed, though moving very slow.

And lastly there was the newest light, one lone small steak of fire, coming closer.

Ndrita

"Kidji, get up," Ndrita pressed a grease stained, callused hand over Kejda's shoulder and shook her urgently.

Kejda started and leapt onto her haunches, peering into the dark, "what's going on? It's not morning…"

"No, Kiji, it's a revolt – looks like some of the girls have been plotting this a while…"

"What the hell are we s'posed to do? We ain't got weapons!" Kejda hissed as they hit the mud and lay flat against the sodden turf. "Lie low and wait to see who wins?"

"Sihana will win, Kiji, whoever has the power always wins you must know that by now."

Anika

To the old folki, like Ma, anything they can't explain must be magic, must be spirits, must be the souls of the dead. I didn't disrespect her for it, I just prefered to base my own beliefs on experience, and in my experience where there's light, there's people and where there's people, there's water. I followed Ma's 'Mulo' and they lead me to the farm.

Aleksa

In the end I knew that One Light was coming for me and I welcomed it; whether it was an angel speeding to take me to my rest or a demon coming to devour my soul I didn't care. Everyone I knew or had ever loved was dead, so what fear could there possibly be for me in the company of ghosts?

I made what I knew must be my last round of the farm, every step an act of sacrifice in the cyan sunset, and this time the taper lights were not to ward off the Mulo, but to welcome them.

Ndrita

Bodies and piles of dust that had once been human littered the soft ground, ready to be claimed by mist and mud and add their own venom to the toxic Indigo Marsh.

Ndrita knelt beside Kejda and cradled her dirt-stained cheek in her rough palm. "I'm sorry Kiji," her throat burned with regret but if tears needed to fall they would come later, if she lasted long enough. She tightened the straps that lashed the stolen water tank to her back, then cursed as something snared her ankle from behind and sent her sprawling face down in the mud beside her friend.

She twisted round.

"Wait!"

It was Sihana. Blood matted her hair and ran down her right temple.

Ndrita kicked her leg free of the woman's grasp and got to her feet.

"Wait!" Sihana choked, "You can't leave, Girl, people are counting on us; families, children, someone has to get that water through to Indigo." She choked again and spat blood into the mire. "I know your story, Ndrita; I know how many lives you've stolen for your own selfish gain. For once in your life, don't you want to help someone other than yourself?"

Anika

"Are you Mulo?" Sweat soaked the child's hair and beaded on her sallow skin, her once-fine frock and shawl were streaked and stained and her eyes were wild and wide with fever.

I looked around the richly furnished parlour; neat-swept, clean and stinking of death.

"Have you come for me?" She took a trembling step forward and as she fell I dropped Papa's rifle and caught her in my arms. I didn't come for her; I came for my own chavies, not for the spawn of those who keep us under their boot.

I held her and rocked her and smoothed her damp hair and walked over to the big bay window and looked out into the cold starless dark. No Mulo tonight, only the small ring of bottle lanterns she must have set herself around the farm boundary. A chill went through my bones, if we could see her lights, then why couldn't I, now, looking back, see Ma's campfire?

I strained my eyes, fearless of ghosts, desperate now for that one small sign of life – and then I saw it, not a campfire but a smaller flame, a tiny green-gold lantern light, moving closer through the dark and I knew she was coming for me.

Ndrita

"Hello? Anyone here?"

The door creaked open and the startled look on the young woman's face, as she cradled her child in her arms, told Ndiitra she'd been expecting someone else. But then who would be expecting a shaven-haired, muscular woman with prison numbers tattooed across her scalp and hands?

The woman backed away; searching for the rifle that they both knew was beyond her reach.

"It's ok, it's alright, look…" Ndrita quickly unlashed the water tank and let its crippling weight slide to the wooden floor. "This is just one tank, there's more, a year's supply, I couldn't carry it on my own but…"

She was crying.

Together they held the child so that she could drink; tiny sips so she wouldn't vomit it back out again.

"There's more of us, my family are back there in a caravan across the marsh, not far. Let me take this tank and I can bring them all back here."

Ndrita must have looked confused, "You're not her mother?"

The woman looked at her like she was mad. "Of course not, look at me."

Ndrita looked; taking in her ragged patchwork clothing for the first time in comparison to the child's soiled but well-tailored dress. "This water is for the farm folk, it's a convoy from the city to the new farm settlement at Indigo…it got delayed but…it's for them."

The joy drained from the woman's features and she chewed her lip and nodded slowly. "Right. But they're all dead, except this little girl," She looked at Ndrita for a long time, "are you telling me you have to 'obey the rules'?"

Ndrita looked at the palms of her hands, covered in so many numbers and brands, unshakable proof that she had never been one for that game.

Sihana's words echoed in her mind, she'd wanted her to help the people of Indigo, she would have thought the Travelling folk beneath her concern, and she was right that Ndrita had always been selfish, always done as she pleased, followed her own path. She was right, too, in thinking that

Ndrita wanted to change, to make-good as they say, to make a new start as soon as she got the chance.

But a new start didn't have to be on Sihana's terms, and her definition of 'good' certainly didn't have to be Ndrita's.

She rose to her feet, picked up the water tank and filled some jugs on the side board. Then she turned and handed it to the young woman. "Take it, if you walk for a few miles in a straight line to the south west of the barn back there, you'll find more. More than I could ever carry here alone. Take what you need."

"Thanks." She didn't gush with joy, the fact that it'd taken Ndrita a few seconds to judge the worth of her own family against the worth of these displaced city folk was a bitter pill and Ndrita felt wretched.

The woman took the water tank, strapped it to her own back, and made for the door.

"What about the child?"

"You better take her back to the city."

Ndrita shook her head, "I can't do that."

"Why not? There's nothing for her here anymore and those city folk need to know that their plans to drain and farm here aren't panning out."

She was right, Ndrita knew it, the child did belong back in the city, but a wanted fugitive couldn't be the one to take her there. She must have read Ndrita's thoughts because she said, "better you than us though – anyone who sees a caravan of Travellers with a city child in their midst will assume we kidnapped her."

Ndrita nodded slowly, feeling this was an argument she couldn't win and didn't have time for, "Sure, I see your point."

"You'll take her then?"

She smiled grimly.

The young woman had obviously seen that kind of smile before because she paused and looked back at the girl now sleeping fitfully in the little armchair. "Alright," she said at last, "we'll take her if you won't. But you have to stay with her while we bring the caravan back here with the water too."

"Sure."

Anika

When I got back she was gone and so, in the end, it was just me who dropped little Aleksa at the gates of the big city, with a bunch of deeds and papers proving who she was, and the address of some aunt who, she was sure, would take her in.

We'd left the caravan full of stolen water safely hidden in the woods and I walked back to it slow, feeling hollow and so very, very alone.

Aleksa

Here in the city there are many lights; the light Aunt Lillibeth leaves burning on my bedside table, the gas lamps flickering in the street outside, but the lights that I hold in my heart are the Mulo Lanterns of Indigo.

Baba told me that the word Mulo means 'Demon,' but I know now that the translation isn't quite correct. Mulo are 'The Wind People' – the light carriers who blow into our lives for a single, brief and beautiful moment, just long enough to do what is needed, and then they are gone and we never see them again.

My Mulo brought light into my darkest hour and wherever they are now, I thank them for it and I remember them. Perhaps one day I will have the courage to carry my own lantern across a cold dark space to where light is needed.

THE END

The Wizard's Quandary

Jaq D. Hawkins

Lesana peered carefully into the crucible, closely observing the swirling, black mass within.

"If that pops, you could lose an eye." Khadri, Lesana's miniature green dragon companion, hopped onto Lesana's shoulder, causing her to brace herself against the weight of an animal the size of a full-grown wolverine. He glanced at the churning elixir.

Lesana pulled her head back a little, but continued frowning at the crucible.

"Your eyes see more colours than mine," she stated aloud. "Can you see any hint of vermilion?"

Khadri danced around on his shoulder perch, pretending not to notice when Lesana steeled herself against the new claw punctures in her partially healed, damaged skin.

"I see the red glowing crystals forming rapidly, as always. You've never failed in your efforts to make the Philosopher's Stone to my knowledge."

Lesana smirked.

"You should have seen my early efforts, when you were just a hatchling," she replied. "It's more by luck than judgement that I never blew up the entire tower."

"It's a dangerous business," Khadri acknowledged. "I don't see why the king doesn't just send you to Egypt to retrieve the cinnabar from mummy wrappings."

Lesana guffawed, pushing herself away from the table where the crucible continued to send sulphuric vapour into the close space of the uppermost tower room where she kept her laboratory, just in case. Fire and explosions tended to travel upwards.

"I can just see the Egyptian Department of Antiquities allowing a foreign wizard to help herself to the preservatives in their precious national tourist industry. Last I heard they didn't even know the nature of the red ochre. I'd rather not be the one to explain that they've had the key to immortality within their relics all this time."

She wandered to the arched window that looked out over the dead forest to the north. The elevation provided by the fifth level tower room allowed Lesana to see the Crystal Mountains in the distance. A wistful note entered her voice.

"Besides, if I ever leave the king's employ and travel somewhere, I'd like to go back to the Crystal Mountains."

"Where you found me?" Khadri gasped. "The dragons would eat you!"

"Perhaps," Lesana admitted. "But they didn't before. I felt something while I was there. Something... magical."

She turned to watch the colour change progression in her elixir. The black had already given way to white, then it moved onto the yellow stage as expected. Lesana nodded in approval.

"It's been easier since you started helping me in the lab, Khadri," she reflected. "The process works so much better with a balance of male and female energies." She gently stroked the little dragon's neck.

"That's why Paracelcus repeatedly failed," she added. "The most famous Alchemist in history couldn't even make Philosopher's Stone."

She frowned again.

"It does seem to be taking a long time to get to the red stage."

"Throw in some yellow wax," Khadri suggested.

Lesana opened a narrow drawer in the table and took out a lump of wax. She held it carefully over the concoction, then simultaneously dropped it and stepped back, withdrawing her hand as if she expected an explosive reaction. The liquid bubbled and steamed above the crucible, crackling from potentially scalding heat. Then it settled down and began to turn the colour of cinnamon. Lesana smiled with satisfaction.

The smile dropped when a sudden pounding on the ground floor door made her jump. Khadri leapt from her shoulder to a nearby shelf, leaving blood-moist scratches on the flesh beneath Lesana's thick cotton tunic. Lesana looked out the window and frowned at the man in king's livery standing in front of the ground level door. He pounded his fists against the solid oak again, then shook his hand and swore.

"On my way down!" Lesana called down to him. She hurried down the spiral steps, keeping her fingers on the rail in case she should stumble on the worn stones in her haste. She began to open the door with a question on her lips, but the king's lackey shoved it open the moment the latch was released and stomped into the plainly furnished room where Lesana normally received the occasional visitor or messenger.

"Where do you make your potion?" he demanded. "The king wants an inventory, all equipment and ingredients."

Lesana glared at the rude intruder and placed herself between him and the stairs.

"My laboratory is private, but I will be happy to write an inventory for the king's pleasure." Her stern tone belied her polite words.

"I have my orders," the kingsman growled. He physically pushed Lesana aside and hopped up the stairs as if it were no effort whatsoever.

A soldier, then, but disguised as a messenger?

There was nothing to do but to follow him up to the laboratory. The sound of his steps hesitated only briefly at each level. A quick glance is all it would take to assess living quarters, library and other rooms. She caught up to him just as he stepped into the laboratory.

The potion, left on a slow simmer, swirled with orange-cinnamon promise. Lesana turned off the heat to allow it to cool and solidify. Khadri stood as still as stone on the bookshelf where she had last seen him.

The incognito soldier examined the equipment and the vials of various substances along the laboratory shelves, briefly skimming the titles on the book shelf. His glance scanned right past the dragon 'statue'.

A soldier who can read... interesting.

"This will all be collected," the soldier stated. "Equipment, books, ingredients... and you. You are to set up your operation in a designated room within the castle grounds and teach the king himself to make the potion that keeps him young."

Lesana felt her stomach drop.

"But this stuff is dangerous," she argued. "Explosions and fire are not unknown!"

"It is not for you or I to question the king's orders," the man countered. "A horse-drawn cart follows behind me. Prepare your instruments to be transported. You are not to leave this tower until the cart arrives. You will accompany us to the castle."

The man turned and stomped down the stairs. Lesana watched outside the window until he emerged and took up a guard's position in front of the entrance.

"Well, that's a turn-up," Khadri jeered, moving from his perch at last. "Who does this king think he is? An Alchemist?"

"Apparently that's his intention." Lesana mused for a moment, then continued. "I've kept him young for three generations. Suddenly he wants to make me obsolete. He would want *you* if he knew you existed. I'm always amazed at your ability for absolute stillness when visitors surprise us."

"My kind hibernate." The dragon hopped onto the window sill and curled his tail around her arm. "A full-sized dragon can become part of a mountain, undetected for centuries."

Lesana nodded. She knew much of dragon lore, but often wondered how her hatchling had learned of his own species, having grown up isolated from them.

"Just as well. He would no doubt separate us." Lesana had never had delusions about the king's benevolence or respect for the property of others. She had often expected him to demand she marry him to keep her under his control. It was because of that fear that she had long since prepared for emergency measures.

"I think it's time to use the tunnel," Lesana muttered, gazing out at the Crystal Mountains. Despite her frequent fantasies of returning to travel further into the mountains, the suddenness of events left her feeling fearful and unprepared. "I wonder how much time we have."

Khadri gazed out across the winding road for a few moments.

"I see nothing on the road as far as the rise before the Tor. After that the hills block my line of sight."

"Your far-seeing eyes will serve us well on our travels. I don't suppose you could fly out and see exactly how far this cart has still to travel?"

Khadri immediately stepped backwards, further into the room. His tail unwound from Lesana's arm and wrapped protectively around his own body.

"I... I've never flown further than the clearing between us and the dead forest. The guard below might see me! Other people might see me! It's so... so *open!*"

Lesana looked quizzically at her dragon friend.

"You're afraid of open spaces?"

Khadri dropped his gaze to the floor.

"After all, my kind are cave dwellers. I've never known the open sky. There are eagles bigger than me out there!"

Lesana thought about this new information for a moment. Her dragon had never known the open sky where the full-sized dragons could swoop down on prey from a great height, undetected until the moment of the kill. She had kept him sheltered all of his life. It was no wonder he would fear the expanse of nothingness in unsheltered skies.

"This could be challenging for you, more than me," Lesana admitted. "But the alternative is to be taken to the king, and I think neither of us can expect a satisfactory fate there. We must be daring and explore the unknown. The known... is about to collapse in on us."

Lesana tried to relax the tight feeling in her stomach. It wasn't as if she were unprepared. The tunnel she had dug under the tower would make their escape easy. She had even prepared a secret alcove for hiding things she wouldn't be able to carry with her.

"Then adventure it is," Khadri agreed. "But you'll keep me close to you, won't you? Until I get used to the outside?"

"Of course I will!" Lesana smiled and wrapped her arms around her friend, hugging him just tightly enough to show her affection without squashing his delicate flesh. "We're a team, you and I, as we have been since the day I found you. No one, not even a king, will ever come between us."

Khadri returned to the window and watched for any sign of an approaching cart while Lesana examined her books, choosing which ones were to be taken with them. Practicality decreed that few such items could be carried in a satchel and travelling light would be essential if they were to put distance between themselves and the king's laws.

The lab equipment she left in place. Let the king try to work it out himself as best he could. As an act of revenge, she took a notebook out of a drawer, saved for just such an occasion, and placed it on the shelf. It contained notes similar to her personal Alchemical notebook, but over time she had changed some of the information in a way that would increase chances of something blowing up. She smiled, imagining the first experiment that would likely explode in the greedy ruler's face.

Many of the books and some of the more exotic ingredients she definitely didn't want him to have. Though she couldn't carry them with her, the alcove in the tunnel would be hard to find even if the tunnel itself was eventually discovered. She gathered the items into her arms and left Khadri watching for the cart while she carried them down through the secret passages.

The freshly finished batch of Philosopher's Stone, meant for the king, cooled while she made her preparations. After about an hour, Khadri told her that he could see the cart approaching in the distance. She would have to hurry now. She warmed some soup and took a mug out to the guard at her door, offering it to him with a smile as if she had no objection to his former rude behaviour. He accepted it gladly, apparently never suspecting that a sedative might have been added to it before serving. She returned inside and bolted the door behind her as quietly as she could manage.

She then collected the items she had deemed essential for travel, along with Khadri and a sword that normally hung above the mantle, and threw a rope out a south-facing window to provide an explanation for how she had got out of the tower when the door was bolted. The sedated soldier had already fallen asleep. Lesana didn't envy him the punishment that would likely await him, but his treatment of her merited a little petty revenge.

The entrance to the secret tunnel was well hidden. Rather than putting a hatch in the floor like most people would do, Lesana had built a false wall that hid a door to another spiral staircase that led down into a secret room beneath the ground level. This room had a bookcase filled with nonsense occult books that any discoverer could spend years studying without learning anything of use. Only someone actually looking for a second hidden door would find the fissure at the edge of the bookcase in the dim light of a torch in the windowless basement.

Lesana tripped the hidden switch that opened the bookcase-door and descended the steps to the tunnel itself. Khadri clung to her satchel, slung across her back. With the bookcase door closed, there was no light whatsoever. Lesana had practiced going up and down these stairs in the dark many times, as well as moving through the tunnel. She knew all the false passages by touch and could move with the confidence of a blind man in familiar territory.

Outside in the forest, the afternoon sunlight dappled through the trees. The end of the escape tunnel was concealed by creeping vines within an outcrop of trees, blocking much of the light from the tunnel, but Lesana's eyes had adjusted to the complete darkness so well that the dim glow when she took the last turn towards the opening seared into her widened pupils. Her eyes squinted in the dappled daylight when they emerged at the foot of the mountains, but she knew the route into the forbidden lands from there well enough to find the way blindfolded. She had only to climb upwards.

There was no path, as humans had avoided the Crystal Mountains for hundreds of years. The incline, however, was not overly steep. Lesana felt grateful for the good leather hiking boots she always wore. Her sturdy tunic and breeches would retain warmth as well as protect against the sharp edges of the quartz boulders that gave the mountain range its name. She climbed until darkness fell, making the footing more treacherous. Lesana and Khadri ate some of the cold provisions packed in the satchel rather than catching anything that might need cooking at this early stage. Chances were that a fire would be visible from her own tower and there were probably kingsmen swarming over every inch of the place by now.

"Tell me again how you found me here in the Crystal Mountains," Khadri pleaded. "I never tire of the story."

Lesana smiled.

"I was very young," she began. "Though I'm not so old now. But I was headstrong in my teens, and though the law forbade traversing the Crystal Mountains, the stories of wondrous magic that were told in my childhood captured my imagination and I thought it wouldn't hurt to go a little way up the first mountain."

"Further than we are now?" Khadri asked.

"Half a day's walk further, though I was less strong then."

Lesana ruminated for a moment, remembering the day as if it had been yesterday.

"I passed a large crystal boulder and had begun to think I should turn back, when I heard a loud trumpeting."

Khadri moved forward, nearly into Lesana's lap.

"It had a bestial quality and I knew... I knew it could only be one creature. That the tales were true."

"A dragon!"

"Yes, a dragon," Lesana confirmed. "I ducked into the shadow of the boulder, trying to hide. That was when I saw the egg."

"My egg!" Khadri chirped. His child-like enthusiasm brought another smile to Lesana's lips.

"Yes, your egg. I was afraid that taking it would anger your mother dragon, yet it felt out of place, like it had rolled out of a nest and no one was there to care for it. I couldn't leave you there to hatch alone and possibly die. Newly hatched creatures must eat quickly, whether it is chickens or reptiles."

Khadri laid his head on Lesana's thigh, purring with affection.

"So I wrapped the egg in my scarf and made my way back down the mountain, ducking from one boulder to the next to stay out of sight of the dragon I had heard. I kept you warm, and I kept you secret. I knew the king would take you from me if he ever learned of your existence. Then when I was given the tower to practice my Arts, I took you there and have kept you safe ever since."

"And I learned to be very still whenever people visit, so they think I'm just a statue!"

Lesana nodded.

"It's a great skill you have there. I'm sure it saved us many times."

Lesana wrapped her cloak over the little dragon and leaned back against the boulder where they had sheltered.

"We should sleep now and hope it doesn't rain. There was no time to pack a folding shelter, and it would have slowed us to carry so much."

They slept curled up together, though every noise in the night caused Lesana to wake enough to identify the noise before drifting off to sleep again. At first light, they awoke and prepared to continue their journey. They ate sparingly of their remaining provisions, knowing they would have to crest the first peak before risking a fire.

They hiked ever upwards, speaking little. Eventually they came to a large crystal boulder that stood taller than the others around them and Lesana stopped, stroking the smooth quartz rock.

"This is the one!" she announced. "The crystal I hid behind... where I found your egg!"

Khadri regarded the massive rock, reflecting the late morning sunlight.

"Then this is where my story began..." Lesana heard a wistful note in Khadri's voice, but the next words they heard were considerably coarse and loutish.

"And this is where it ends. I reckon the king'll reward me plenty when he sees what I found here!"

The kingsman whom Lesana had left sleeping off her drugged soup looked at Khadri with the gleam of pure greed in his eyes.

"You didn't think I'd really drunk your soup, did ya? Why, that's the oldest trick in the book. I poured it out as soon as you was in the door and pretended to sleep so's you'd try to get past me. Only you never came out. How did you slip by, I wonder? And where did you find that young fella?" He gestured towards Khadri, probably mistaking him for a baby dragon, Lesana speculated, worth a small fortune as no one was mad enough to breach the realm of the dragons, even for greed.

"Wizards have their secrets," was all Lesana offered in response.

"Not for long," the man growled. "The king wants *all* your secrets and he has his ways of getting them."

Torture! Lesana kept the thought to herself. There was one way out of this. She drew her sword. He was one man, though others would no doubt follow soon. Lesana was tall for a woman, but chances were the trained swordsman would underestimate her skills for no other reason than that she was a woman. It might even the field for a self-taught swordswoman.

The man laughed. *Good*, Lesana thought. His dismissive attitude might well spell his doom. Khadri flitted from her shoulder to a perch on the crystal boulder, still eyeing the open sky suspiciously.

With her arms free to swing now, Lesana felt emboldened.

"Let us pass or die!" She tried to make the threat sound convincing, despite the kingsman's laughter. She took a defensive stance, unwilling to make the first move.

"You will do neither," he jeered, deliberately misinterpreting the sentence. "The king wants you alive." He stepped forward and reached as if he would simply take the sword out of Lesana's hand. That level of condescension nearly lost him an arm when Lesana swung the weapon with all her strength. The move changed his attitude quickly. He crouched and brought his own sword up, blocking her swing. Lesana, anticipating the block, adjusted the trajectory of her heavy blade into a circular motion that rang loudly as the swords connected, metal against metal, and gave her the chance to step uphill from him as the blades released each other.

It wasn't so much the advantage of high ground she sought as having got past him, even a few steps away. Khadri could fly to join her if only they could rid themselves of this human obstacle. As if he heard the thought, Khadri breathed flame onto the back of the man's helm. He couldn't make much of a fiery stream, but it was enough to heat the metal and distract the man while Lesana took a few more steps up the mountain.

He turned and took a swing at the little dragon. Lesana nearly panicked at the danger to her friend and took one step forward, her eyes wide in fear. Khadri launched from his perch and flew in an arc, landing back on Lesana's shoulder. The pack with the few items they had brought still lay on the ground, unregarded, but getting away from this man took precedence over everything. Lesana's only regret was a notebook with her most important Alchemical recipes in it, but at least it was in code and no one would ever be able to read it.

The man threw the heated helm off, revealing a few scraggly hairs, thoroughly singed. The murderous look he gave Lesana and Khadri chilled her, but she took a defensive stance again as he charged up the hill, shouting in some sort of guttural Berserker roar. She knew she was outmatched, but still she brought the sword up just a little higher, preparing to swing.

Suddenly the man stopped. His eyes widened and his jaw dropped. At the same moment, Lesana heard a sound that hadn't assaulted her ears since that day when she had found Khadri's egg. Only this time it wasn't distant. The trumpeting dragon sounded as if it were right behind her.

The stench of excrement permeated the morning mist. Lesana wasn't sure if it was coming from the man or herself. All she knew was that she had a primal urge to *run!*

Don't move. The voice inside her mind was unmistakably Khadri's. Despite the instruction, Lesana slowly lowered her sword and turned. She kept her feet planted in place. The massive bronze creature sat further up the mountain than Lesana expected. The sound of its voice had carried so efficiently that the mountain had gone still, completely silent. All the wild creatures had either hidden or run away. There was no time to determine which.

The kingsman dropped his sword as if it burned his hands, then he turned and ran, whimpering like a frightened child.

Don't move. Khadri's voice repeated inside Lesana's mind. She saw the majestic dragon launch from its perch into the sky, then it plummeted directly towards the man running down the hill. The unpleasant stench had receded with him, to Lesana's relief. She didn't want to die with the indignity of soiling herself.

One gulp later, the man was no more, but the dragon wheeled about in the sky, returning to Lesana's position.

Trust me, Khadri voiced inside Lesana's head. *Stay right where you are.*

Lesana obeyed, resisting her instinct to hide or escape. Then she looked around herself, her gaze attracted by the glitter of scales. More dragons had appeared while she had watched the kingsman's doom. At least twenty, maybe more, perched in a circle among the outcroppings of the Crystal Mountains. Lesana felt her vulnerability in the centre of their formation, yet she couldn't help appreciating their beauty.

The dragons varied in colour, ranging from reds to greens and even an iridescent purple glint from a dark dragon who looked almost black. All of them glittered in the morning sunlight. Lesana was painfully aware that no human had ever seen such a magnificent display and lived to tell about it. This, at least, presented a suitable vision for a magician to take to her grave.

Suddenly Khadri trumpeted, much like the big dragon, far too close to Lesana's ear. She cringed in pain from the sudden volume.

Sorry, the apology came unspoken.

How do I hear you in my thoughts? Lesana was not sure Khadri would hear her, but it was worth a try.

I have always heard your thoughts, Khadri responded. *As do they.*

Lesana tucked that piece of information away for later, in case there might be a 'later'.

I won't make much of a meal for so many, she thought towards her dragon friend.

You're my human. They won't attempt to take you from me. It's time to move to higher ground. Men are coming. Get the pack.

Lesana had to fight every instinct she had to follow Khadri's instructions, but her perfect trust in him compelled her to pick up her satchel and pretend to herself that it was perfectly alright to be surrounded by dragons on the bare face of a quartz mountain where no place to hide was likely to present itself. More difficult was the act of walking uphill, towards the waiting dragons.

That impediment resolved itself when the sound of a mob of shouting, angry men coming towards the mountain brought a concerted reaction from the gathered *Draconis Maximus*. They launched as one, trumpeting their battle cry and flying into an aerial formation that gave the impression of a well-practiced manoeuvre.

Lesana didn't turn, but kept walking up the mountain as fast as she could without exhausting herself. The thought that the dragons would come back, probably soon, made her falter once. She stumbled sideways, nearly falling.

You won't see them. When those screams of dying men fall silent, my brethren will not allow you to see them again.

They're going to let us pass?

I've explained you as a sort of pet. They don't exactly approve, but they won't interfere.

Later, after the day's walking took them beyond the crest of the first mountain, Lesana and Khadri stopped and made a camp fire. Khadri hunted and caught a wild rabbit for Lesana to cook.

"Why have you never mentioned you could read my mind, Khadri?" Lesana turned the roasting meat on the metal spit she had brought for just this purpose.

"It was just something normal to me," Khadri replied. If a dragon could shrug, Lesana had the impression that Khadri just had.

"But speaking mind to mind.."

"Useful, isn't it?" Khadri interrupted. "I didn't know I could do that until the big dragons showed me."

"Oh, I see." Lesana thought about this for a moment. Khadri had, after all, grown up apart from his own kind.

"I hope I didn't..." she began, then rephrased her thoughts. "Have you ever wished you could live among the other dragons?"

"And not have you?" The answer was so quick that Lesana couldn't doubt the little dragon's sincerity. "They invited me, but I don't think I would fit in with them."

"Because you're little?"

"No, because of what the bronze dragon said to me, mind to mind."

"Do they speak our language?"

"Not exactly," Khadri tried to explain. "The concepts are the same, but it comes across more in visual thoughts."

"What did the dragon actually say to you?"

"Well..." Khadri prevaricated, pretending to look for the right words.

"Go on," Lesana insisted. "I've faced my potentially messy death today. I'm not going to be sensitive about how a dragon phrases things."

Khadri turned and looked Lesana in the eye.

"If I were to put it into words, basically what he said was *'Eat the human and be welcomed back among dragon kind.'* I politely told him no thank you."

Lesana felt the blood leave her face. Though small for a dragon, Khadri was big and heavy enough that he could no doubt overpower her if he had a mind to do so. It was only the love and trust between them that had kept her from becoming dragon lunch long since.

She took a deep breath and remembered that love and trust, as well as the fact that he would have seen her momentary reaction in her mind.

"I'm glad you were polite," was all she said.

They curled up together to sleep after sharing the rabbit feast, all thoughts of danger forgotten. Whatever future they faced, at least now they were free.

THE END

Count Vlasko's Curse

Paul Michael

"So Miss Henderson, were you in domestic service before your time with the Jennings family?" asked the man behind the huge desk.

"Oh no, Mr Smith," said Miss Felicity Henderson, "that was the first time I was domesticated."

The man who was taking notes looked up at this and glanced at Mr Smith.

"I see," said Mr Smith, with a look of mild confusion, "and may I ask why you wish to leave, as by all accounts it sounds like a very agreeable position?"

"Oh, it surely is," said Miss Henderson, "but I dream of bigger things. A chance like this, to be a maid in the great house of Count Blasto…"

"Vlasko," corrected Mr Smith.

"Vlasko," continued Miss Henderson, "would be truly exciting for me."

Mr Smith sat back and his partner stopped writing.

"Miss Henderson," said the man cautiously, "it is 'miss', isn't it? I have a slightly delicate question. Do you mind if I ask?"

Miss Henderson nodded approval.

"We have had situations where girls have joined the staff and have then, er, become attached to men," said the man. "They then marry and leave us bereft. So forgive me, but I need to ask about your marital situation. Are you… do you have an understanding with a gentleman?"

Miss Henderson looked down.

"It is true to say that I have a good gentleman friend, who does from time to time take me to nice places. But," she hesitated, "...but I have to say that we are not presently, or indeed ever likely to be, understood."

"Well, Miss Henderson," said Mr Smith, "do you have any questions to ask us?"

"Yes, if I may be a trifle forward," said Miss Henderson, "I have heard that Count… Vlasko is troubled by daylight, is that true? I'm only asking to make sure that I don't make any mistakes if I were lucky enough to receive an offer."

"Count Vlasko is, tragically, afflicted with a rare disease that affects his skin," said Mr Smith. "He cannot bear even the smallest hint of daylight. Also, he cannot be near garlic, for he is allergic to that. But Miss Henderson, whilst your concern to your service does you credit, there is no need to be alarmed. Full and proper training will be provided."

"Thank you Mr Smith," said Miss Henderson. "I have no further questions."

"Then we are pleased to say we can offer you the role," said Mr Smith. "Please report to this office on Monday."

Just then, a girl came in with a tray of water glasses.

"There's no need, Jane," said Mr Smith snippily. "We've just concluded here."

"But the lady may be thirsty," said Jane with a trembling voice.

She moved directly over to Miss Henderson and passed her a glass. Her hand shook a little as she did and she leaned forward.

"Go! Leave this place," Jane whispered into Miss Henderson's ear. "Go and don't ever return."

§ § §

Next Monday Miss Henderson was in a room in the Vlasko house with another girl. They had both been fitted out with maids' uniforms although Miss Henderson's was a little small for her. Apparently, they didn't usually recruit maids of Miss Henderson's height. A young woman walked into the room wearing a dark dress.

"Now then girls," she said breezily, "My name is Miss Shaw, although you may call me Gertie. I'm here to train you girls up. You see, you may be used to domestic service, but you will have to learn the ways of the Vlasko household."

They spent the next couple of hours walking around the giant house. It truly was one of the finest in London, although Miss Henderson noticed that they only seemed to see part of it. They walked round in a big circle and Miss Henderson felt sure that there was a central part they hadn't seen.

"Are you alright, Felicity?" whispered the other maid being trained, a pale girl called Alice. "You look like you're limping."

"These stockings are a little tight," said Miss Henderson. "It makes it a little difficult to walk."

As the trainee maids continued their tour, Miss Henderson saw Jane from the interview coming towards them. Miss Henderson gave a discreet wave to the girl, but she passed by ignoring the gesture, looking glassy eyed and listless.

Gertie coughed loudly to get the attention of the girls. She stood in front of a large, black, ornate door facing into the centre of the house. On either side of the door were huge internal windows obscured on the inside by black drapes.

"This door," she said, "is the entrance to Count Vlasko's private quarters. This area is completely off limits to you girls for now. Well, that completes our tour. Please return to the servants' office for further training and I will see you later."

As Miss Henderson and the others headed back the way they came, a tall, pale man with a square forehead opened the gigantic black door. From inside the room he gestured to Gertie to come in.

"No!" said Gertie, "I mean, I'm doing the training. I was promised… Not now, please."

The man gestured again. Gertie swallowed hard and went through the door.

Alice giggled.

"What was that about?" she asked.

§ § §

The next day Alice and Miss Henderson were starting the job in earnest. They found themselves on dusting duty, wandering along the corridors.

"Such a grand house!" said Alice. "I've never seen such a place."

"That's probably why they need so much staff," said Miss Henderson. "The advert is always in The Evening Standard."

"I know!" said Alice. "I was going to ask about that, but I thought I'd better not. They sort of told me anyway, apparently a lot of the girls get married. They even asked me about it in the interview."

"Me too," said Miss Henderson, still limping like yesterday. She knocked into a table and there was a sound of a metallic chink. Alice's eyes widened.

"What was that noise?" she asked.

"It's nothing," said Miss Henderson. Alice quickly ran round her new friend and tapped the side of her maid's outfit. There was a metal ring.

"Is that - a hip flask?" whispered Alice grinning. "They'll throw you out if they see that."

"It's just water," hissed Miss Henderson, "in case I get thirsty."

"Is this your first house?" asked Alice. "I mean were you in service before?"

"I was," said Miss Henderson, "but in a much smaller household. It was just me, a part-time cook and a vacancy for a parlour maid that never got filled."

"Why didn't it get filled?" asked Alice. "It seems easy enough to find domestic staff."

"Well the family was away a lot on… business," said Miss Henderson. "How about you, this isn't your first time I think?"

"No," said Alice, "I was in a grand old country house with a very wealthy family. But my sister just gave birth to her first one, and her husband is away in the army. So I came back to help. She can use both the rent and the spare pair of hands."

"You're a good sister," said Miss Henderson.

"Anyone would do it," Alice shrugged.

"Do you miss the country?" asked Miss Henderson.

"A little, but this is such a glamorous job and I like seeing my little nephew, so I don't mind so much," said Alice.

The pair found themselves outside the ornate door.

"Bit creepy, ain't it?" said Alice.

Miss Henderson looked closer at the carvings on the black wood. There was a strange tableau of demonic faces, peculiar creatures and cowering humans.

"A bit," she said. "Alice, why don't you dust over there, away from the door a bit. I'll do it here."

"You don't have to ask me twice!" said Alice and the two women started dusting quickly, glancing nervously at the door from time to time,

Presently the door swung open and both maids jumped. The same tall man that had appeared the day before stood behind the door and said, "You." Alice looked round to see the man pointing to Miss Henderson.

"In," said the man. Miss Henderson looked at Alice.

"Wish me luck," she said before going into the room. Alice dusted as quickly as she could to get away from the terrible door.

§ § §

The room was vast. It was so dark it was hard to see how vast, but Miss Henderson reckoned it must have taken up half the house. There was a smell of dirt and the sound of strange groans. In the center of the room was a large white throne on which sat the Count. Surrounding it in all directions were young girls in a state of undress, writhing and moaning. Miss Henderson looked around and one face caught her eye. She looked back to the throne and saw the Count beckon to her. Miss Henderson walked over to the throne.

"Hello, my pretty one," said the Count. "You're nice and tall, you'll fit in well with my brides."

His hand gestured to the sea of women.

"Yes," said Miss Henderson, absently.

"Come closer," he said, "so you may join them. Come closer so you may receive my gift."

"Yes," said Miss Henderson again and walked slowly over to the throne. The Count took the front of her dress and ripped it open to expose her neck and shoulders. Two sharp fangs grew in his mouth and saliva dripped from them.

"It is time," he said, staring into Miss Henderson's eyes and glanced down at her neck.

"What is that?" he said, looking at a small pendant.

"It's a surprise," said Miss Henderson. "As is this."

She reached under her skirt and produced the hip flask. With a quick turn of her wrist, the top came off and she threw the contents at the Count. He screamed as the water steamed and burned on his face.

"And good things come in threes," said Miss Henderson, "so here's another surprise."

She pulled a wooden stake out of her stocking and plunged it into the Count's heart.

"No!" he screamed as she gave one final push. There was a bright flash of light and when it had gone all that remained of the Count was a bleached white skeleton.

Voices started screaming round the room so Miss Henderson headed for the wall. She found one of the drapes and pulled hard. Sunlight flooded the room and she saw the tall pale man and others like him burning in its light.

Miss Henderson ran around the room flinging open the drapes. The girls in the room were emerging from their trance.

"What the bloody hell's going on?" said one.

"Where am I? Where are my clothes?" said another.

Miss Henderson found the face she had seen earlier and grabbed the girl by the hand.

"Come on Elsie," she said, "We're getting out of here."

Miss Henderson pulled her friend to the big ornate door and out of the room.

"Felicity?" said Elsie. "What's going on? What happened?"

"I'll explain later," said Miss Henderson. "We need to get out of here before people arrive and ask questions. But we're making one stop first.

Miss Henderson took her friend down to the servants' office. Mr Smith was there frantically loading a pistol. He looked up at Miss Henderson and her friend.

"You!" he said, "I might have guessed. Well, Missy I have bad news for…"

He didn't manage to finish the sentence as Miss Henderson punched him in the head, knocking him out cold. She then rifled through the desk drawers.

"What are you looking for, Felicity?" asked Elsie.

"This," said Miss Henderson, pushing a wad of money into her friend's hand. "Back pay."

Miss Henderson looked at the drawer again, shrugged and took a smaller sum.

"And severance pay," she said before taking her friend's hand once more. However, Elsie stood stock still.

"Felicity Henderson," Elsie said, "you tell me what is happening right this instant or I ain't going nowhere."

Miss Henderson sighed.

"So three weeks ago we were having a nice cup of tea and you were telling me about this wonderful new job you had with this Count Vlasko chap."

"Three weeks?" said Elsie. "No that were…"

"Three weeks ago," said Miss Henderson. "Whatever it seems to you. Then I heard nothing from you. Not a sausage. So I did a little research, and a little thinking and made a few acquisitions. Some holy water, a stake, some other little things. I got a job myself and I came looking for you. It seems you've somehow been hypnotised or mesmerised and you've spent some weeks as one of the so-called brides of Count Vlasko who is, or was, a vampire."

"Oh my gawd," said Elsie.

"And so now I've disposed of the aforementioned villain, and his henchman, have acquired suitable back pay for you and am trying to get you out of the building before the coppers come along and your reputation is in as many tatters as your clothes."

Elsie looked down at her outfit.

"Oh my gawd," she said.

"So can we go now, please?" said Miss Henderson.

Elsie nodded once and they ran out of the building.

Sir John and Marie Jennings were entertaining their acquaintance Detective John Symonds in the drawing room of their modest Southampton Row house. Miss Henderson came in with a tray of tea for everyone.

"Feli... Miss Henderson," said Symonds. "So good to see you! How was your trip to Cornwall, did it rain much?"

"Oh no, the weather was very fine..." said Miss Henderson.

"Oh, the paper said it was foul," said Sir John.

"...last Tuesday," finished Miss Henderson. "For an hour. Or so."

"Well, it's rather pleasant to see you back Feli... Miss Henderson," said Symonds. "Might you be free this weekend for a little jaunt on a boat?"

Miss Henderson and the detective both looked at Sir John, who looked puzzled. Marie gave him a little kick.

"Oh yes, of course!" he said.

"Oh, by the way," said Miss Henderson, "I found that pendant that you were looking for. It fell down the back of the dresser."

"Oh bravo, Miss Henderson," said Sir John, before turning to Symonds. "It's reputed to be able to repel mind control. I'm not sure how we test that theory, though."

Sir John glanced down at the newspaper. On the front page was a story page about mysterious goings on at Count Vlasko's townhouse.

"Do you know anything about this," said Sir John, "the paper is full of hints of all kinds of strange behaviour but no detail."

"Didn't your friend work there?" said Marie to Miss Henderson. "Elizabeth?"

"I believe Elsie declined the offer in the end," said Miss Henderson. "The pay was beneath her expectoration."

Sir John looked puzzled.

"The problem was her expectation?" he asked.

"No," said Miss Henderson, "her health is fine."

"That's a stroke of luck for her," said Symonds, "I wasn't on the case, but it's all over Scotland Yard. I heard the most fantastic stories..."

He leaned forward as if to speak but then glanced at Marie and Miss Henderson.

"Although, perhaps, another time," he said.

Marie smiled and sat back with her crochet as Miss Henderson took the empty tea tray from the room.

"Oh," said Miss Henderson as she walked out the door, "I've found a suitable parlour maid for the household. A Miss Alice Cribble. She comes highly recommended."

THE END

Red, the Wolf (Part 1)

Leslie Conzatti

Deep among the craggy peaks of a mountain, far enough to be out of the range of normal human hearing, a young woman dragged herself into the safety of a secure cave. Wounds on her arms and side oozed blood. Anyone in her condition would not be able to move very far, but she did. Sinking with a heavy sigh onto a pallet of pelts, she pulled a squat jar out of a cleft in the rocks and scooped some of the healing ointment onto her fingertips. She spread it over the wounds, gritting her teeth against the searing pain. She kept going until every scratch and scrape had been tended, and only then did she allow her body to relax, curling up in the pelts and closing her eyes to rest and heal from the day's ordeal.

§ § §

The village of Queston sat well-protected in a wide, flat valley in the midst of tall mountains. Many tradespeople and farming folk lived there, raising their families in relative peace. They were dependent on people from the villages below willing to travel up the crags and slopes for the things their own hands and skill could not provide.

One such traveler was Schoolmaster Remani. The tall, lean scholar made the trek up the mountain every year just after harvest time. He taught the children how to read and figure for six months while the winter prevented him from leaving, and then headed back down to his own village when the paths cleared.

Today marked the Schoolmaster's return to Queston, and the whole town buzzed with excitement. No one knew the precise hour, but he had sent a letter ahead from the inn at the bottom of the mountain. It informed them that he hoped to arrive at midday, so everyone desired to be ready for him.

The wives and older ladies set out a sumptuous array of pies, cakes, cookies, and sandwiches upon tables the men had built. Young women decked the walkways and windows with flowers. The young men climbed ladders and drove nails to hang colorful streamers and a banner that read WELCOME SCHOOLMASTER!

Red favored her sore hip and arm as she milled about the town. She didn't care to interact with the villagers on a regular basis, leading them to depend on one another for wildly-exaggerated stories of her prowess and valor. (Not that she minded what they said about her in her absence, but she tired of refuting it in person.) In spite of this, every so often she liked to take a quiet, close-up inspection of the town she guarded so carefully. Those who had interacted with her in the past gave a subdued smile and nod, while the others mostly left the strange, caped figure alone.

The town had been built along and around many of the natural cliffs and mountainsides, and the valley floor served as a sort of central square for the residents. Everyone climbed up and down the narrow pathways that would seem treacherous to anyone who hadn't lived here their whole lives

The 'Town Square', as it was known, had nearly filled with tables and chairs. There were all manner of well-designed boards for games, such as a bean-bag or ring toss. There were horseshoe-tossing games, wool crafts, painting displays, and a set of raised platforms where the older children were just warming up to sing their welcome song for the returning Schoolmaster.

Red wandered over to the refreshment tables, where she saw the familiar, warm, round face of Mrs. Garrity, a peace-loving goodwife who never hesitated to treat Red as one of her own daughters.

Now, she unloaded baskets of clean linens and heavy silver serving dishes, getting ready for the food that came down from the cliffs in small groups. She stopped in the process of setting out a collection of pewter drinking cups next to an assortment of metal pitchers and crystal punch bowls to greet the red-caped woman.

"Oh, Red, dear! So good to see you up and about. Word has already gotten around about what you did for Burch and his boys this morning. Facing off against the white wolf, yet again! He didn't scratch you this time, I hope?" Her practiced eyes traveled down the long cloak concealing Red's body.

Red grit her teeth against the pain and smiled for the old woman's benefit. "Not too badly, I'm glad to say--just a few nips here and there. I came down to see if you had any more of that magical salve you gave me last winter." She reached into her pocket and pulled out the jar she carried there. "I have enough for today, but I'll need more, for the next time danger strikes."

Mrs. Garrity nodded emphatically. "Oh, indeed! I'm sure I still have plenty of tins in my larder. I can spare one or two for our resident guardian" She chuckled and moved over to another basket, unloading the odds and ends and placing them on the table

Red's nose twitched as she picked up a whiff of something important. "What about you, Mrs. Garrity?" she began casually. "How are things at home? You seem quite a bit more tired than usual."

The blue eyes came up twinkling. "How did you--oh! Never you mind!" Mrs. Garrity waved a hand and let her trembling hands fidget with her apron. "I'm all right, the house is just as lively as ever!"

Red smiled, and took the matron by the hand. "Deborah," she chided her as a peer, not a parent, "I can *smell* your fatigue. Don't try to hide it from me."

Mrs. Garrity gave a nervous giggle. "My, my!" she clucked her tongue, "What a keen nose you have there, Lady Red!" She pulled away and returned to the basket on the table, carefully counting out each item she retrieved.

Red came to stand next to her, placing a gentle hand on her shoulder. "The better to sniff out signs of distress or danger, my dear," she murmured softly. "Tell me, why do you push yourself so hard?"

The older woman set down the silver cruet in her hands and gave a sigh that weighed on her whole body. "If you must know," she said softly, "it's Henny. She's not a problem, don't look like that! It's just that... Well, you know how she was always my right hand, always waiting at my side and helping with absolutely everything I did--oh, it gave her such pleasure to be working along with me! But since she graduated from the Schoolmaster's lessons, last harvest season, she applied for an apprenticeship at Bethany's dress shop. learning about designing and materials and all manner of sewing and tailoring."

Red's brow creased. "And this troubles you?" She didn't see anything wrong with a young woman learning the skills for a profitable trade.

"Not at all," Mrs. Garrity wagged her head. "It's just that she spends so much time at the shop, and I don't want to interfere with this good work she is doing, but at the same time, I've got the young ones to tend to, as well as the duties of the house, and all the other things--I really miss her sometimes!"

But she said this last with a small laugh, letting the younger woman know that it really wasn't a terrible situation, but a frazzled one.

"Ah, here we are!" the goodwife cried, pulling out a small crock of a thick, golden paste. She handed it to Red. "There, dear--that will keep you right as rain till after the festival, when I can get more for you."

Red took the crock and tucked it away in the pocket of her cloak. From the way her side was beginning to ache again, she would need to reapply soon. "Thank you, Deborah," she murmured. "I hope all goes well for your party."

Mrs. Garrity's mouth bent into a small frown. "Why, aren't you going to stay?"

The cloaked young woman chuckled. "Only you could ever convince me to forget my disdain for socializing!" she mused. "But I think it would be best for me to rest and heal while everyone is happy and peaceful, so that I can be ready for the next time danger strikes."

Mrs. Garrity gave a wistful sigh. "Oh, you and your Lone Wolf ways!"

Red reached out and took the old woman's hand. "At least I always know exactly where to go when things get too lonesome."

Her words brought a smile to Deborah Garrity's face, and Red took her leave.

She ducked into the alleyway beside the dressmaker's store--and nearly pitched head-first as she tripped over a body laying there.

"Oh my!"

"Watch out!"

Make that two bodies. Red sprawled on the ground, but her reflexes allowed her to gather her feet under her at least. Only her wrists smarted from where she had banged them on the rough corner of an empty crate used for transporting materials

She gathered herself and turned to face the two people in the alley as a young man helped a young lady to her feet

"Henny!" Red gasped, recognizing the woman.

Henny Garrity bit her lip and ducked behind the dishevelled young man--Red recalled seeing him up in the pasture only this morning. What were they doing here?

"Hullo, Lady Red," Henny murmured politely.

"Why don't you watch where you're going?" growled the man. "We'd like a little privacy, if you don't mind! Be on your way!"

Red detected something in the edges of his voice, and she studied him closely. Did he not realize who she was? Just how much 'privacy' did they think they would have in an open alleyway where anyone might choose to walk?

"Marc!" Henny murmured, tugging on his sleeve, "Let's just go..."

A warm, heady scent wafted off of the two young people, and Red grew keenly aware of the sheen across their faces. Come to think of it, she recognized his scent, from previous visits to the village--among other places. Her hackles rose. Privacy, indeed!

She glared at Henny. "*So this* is the tailoring business you've been spending all your time at, while your *mother*, bless her soul, is working herself to the bone so that you might be able to make something of yourself!"

Marc's face twisted into a scowl, and he stepped forward. "Now see here--"

"What I do is my own business, thank you!" Henny piped up, lifting her copper-brown eyes defiantly to meet Red's gaze. "You don't know anything about how hard I work, nor how much Marc cares for me!"

"*Cares* for you?" Red grabbed the man by the arm and shoved him aside, not quite throwing him, but hard enough to separate the two. "If you think that, girl, then you're fooling yourself. I can tell just by *looking* at him that he means you no goodwill!"

Marc tried to interfere, but Red arrested him with an upraised hand.

Henny, meanwhile, gave a harsh laugh. "Oh my! What sharp eyes you have, to see such horrible flaws in people!"

Red didn't break eye contact with the defiant maiden. "All the better to see through a predator's lies, my dear," she quipped.

"Who are you calling predator?" Marc retorted, reaching for Henny's hand again. "Don't listen to her, Hen. You know me better than anyone, I will always--"

Red grabbed him by the arm, and this time, she didn't bother holding back her strength. He grazed the side of the building and tumbled into the stack of crates. "Spare her the deception, you dog. This is not the first daughter of Queston you've tried on in the last few years, any more than you're her first 'trim on the side'!"

"How dare you!" Henny squealed, but Red kept going, pointing at the two of them, on either side of her.

"Don't think I don't know everything that goes on in these trees! What would Burch say if he knew--"

Marc arose with clenched fists. "I don't see how it's any of your business!" He planted his feet, crouching into a fighting stance.

Red folded her arms. "Everything to do with Queston is my business!"

She didn't bother bracing, standing defiantly before his threatening posture. "So, what did you promise her this time? A tiny flock, a quiet home, faraway in some other valley where you will only have yourselves to look after?"

The events of that morning returned to her mind in perfect detail: the specks she found on the wool of some lambs, but not others--most likely paint or ink, and *not* a coincidence. In fact, now that she thought of it, the herd did seem to shrink every time the white wolf struck, even when there was no sign of an attack at all. "How many of the village lambs have you already marked for yourself, poacher? Too bad that wolf killed the bellwether this morning, or you would have been able to abscond with half the flock before anyone no--"

The heavy fist launched toward her face while she was still talking. Red ducked a little too late, so the blow aiming for the center of her head caught her in the cheek, knocking her backward.

Henny screamed, *"Don't hurt her!"*

"That's enough, meddling shrew!" Marc snarled, standing over the red-caped woman. "You might have the whole of Queston eating out of your flea-bitten hands, but I'm nobody's fool! I'm getting what the old man owes me!"

Red braced herself with her hand and pushed back onto her feet. She wiped the trickle of blood off her lip with the back of her palm. "If you think that, then you're the biggest fool of them all!"

Outside, in the square, the band struck up and people raised a cheer for the long-awaited arrival of Schoolmaster Remani. The noise out there covered the sounds of the scuffle from the alley.

Red pushed off with her legs and launched her body right at Marc's center of gravity, slamming him into the building. He threw another punch, but she dodged it and sent him a blow of her own, catching him full in the side. He grabbed her hood and yanked it off her head, but that only exposed her infuriated face and gave her greater advantage to be able to shove him again. Back and forth they wrestled, Marc having the advantage of height and weight, but Red able to evade him thanks to wolf-like reflexes and a cunning knowledge of the most vulnerable areas to hit.

Henny crouched behind a large crate, shaking and blubbering. Red had shed her cloak, for the sake of the valuable jar in her pocket. She focused on evading Marc's blows and wearing him down with small, close hits while he flailed angrily. The fight changed when he produced a knife from somewhere and faked a lunge that Red followed. This mistake left her shoulder exposed to the blade.

Red roared with the pain as blood spread from the tear in her sleeve.

"Ha!" Marc grunted. "The fabled super-wolf-witch *bleeds* like an animal, too! Guess you aren't as all-powerful as--"

With a snarl, Red reached over and pulled the blade out with her opposite hand, gritting her teeth and grabbing the hilt in her injured hand. She howled with rage as she sprang toward the man, slamming her good arm against his throat. In two quick movements she slashed the side of his leg, and shoved the blade straight in, perilously close to his side--but it only caught his shirt and bit deep into the wooden siding behind him. He squirmed and gurgled as she pressed on his windpipe, but he couldn't move.

Red scowled at him and spoke slowly, through bared teeth. "Get. Off. My. Mountain. If I ever see your tracks around here again, if I so much as smell your stench on a westerly wind, I will personally hunt you down and then we will see how you stand against a *real* wolf!" She stepped back and picked up her cloak, tying it around her shoulders with one hand as she let her wounded arm hang still by her side.

Marc gasped and coughed as he recovered from the chokehold, and it took most of his strength to rip his shirt away from the blade--and yet it never moved, sticking there with a piece of his shirt hanging from it. Red didn't tear her eyes away as Marc stumbled off into the hills, away from Queston.

Her shoulder felt like it was on fire, but Red knew there was one more matter of business to attend to.

She turned to the quivering, snivelling girl still huddled behind the crate. "And as for you, Hepsibah Moriah Garrity--"

Henny sprang out of hiding at the sound of her full name. She couldn't even stand upright, but she grovelled at Red's feet, reaching for her hand.

She pled, with tears running down her face, "Oh, please don't hurt me! And don't tell mother--I'll do anything you want me to!"

Red put her good hand on her hip and snorted. "Seems to me you are entirely too eager to do things for other people, when they don't require too much effort from you!" She shook her head and held out her hand, helping the young girl to her feet.

"As a matter of fact, Henny," she continued, "this is what I want you to do: you will walk straight back into the dressmaker's shop; you will apologize to Bethany, and you will do everything she asks; when you are finished there, you will go straight home and apologize to your mother also--and you will do whatever *she* asks of you, and give her the rest she deserves. This will be your life for the rest of the year, and I had better not see you anywhere but exactly where you ought to be..."

Henny's eyes widened, and her mouth dropped open as Red listed the requirements. She cringed as Red delivered her ultimatum.

"Or what? Are you going to hunt me down like you threatened to do to Marc?"

Red gave a thin, firm smile. "No; I'll simply tell your mother *and* your employer exactly what kind of 'tailoring' business you've been running behind their backs this whole time."

Henny gasped and clapped both hands to her cheeks. "You wouldn't--you *cannot*--Oh!" She pulled a pouting frown and stamped her foot. "What big teeth you have, you savage *wolf!*"

Red grinned, showing all her teeth, adding special weight to her words as she replied, "All the better to deal with anything and anyone that would threaten the safety of this village... *my dear.*" She said this last in a deep, rumbling growl.

Henny scurried out of the alley as fast as she could go.

Only when she stood alone in the alley did Red allow her face to display the grimace of pain that had remained just below the surface. Her shoulder screamed at her, while her back threatened to seize up, with the strain she put on the still-fresh wounds. She limped over to her discarded cloak and picked it up to grab the jar secreted within. She applied a small daub of Mrs. Garrity's ointment to the wound and tore a small strip of her own tunic to bind it. She would need to return to her cave right away to bind it better, but at least this would hold long enough for her to get there.

Behind her, the townspeople celebrated, sang, cheered, and chatted with one another as the party swelled to full strength. Red allowed herself a small smile of satisfaction in knowing that they could revel in safety, thanks to her.

THE END

Red, the Wolf (Part 2)

Leslie Conzatti

While Red confronted the couple behind the dressmaker's shop, a commotion at the valley wall attracted attention that way. All eyes watched as a boy burst into view, running full-tilt and waving his hat as he shouted.

"Wagon, ho! I saw a wagon! A wagon is coming this way!"

A wave of excitement rippled through the townspeople.

"Is it the Schoolmaster already?" one woman asked another.

"I hope not! The cakes aren't quite finished yet!" her neighbor responded.

Gradually the noise ceased as everyone caught the rattle and creak of a wagon echoing off the cliffs of the mountainside, and the noise settled so that a clear, ringing voice was heard.

"*...and the maiden fair danced light and free, and the maiden fair danced free!*"

The horse trotted into view, and a few villagers turned away with disappointed sighs. Others resumed their tasks with sighs of relief. It wasn't Schoolmaster Remani after all, but one of the regular peddlers who trekked up the mountain, a rover by the name of Justin. Though he only passed through the mountain villages a handful of times per year, Old Justin was as much a staple among the people of Queston as the swarthy band of shepherds. He kept his beard only a small patch of hair at his chin, and an impressive, slender mustache that spread straight out over his lip, and his twinkling eyes betrayed no guile as he politely nodded to everyone he passed.

His presence never failed to excite the children. They came running as he pulled his wagon to a halt.

"The Peddler! The Peddler!" they cried

"Have you brought us new toys?" one eager boy asked.

Justin chuckled as he climbed down from his seat. He held out his hands to greet the children.

"Have I?" He answered the little boy. "Let me tell you, the whirligigs I've collected in my wagon are guaranteed to give you *hours* of fun!"

He pulled an object out of the back of his wagon. "Let me show you," he said, kneeling in the dirt. He placed the thing on the ground before them, a metal object shaped like some four-legged monster with a key in its back. Justin gave the key a few twists, and something rattled inside the monster. With a series of stiff jerks, the monster began to move by itself, waving its claws in the air. It pinged and crackled as tiny sparks burst from its jaws.

"A dragon!" Squealed a young boy, and all the children laughed and clapped.

Justin rocked on his heels and gestured to the decorations.

"This looks mighty auspicious!" he declared. "What's the occasion? You weren't expecting this much of me, I hope!" He laughed and winked at the lass standing near him.

"Oh no," she said with a blushing smile. "Our Schoolmaster is returning from his time in the city, and we're getting things ready for him."

Justin smiled. "Lucky sort, that is! What I wouldn't give to have a place of my own in every village I pass through!" He sighed, still staring at the maiden. "And whom do I have the pleasure of addressing?"

The young woman gave a curtsey. "They call me Wendy, if you please, sir."

Justin nodded. "Well, Miss Wendy, can I interest you in the latest beauty trend, straight from the King's court?" He reached into his wagon and pulled out another set of cases.

Wendy leaned over, eyebrows raised in curiosity. "Oh? What is it?"

Justin flung the lid back, aware now that he had the attention of several young women.

"I have combs," he said, lifting them up and letting their shiny surfaces catch the light. "Beautiful combs that are all the rage in the king's palace! And dresses! Just look at these," he opened a chest and brought out garments of fine, brilliantly-hued cloth. "I went to a party at the Duke's *palais*," he said the word with a refined accent, "and I swear every high-born lady there was wearing this very style, along with these shoes." He threw more boxes open, "and if I could have the attention of you men--long coats and baggy sleeves are out, don't you know! That's peasant-wear; you want to look like a classy gentleman, you wear *this*!" he pulled out a puppet decked in a sleek waistcoat and a shirt with close-fitting sleeves. Handing it to the nearest villager for a closer look, Justin pulled out a few items to demonstrate that he had normal-sized versions of everything the doll wore. "Doesn't that look a treat?" Justin asked the growing crowd with a wink. "No more catching your sleeve on anything or dragging it through the dirt and dust of your everyday life. Your wife will thank you when you *don't* smell like you've been in the trough all day!"

He winked, and a few of the villagers laughed at the joke. He brought out a small stool and stood upon it, so that his voice could carry over the heads of the gathering crowd. "Step right up, folks! I have plenty of items for bartering! Bring your things, and let's strike a deal!"

From the far side of the Town Square, Red watched from her perch on the steps into the dress shop as she rubbed Mrs. Garrity's ointment on her newest injuries. She grimaced as the villagers brought out their food preserves and hand-made items to trade for Justin's 'new and very popular' trinkets. Those in

Queston didn't have much need for money among themselves, so they bartered for everything. Two small pots of soup and a skein of wool netted a set of dresses for the whole family. Half a cow of dried and cured meat got a set of pans that looked like tin, but Justin promised they would last far longer and hold up longer against the flames than their usual hammered steel dishes.

Red observed every transaction, as farmers traded gardening tools to buy their children one of those new, key-wound toys. She listened as Justin presented a new kind of seed that grew a unique plant that had never been seen before. He claimed it grew in any kind of soil, needed very little care, and promised to keep a family of five fed and happy through the winter months. She saw a village woman offer beautifully-embroidered pillows and garments to Justin, who barely glanced at them with a shrug.

"Well, I hate to say this, Mrs. Haben," he told the woman, "but with the advent of machine sewing in the big cities, there just isn't much of a market for this kind of novelty needlework anymore."

The woman's chin trembled, and her eager eyes dimmed a little.

"Oh," she murmured, "but I would dearly love to have a set of those combs! And this is all I have to barter with!"

Justin patted the woman's shoulder. "What can I say? You've won me over. I suppose I can let you have the combs, and I'll take these," he deftly removed the whole pile of cloth from her hands, "and see what I can do with them, how does that sound?"

Mrs. Haben squealed as much as the children as she picked up a set of the combs. She set one in her hair and admired her reflection in the tiny mirror built into the lid of the box. "My!" She gushed. "Don't I look fine!"

Red snorted. The woman's hair was already too thin--the comb looked as if it would fall out at the first sign of a breeze, but Justin replied, "I declare! You look as much like a courtesan as I've ever seen!"

He extended a hand and raised his voice to the women whispering behind her. "This goes for anybody who wants to trade for me, as well: I'll take what you're willing to barter with--it might not have much of a market, but I didn't get to be a traveling peddler by being choosy!"

Red rolled her eyes. She'd seen enough. The peddler made a few more trades before finally getting himself invited to the festival. Red chose the moment when everyone's attention focused on the refreshment tables and colorful, loud amusements to slip away from all the gratuitous indulgence. Justin had once again created a sense of discontent and desire in the hearts of the villagers, one that would fester and grow until he was gone, and only then would they remember the benefits of their simple way of life. A sharp pain in Red's shoulder reminded her not to start another fight when she was still healing from the first one. Her best option was to wait for a better opportunity to ensure Justin's prompt departure. She draped the hood of her cloak low over her face as she slipped out of the alleyway, heading for the small trail that would lead out of the valley and into the forest.

"Leaving so soon?" called a voice behind her.

Red's hackles rose, and she stopped without turning.

"In other towns, a mysterious figure in a cape who chooses to skulk about in the shadows is usually a thief or a killer," continued the speaker, "but it would be hard to prowl about undetected in a color as bright as that!"

The footsteps crunched to a stop immediately behind her, and Red finally turned to face him--Justin the peddler, standing there with his thumbs hooked in the shiny leather suspenders, a wide grin on his face.

"Oh my!" he chuckled. "You must be that notorious Crimson Hood everyone always talks about, the one that comes from Queston. Begging your pardon, but I've heard such stories that I truly consider it an honor to have seen you." He held out his hand and bobbed his head in respect.

Red didn't stir. She continued to watch him without making a sound.

Justin coughed and dropped his hand. "Well, ah," he stammered, "if you're here--will you be joining the townspeople this evening? May I escort you to the festivit--"

"Let me make one thing very clear, peddler," Red cut off his chatter with the steel-hard edge in her voice. "The people of Queston are under my protection. The entire mountain is within my jurisdiction. Everything that happens here is my business. Do not take my authority lightly, for it is by my leave that you were able to enter this village at all."

Justin's eyebrows raised. "Well now, let's not get all bent out of shape; I assure you I mean these good people no harm--"

CSpare me your platitudes," Red retorted. "I know your type." She scowled and stared deep into his eyes. "I know your ilk; you plead and you parade, you boast and you bargain--all the while seeking to get as much as you can for yourself and giving very little in return."

The sheepish modesty gave way to an indignant frown. "Now, wait just a moment! I am no mere shyster, Milady! I am a businessman--"

"And your business is the fruit of other people's labor?" She pressed again. "I have seen the deals you make--the culmination of decades of skill and training and practice, exchanged for some paltry trinkets and glittering baubles that catch the eye and accomplish little else."

The peddler lifted his palms in a shrug. "So what, if the innocent toys and dresses serve little purpose except to bring joy? Is that not a sufficient goal? My prices are fair, Madam Guardian. I take no more than my goods are worth."

Red folded her arms, steeling herself against the pain it caused in her side. "Then you will take no more from these good people. You have trespassed on this mountain long enough. Doubtless they will still manage to survive the year, with or without your assistance."

Justin rubbed his chapped palms together. His eyes still held a small twinkle. He smiled at the caped woman. "Oh come! I've traveled all this way... At least let me rest my horses--"

Red sighed. "You may stay one night. I want you gone by tomorrow."

He nodded profusely. "That's fair, that's fair; I'll just-- ahem--stop by on my way out to see if any others might want--"

"No." Red cut him off flatly. "You will not stop. Tonight will be the last time you see Queston. I want you off the mountain by the time the sun hits these peaks over us--or you'll find this mountain a very *unwelcoming* place."

She never stirred, but the weight of her voice sent Justin reeling back a pace. "A-a-are you threatening me?" he spluttered, eyes wide.

"Do you feel threatened?" Red tilted her head up so that he could see her smile underneath the edge of her hood in the muted light as the sun dipped behind a mountain peak.

Justin huffed deeply and clenched his fists. "Now that you mention it," he grumbled, "yes."

Red felt the rush of dizziness that said her wounds were about to get the better of her. She needed rest and healing. No more time for games.

"My work here is done," she stated simply. "Fare well, and safe journey, Peddler."

She left him standing there as she slipped into a thick patch of overgrowth, the dark branches hiding even the bright-crimson of her cloak. She waited, motionless in the thicket, until Justin gave up and wandered back toward the festival, wringing his hands and muttering to himself the whole way.

Had the unscrupulous man turned back just then, he would have seen a common she-wolf emerge from that same thicket. In her animal form, Red the shape-shifter smiled to herself as she climbed up the sheer path with sure steps. All in a day's work for the Wolf, Guardian of Queston.

THE END

Miss Hattie and the Hoppers
Mary R. Woldering

Hattie. I see you. In my lazy afternoon dream, I pictured my sister Caddie standing in my empty schoolroom as if she had magically appeared, laughing and twirling as if she was showing herself off to me. Her long caramel-color hair floated past her shoulders and down her back unbound. *Is that hat on the shelf behind you the latest style? Looks silly!* I knew she was talking about my felt day hat with feathers and flowers on top.

See how I look? Where I live I can wear my hair down and full of flowers like we did when we were children! She wore a loose red and gold patterned gown that looked like it belonged on a Greek Vase. Everything about the way she looked whispered freedom and seemed almost naughty, but I knew it was a fantasy. She had died while I was away at school studying the sciences, classics and the French language, but I had never accepted it.

I usually experimented with dreamer-controlled or "lucid" dreams on boring and hot August nights when the doldrums of a too-hot summer sweltered, and the cicada song rose to a scream outside my bedroom window. This afternoon I wasn't at home. I was at the schoolhouse and it was the last day of school before summer.

After the end of the year picnic, I had stayed behind to mop and lock up. That task done, I realized something I had eaten had given me indigestion. Hoping the misery would ease before I went home, I put my head down on my empty desk and drifted into a dream to contemplate my sister's disappearance once again.

I still wish I knew what really happened to you, Caddie, I mused, wondering if I would face yet another lonely summer of unanswered questions. *I never once believed you got killed by some wandering stranger down in the caves. That's what everyone told me.* I'd been away at school, but just as I graduated, news of Caddie's disappearance followed by my mother's sudden death cut short my hopes for the future and further study. I now had a house and land to tend and no husband, so I decided to return to Wolf's Landing, Tennessee to live and earn a living as a schoolteacher.

Except I'm not dead and you know it. I just couldn't get back yet. I left my stars on things, the way I used to leave them on notes as children. Her voice faded out, edged with a laugh. *But you—*

Wait. Come back! I excitedly ordered her image in my thoughts. It was a way of dreaming I'd read about in "Dreams and the means of directing them: practical observations" – written by Marquis d'Hervey de Saint Denys. I had studied the technique and had been practicing it regularly with some success.

This afternoon, however, the pain in my stomach distracted me. *Perhaps I'll try again tonight when it's cooler, unless the latest story by Mr. Jules Verne has come in the post. I've read every one!* For now, only what my sister said about leaving clues stayed with me.

Wait a minute. I sat straighter in my chair and stared into the empty room, now fully awake. I reached into a secret compartment in my satchel where I kept Caddie's last weepy letter from five years earlier. Unfolding it, I stared at the part in which she said she was leaving Wolf's Landing as soon as she could, because Jimmy Jay had betrayed her.

I regarded the ink blot in the crease. At one time I had imagined it looked like the eight-pointed star of an ancient goddess older than Athena or Diana.

Harriet Adeline Douglas! I cautioned myself with my full name. *Hattie, be sensible. It only looks like a star because you want it to look like one. It's just a tear-stain.*

Refolding her letter, I went about the last task of the afternoon. I tugged the heavy crate of locks on the high back shelf forward and then eased it down to my desk. I could have waited for the Schoolmaster from the upper school to come, but knew he'd complain about his back the whole time. I didn't want to hear it.

Men! It's done though. I opened the lid. Inside were the dozen iron and brass locks for the doors and shutters to be used at the end of each school year.

I slammed books and papers into my satchel, lay it on top of the box and then trudged outside with the locks to fasten everything. When I dug the big skeleton key out of the box, I saw something I knew hadn't been there before. It was a mark identical to the one on the letter I had just opened - a little eight-pointed star.

This one was no accidental mark. It was as deliberate-looking as if it had been stamped with a press. *Caddie was just talking to me about clues. The letter a moment ago and now here's another. I wonder how it got there? I'll just take the key home and think about it some more over the summer.*

After I locked the doors and windows, I fetched my mare Mabel out of the grassy shade, hitched her to my buckboard and drove toward the edge of town.

§ § §

By the time I came out of the telegraph and postal depot with the latest story by Mr. Verne, some fine nonsense was going on at the nearby Cates Inn. I heard Jimmy Jay's hilly twang rising above a gathering crowd. I couldn't tell what he was fussing about, but by the time I hitched my horse at a water trough, a crowd had gathered outside the front door in a semi-circle. Men ran up each moment and behind them clustered curious women and children. All of this created a jam in the road and wagon drivers paused to stare. The late afternoon train to Knoxville grunted, hissed and puffed up to speed as it pulled out of the station. After the noise faded, I heard:

"Y'all ain't from 'round here, I can tell, but I don't want no trouble. Now you fellas go on around to the back to do your business. Someone will see to you there." Then a moment of silence was followed by: "You speakee English? How 'bout him? Do he speakee English?"

Someone in the crowd called out. "Hey Jim--here comes Sheriff Poe. He'll sort this out."

Oh brother. This is not good. Someone had to get the sheriff. I pressed through the crowd to see just who the troublemakers were. When I saw them, I thought they were the oddest-looking fellows. I hadn't seen gentlemen such as these anywhere other than in a big city like Macon or perhaps described in one of Mr. Verne's stories. One was tall but sturdy looking and darkly tanned. His long and wavy sun-brightened hair made him look like a whiskerless version of General Custer. The other man was a burly-looking dark fellow; most likely a 'Hindoo'. They were well dressed, but wore only shirtsleeves, weskits and hats. The tall one was carrying a heavy carpet bag. He noticed me and said something to his friend, but Sheriff Poe put his hand on the darker man's arm and said:

"Come on, boy. You fellas need to come on over to the--" which was followed by a "What the Hell?" because his hand was snatched firmly away, and the darker man appeared to growl. I thought a fight would start right then but the lighter haired man said something to his friend to get him to calm himself. The dark one complied but was scowling mad and looked as if he wanted to punch someone. From the little I could hear; their words were no language I understood. The deputy came up with some manacles, but Sheriff Poe waved him away and began to lead them up the road to the jail. As they passed by me, I noticed the Custerish one staring. His glance both startled and charmed me; as if he was looking into my soul. *He has the lightest blue eyes*—I thought, *and light brown skin—odd combination.*

As if my expression satisfied him, he touched the brim of his cap like a perfect gentleman.

"Hattie." I thought I heard him whisper.

"Huh?" I couldn't mistake the next thought that came to me. *Strangers who know my name? Are these Caddie's strangers?* I wanted to call out to Sheriff Poe to wait and let me talk to the men, but they were bustled up the road with remnants of the crowd trailing them. Soon enough the excitement died, and the crowd thinned to go about their business.

I walked up to the front door of the Inn to see what had happened and found Jimmy sweeping the entryway. He looked up at me, then mopped his brow.

"Evening, Miss Hattie." He drawled.

"Evening." I began. "Are you alright? I saw the end of that."

"Oh, uptown nigras and carpetbaggers. Sheriff Poe will set them straight." He went back to sweeping but added: "Don't bust your pretty head over it. It's handled."

Don't bust your pretty head! I snorted, inwardly. *You and all the men here are so eager to point out how I'm suddenly too smart and "city-minded" now that I have an education — that I'm not a regular woman. No matter. At least I can teach your children without having to bow to some fool man and play simple-minded. And I can put my feet up—all day tomorrow or all summer if I wish— and read the latest story while I see if something comes to me about these marks —* I waved goodbye and returned to the wagon for the drive toward my house on the river.

The sun filtered through the trees in the woody places down by the flood creek. It was a peaceful ride home to an empty house, but the whole way I was haunted by thoughts that after five years of wondering I might never solve the mystery of Caddie's disappearance. I was just fooling myself about stars on things and trying to make something real out of a dream. Still, I couldn't let that mystery rest, especially since she mentioned these star marks. The men I had seen in town had been an absurd distraction, but best regarded as nothing more than a sudden flash of summer evening lightning: here, gone and not even producing beneficial rain for the fields.

Maybe I should *move to the city — maybe work as a governess to a couple who travel. Maybe that would be a way to get to Paris and later seek my own way. Maybe I could meet Jules Verne. I'm twenty-six years old. I could have adventures like going to the moon in an airship and seeing moon men or going into the center of the earth — or around the world. This is my home, but I know I'm wasted here.*

I had just turned a corner where it cut off and drove toward the rickety old bridge over the river when I noticed two men sauntering along the side of the road ahead of me. Though I had barely seen them earlier, I knew I had just entered the realm of the impossible.

Them. Incredible. I thought. *Now how did they get out of Sheriff Poe's office or perhaps the jail and all the way down by the river? Magic? Ridiculous. There must be an explanation; a trick of the eye. Keep on driving by them. Pass them up. Don't look and don't stop.* My heart beat faster as I slipped by them, glancing briefly. It wasn't a mistake. They were there, shirtsleeves and no coats. The dark, muscular one had removed his weskit and loosened the mass of plaited hair that had been tucked under his leather top hat. The taller one carried his bag but had stuck his folded squash hat under a suspender strap.

I snapped the reins to get Mabel to pick up the pace as I hastened by them, still amazed that they had arrived on this road ahead of me when not a half hour earlier they had been in town and were being taken to the jail in the opposite direction. *Don't turn around. Don't look,* I urged myself.

"Hay–" one of them shouted.

"Hair-ee-yet-ahh-duh-line-dug-less–" a full and rich man's voice called out. "Hair-yet. Dug-less, Had-tee." A second voice came from the other "Hay! Sdop dis horz, wo-man–"

Against all rational thought, I pulled on the reins, turned and looked around to see them running toward me, the dark one flapping his arms as if he wanted me to pick them both up.

Get moving Hattie! My better judgement warned me. *They are up to no good and you don't even have your gun with you.*

I grabbed the handles of my satchel as they ran up, thinking I could smack one of them if they tried anything untoward with me. The heavy books inside might knock one down enough for me to get out into the grass and the bushes, find a big chuck-hole and hide in it until they gave up. I wasn't too far from home.

They reached the wagon, out of breath and looking up at me. In the next moment the light-haired man touched a curious disc shape attached to a pendant at his chest. It looked like an oversized timepiece. When he lifted it slightly I saw a dozen sky-blue gears moving in rhythmic cycles with extending sweeping arms. As they moved, little red and white sparkles blinked on the outside rim. As soon as he touched it and twisted the outer rim, I could hear him speaking clearly.

"Good afternoon, Madame. My companion and I are lost. We've unfortunately distressed your citizenry and your constable before we could fully decipher your language." His face looked up as if he expected approval.

I sat staring, open mouthed. *No English before, and speaking as proper Englishmen from England?* My face must have mirrored both confusion and discomfort.

"You were with Sheriff Poe in town and now—I-I have to go." I turned my glance forward and whipped the reins to get Mabel moving again. *They broke out of the sheriff's office and somehow got ahead of me. Men should be coming down the path hot as warriors. I don't understand what sort of hoodoo—*

The darker man poked at his partner and shook his head, then seized the glittering timepiece-looking thing. He turned the outer rim slightly as if adjusting it.

And why do I think these men have something to do with Caddie…Why did I even slow down? I must be truly ill. The devilled eggs did it, or Jenny Rider's jellied ham that tasted a bit off—

The excitement in town, my long day, the afternoon heat, the mark on the key and the sudden presence of these men came upon me like a sudden case of the vapors. I felt a wave of sick and dizziness rise. My vision greyed. I felt as if I was floating. When the feeling eased, I realized I was lying in the back of the buckboard across a man's lap. A pair of strong, warm arms surrounded me. Dark fingertips massaged my temples and moved to my throat to rub and then gently toy with the button on my collar.

"Shh…" the darker of the men blew a little of his breath on me.

Olive brown eyes. Touch feels so nice, I… I froze. *I am letting a strange man hold me and touch me and I like it. I know he can tell I like it by the look in his eyes.*

"No. Stop. I'm better now." I grabbed his hand and pulled it from my blouse. "Let go. I'm not that kind of woman."

The lighter man sat on the driver's bench, gently driving my horse. He glanced at the timepiece once and pulled ahead. That was all I cared about at the time. The other man was still unbuttoning my blouse. I grabbed his hand and pulled it away.

"I told you to stop!"

"Hatt-ee." his voice sounded low and firm; almost rusty. "I am opening your clothing, so I may take it off you. Then the rib brace – so breathing with be easier for you. You wear too many layers in this climate."

Rib brace? My stays. Lord, he intends to undress me. My thoughts rioted but those feelings were quickly replaced by a wavelike sense of calm. *Smells nice, though—honey and spice hair dressing or something, on his—body. So nice. Have mercy!* I felt the blush turning me red as a beet. "Stop…" I pried at his hand again, wondering if he had used some kind of mesmerism to make me go from the struggle of virtue and honor to swooning in delight.

The man in front slowed the wagon and turned to look at us.

"Maatkare–" he cautioned "Stop that. I *told* you women here won't let you touch them or take off their clothing unless you intend to bed them. –And most will not want you to do *that* either…" he laughed and turned back to his driving.

"Well, is that so?" the dark man shook his head, looking sullen. "This could be a needy journey for me, then."

"We've been over this. Just most women—require—more time. And don't go on instinct again and start things like that fight with the painter in Naples. He shook his head settling between disgust and humorous memory. "Almost had to re-hop–"

"Matt–what?" I sat and hurriedly re-fastened my blouse, knowing my hat and hair must have looked frightening. The lighter man's words sank in. *Naples? A painter? Made them what? Re-hop?*

"Matt Kerry. Traveling magician" the dark one gave me a curious salute, then added, pointing to his companion. "–and he is Jerry Ben Easy, engineer and inventor." The man who had just named himself Matt answered as if he had heard my silent question.

The lighter man turned again, still looking amused, but tired.

"We'll take you to your house, and get you inside, but we must also beg shelter from you if you have—" he paused as if he couldn't place a word, "barn or clean stable loft. We obviously cannot return to the town and seek lodging at that Inn." he paused, expectant, then added. "Perhaps one night is all we will require."

"What sort of work–" I felt woozy again, not entirely aware of what the man was asking. *The name—Matt, as in Matthew Kerry? Irish? A rich colored man or Indian with an Irish sounding name? Jerry Ben Easy? Joke—never heard of a name like that.* The sparkles and blurs returned.

"You see–" Matt spoke again, his voice becoming oddly gentle and calming "Look at you. Your lights will go out all over again until you let me take these tight things off." His hand went forward to assist.

"Don't you *touch* me." I snapped. "No means no! I'll be *fine* until I get to my house and then I will take my *own* clothing off...in another room, behind a locked door. In *fact*, should I let you in my yard you will both wait downstairs, outside on the porch." I was panting heavily by that time and feeling worse because of it. My stomach ached. I couldn't think of anything better than getting upstairs to my room, bolting the door and unfastening myself. After that, I wasn't sure what I would do about strange men on the porch, one of whom was wearing an odd sky-colored device that resembled a big watch.

As Jerry neared the house and turned to drive into the stable, I noticed Mr. Kerry also wore something. The sight of it nearly finished me.

"You–" I freed myself and gripped my arms around my bosoms to shelter them from whatever dishonorable thing he intended to do. That was when I saw the gold medallion clearly. It bounced on his dark, lightly furred chest. In the center was a faceted red stone imbedded in an eight-pointed star.

"Another star, another clue! No!" I squeaked aloud and pointed at it, as "Jerry" hopped down and unhitched Mabel, then gently led her into her stall and fastened her stall door. His companions' arms had returned to hold me in a loose embrace. I tried to keep my thoughts on my sister, but everything about the darker man seemed to be a seduction, as if his thoughts echoed.

Be with me. Enjoy us, sweet one.

What is it about this man? I've been embraced at socials, even kissed once or twice but always maintained my uprightness—I'm no easy— unless. Dear God, I read about this kind of man. An incubus? They aren't real. They're just an excuse hapless women use for having been foolish with a man. I refocused, emerging from the overwhelming sensation of delight.

"That star design, sir." I touched the jewel, noticing it's beckoning warmth and vibrance. "I-I've seen it earlier today on a key that was unmarked before, and before that on a letter from my sister and now on this jewel. Just tell me what it means. And why–" I winced, still cramping from the stomach ache and heat. "I know this is no chance meeting. You two *must* know something about my sister Catherine Anne."

Jerry stretched up his hand to help me down from the wagon, but I declined it and climbed out on my own, desperate to hear his answer but even more convinced that I should put a locked door between myself and these men.

"We call her Kaethera-ahn," a sheepish grin moved over Jerry's face and he shrugged as if I had uncovered a secret ahead of schedule.

"We-e-ell, outstanding!" Matt got out of the wagon and looked right and left like a hound checking a distant scent, then gestured for the fair-haired man to hurry to the porch. "at least *something* has gone right about this cursed journey. Think we threw the posse off our scent for now. Bastards went as far as the caves, but not far enough in them to see anything." A low-pitched noise came from his throat and for an instant I thought I saw two elongated teeth in his mouth that looked like dog teeth.

Did he just growl? My heart jumped. *Mysterious strangers, maybe one is an incubus out to drink my soul through pleasure. Or is he a loup garou in the flesh, Hattie you need air.* I turned in my flight to the front door once to see if they were following me, then opened the screen.

"You gentlemen wait here. I'm not in the habit of inviting strangers into my house."

"Your stable loft then, if we might?" The taller man reminded me I hadn't answered him.

"Make some sweet tea, then—ma-dm." the darker one spat, but I sensed no disrespect in his tone, even though he ordered me as if I was a servant. I knew they were likely hungry, having been turned away at Cates Inn and possibly other places before they arrived at Wolf's Landing. Even though I needed to run them off, the tall one said the name Kaethera-Ahn. – That was Caddie's nickname when we were children.

"You may, I suppose, but wait here a moment." I breathed, beside myself with curiosity but also alarmed. *Mystery men? Moon men maybe? Like in the stories I read? Caddie?* I rushed inside, latched the door and then called through it:

"You fellas go around to the back porch, so no one can see you from the road. I'll bring you something to eat in a while." I strained to hear any comment, but the one called Jerry answered: "Much obliged, ma'am." which was followed by two sets of footsteps leaving the front stoop and a lively discussion rising in the yard as they went to the porch. I paused, nearly witless, by the door, but calmed myself enough to run upstairs, slam my bedroom door and lock it.

I need my pistol. I grabbed the six-shooter from the drawer in the bedside table, spun the chamber and checked. *Loaded. Good. I haven't even used this silly thing for anything other than targets and scaring crows in the corn patch since my Daddy taught me ten years ago. Kicks too hard, but he always said a woman can't have a man at her side all the time*—I listened and heard the strangers on the back porch discussing something in their own language and making rustling noises that sounded as if they might have been going through the Custer-looking gentleman's carpetbag. Then one of them sounded as if he was heading toward the riverbank.

My fingers fumbled with the buttons on my blouse and I loosened my corset until the pinching eased. After a few deep breaths, bending down, water on my face and the gathering of blankets for the men to take to the stable later, I put on a duster and apron with pockets deep enough to hide the gun—just in case.

I silently fussed as I trotted down to the dry pantry to get sausage and cheese and a jar of pickled peppers. All the while I was thinking: *Oh Caddie, if these are the men you ran off with—* I sliced the food and put everything on a wedge of cornbread, followed by two big glasses of tea. *I hope they weren't the ones.*

When I nudged the screen door open with my toe, the light-haired man jumped up like a perfect gentleman and took the tray from me. He set it on a low table while I took a seat on the swing nearby. As they settled, I politely re-stated:

"Kaethera-Ahn is the name my sister used when she was little. She ran off five years ago, but I was told she was murdered in the caves by a stranger. They found bloody clothing by the underground river. I never believed it. I think some of the older folk here wanted to make a ghost story so the young-uns would stop playing there." I paused, wondering if it was right to tell these things to virtual strangers. "Caddie and I were close. I think I would know if she was really gone."

"Aha–" the darker one grinned "I told you so—"

Jerry paused, bread halfway to his mouth.

"You feel her/hear her speak. Perhaps—later we can explain–" he tasted the bread politely, but his partner had already attacked his meal in a more ravenous fashion – as if I had set out the finest Christmas Dinner with all the trimmings.

I had hoped to bring up the subject of my sister, but we talked about mundanities and the early heat of the season. I mentioned teaching and was relieved when they seemed pleased that I had studied a wide variety of things. They mentioned they were travellers and that the food I had just pulled out of the cabinets was wonderful, but nothing about my sister or how odd it was that they had known our names. It was as if they were avoiding the subject.

After stuffing his face with sausage and quaffing his second glass of sweet tea, the one named Matt grinned and reached inside his re-donned weskit pocket for a thin cigar. An instant wisp of aromatic smoke curled up from it as if it had lit itself the moment he perched it on his lower lip. As if he was suddenly "man of the house" he put his feet up on the porch rail and puffed contentedly.

He lit that with his finger— I thought, hoping I could ask them some more, but I noticed the first lightning bugs had begun to pop from the unmown grass. *Where did the time go? Almost dark? How can it possibly*—"

While Jerry finished his meal, I noticed the man Matt's obviously lustful thoughts entering mine:

See something? Like something?

No. I glared back at him. *You, sir, need to be reminded that my courtesy can and ought never be a sign of anything other than civility.*

"Um." Jerry noticed my discomfort, "Pretty place here by the river," he dotted his lips with the napkin, stood and beckoned to Matt Kerry. After a final gulp of tea, he gathered the plates together and looked as if he wanted to carry them into the kitchen but had already decided against it. Then he turned and beckoned sharply for his companion to come along before I could think of any more questions.

"As for your sister, Kaethera, we know her as — a student, you might say. She is near, and she wished to come to you, but not yet." He handed me the tray.

"But where? How did it—" I sputtered as I took it, suddenly distrusting him. Something was insincere in Jerry's tone of voice.

"Perhaps soon as we conclude our business here, but not tonight—" Jerry's shoulders drooped, giving him the appearance of being immensely tired. I frowned, confused.

You're not tired, you're hiding something. And that other one, Mr. Kerry - the way he watches me, like a hunting dog, waiting for me to make a move.

I felt Mr. Easy was searching for answers and walking a line between truth and lie. I was about to demand an explanation, but Matt hopped up from his relaxed position and trudged alongside me, flashing his beguiling smile as I went inside. He opened the screen for me, but every bit of his manner seemed increasingly wicked. My thoughts went back to the way his arms felt and his scent. The glint of his slightly pointed teeth and the look in his eyes was just a little too confident. *I hope you weren't the one Caddie fell for.* I thought, but then I gasped because I had the oddest feeling the beast was standing right behind me. I could have sworn I felt his breath on my neck as I moved to the sink with the tray. I quickly set it down, found the revolver in my pocket, turned and started to draw it out.

"What do you mean—" I snapped but to my horror saw no one was standing behind me. Both men were still standing on the porch, the darker one enjoying the last of his cigar and flashing a knowing smirk in my direction.

"Oh! Impressive!" he snickered. "I knew you had a pistol, woman–But why would you want to shoot me?" he shrugged. "No reason. Now take your hand off it before you fire it by accident."

"I—Mr. Kerry!" I hissed, turned away insulted, and stomped upstairs. *Men! I should just shoot him. No better than these farm boys thinking—thinking—*

Leaning out of the open window I shouted down to the men who were still on the porch. "If I shoot someone it won't be an accident and I will use this gun if either of you come in here after me tonight!" I quickly wadded the bedding I had set aside, then returned with it down the stairs. When I handed the bundle to Jerry, he gave it to Matt; a put-upon stare simmering in his pale eyes.

Matt Kerry shrugged as if he was indifferent to anything I had said and carried the bedding toward the stable. That, to me, was more infuriating than anything that came from his lips.

"Don't be angry with us, Miss Douglas." Jerry stepped between my glare and the departing man. "Mr. Kerry," he explained. "labors with spells of blackest loneliness and will reach out to a woman at these times—for comfort—particularly one fair as yourself."

Fair? Me? Plain looks and spectacles? I laughed inwardly. *Polite joke, of course, not serious. Caddie was the pretty one.*

"I'm not angry." I shook my head. "Not really. It's just – with you two –Land sakes, I'm in such a stir, I can't even think!" I was becoming even more convinced that Matt Kerry or Jerry

Ben Easy must have seduced her years ago. I thought of her pretty face and open caring heart that was so easily broken, unlike me with my studious and analytical nature. Strange men promising a life of adventure – she would have leapt at the chance. Something in me wanted to leap, too – not into their arms but simply away from the world of my own making which was steadfastly closing in on me.

"Well then, off to get some rest for us." Jerry followed Matt to the stable but added. "Still, I thank you for your kindness, and we'll not bother you except for – Kaethera-Ahn— she mentioned biscuits and gravy. Do you make that? The big fluffy ones with heaps of sausage gravy?"

"–and coffee? Tankards of hot coffee" Matt called from the stable, then added "—*two* tankards."

He heard us whisper? I noticed lightning bugs dancing and flashing in greater numbers, then thought of the man's timepiece. I briefly imagined he was controlling their lights. It was getting darker. I didn't want them to go but asking them to stay was nothing a proper spinster would do.

Biscuits, he said. I shook my head. *Some men! What is it about them that when they see a woman in a kitchen their thoughts always turn to biscuits?* I groaned because until these men showed up, I had wanted to spend Saturday alone, sleeping late and just getting by on crackers until I was certain my stomach had settled. *Even If I sleep— old Arlen Murdoch's cows will start across the river at dawn and that rooster I wish to be found by a wolf will crow and that will beget the mules braying. There aren't so many wolves left now. Maybe Mr. Kerry-- Loup garou. Incubus. Imagine.* I snickered, realizing this entire afternoon, though unnerving, was one of the most exciting things that had ever happened to me. I just wanted Caddie to be on the other end of the adventure.

"In the morning, Biscuits, sausage gravy, eggs and coffee, but I still have rules. Breakfast *after* you've told me how I can see

Caddie." I called, watching both men part the glimmer of sparkling insects on their way to the stable. "And wash up. There's a shallow part in the river near the foot of this hill." I blushed at the thought of these two strange gentlemen bathing themselves. "Oh, and don't come to the door unless you see me moving around in this kitchen."

I didn't know if they heard the last thing I said, because they were chattering in their own language once again as they faded into the early dusk. I went out to the porch long enough to bring in some pieces of firewood for the stove, then measured out the flour and put the milk out to sour, covered it and locked everything on the lower level, including the windows and went upstairs.

For long moments after I had washed and put on my nightdress I paced the floor, sat on my bed for a short while, then reconsidered. I went to the window in the unused front guest room to stare outside in the direction of the stable.

Nothing's moving. Good. I thought, *perhaps they've settled, and I should too, since they will be needing a hearty breakfast before they...* I shook my head and sighed *typical, Hattie,* went into my room, sat on my bed with my satchel and took out the letter from my sister, followed by the key. Beside them I opened the copy of the latest story from Mr. Verne.

Around the World in Eighty Days. These two — maybe that's what they do. He said they travel different places. The magic, the strange devices, that Matt Kerry who acts like a wolf, but is constantly trying to wear me, or maybe any woman down. Caddie what have you gotten yourself into? The eight-pointed stars looked up at me as if they were teasing me with arms that wanted to spike and curl. They danced before my tired eyes, daring me to get all the answers in one night. *Perhaps they might stay another day and then I can discover enough to find her myself, not follow the crumbs you fellows decide to leave me.* At that point, I studied the things arranged on my bed: the letter, the key and the copy of *Magasin* opened to the place where Mr. Verne's tale began.

When I read about Jean Passepartout, I thought about Jerry Ben Easy's companion, but Matt Kerry was no valet for a daring adventurer. If anything, Jerry seemed to be the gentler, more helpful soul. Still, I wondered if Mr. Verne and men of his ilk were anything like my visitors. If they were—I knew my entire life here was an understatement and though my education could be simplified and taught to children, it excluded me from all but polite after Sunday church service chatter. *But my home is here.* I felt my own lips tremble. *I buried Mama and Daddy here and even you, Caddie, in a make-believe grave.* In so many ways it didn't seem right for me to take flight as well.

I folded everything on my bed and put my spectacles on the bedside table beside my revolver, then lowered the light. Lying back, I enjoyed the cool night air, even though my thoughts were racing. Watching as the moon showed its full face over the tops of the trees, I drifted, but my eyes suddenly popped open, and I sat. An aromatic scent drifted from a dark shape seated in my rocker across the room. The glowing end of a cigar brightened as the shape puffed on it.

Mr. Kerry is in my bedroom, watching me. My hand grasped the revolver and I fired above the darkness, hoping to put the fear of God in the man.

A thrash, followed by a growling grunt and "Ow, Son of the Great Whore, that stings!" rang through the dark. A shadow that no longer resembled a man at all leapt toward me, across the foot of my bed and out of the bedroom window. I sat with the smoking revolver gripped in both of my hands as if thunderstruck. Then, I darted to look out of my open window. Nothing moved through the underbrush. Only the moon shone quietly on my empty yard. Putting the gun down but within easy reach, I turned up the lamp and searched for the place the bullet struck, a trail of blood, or anything that proved I had not been shooting at the air.

As youngsters, Caddie and I had known of the men who came back from the War of Northern Aggression seeing ghosts of Yankee soldiers. Some would even shoot these visions, putting those they loved in harm's way. *I never saw a battle, though the fighting had been a scant mile away once. I don't have that madness. I'm just a lonely*—I shook my head. I knew I had fired the gun. It was hot when I lay it down, but my guests in the stable hadn't even come out to see what made the noise. For my own sanity, I knew I needed to find evidence someone had been in my room. A tall white quartz spear that had always been on the top of Caddie's bureau was missing.

Her wishing stone? Did he knock it off? I looked around the floor and then noticed a powdery substance that lay there. *Cigar ash. He was here.* Knowing he in some monstrous shape had leapt through my bedroom window and to the yard below left me terrified. Was he outside cavorting like a bad dog off a leash?

In the distance I heard another rising sound: growling and distant chickens squabbling in terror followed by the unmistakable sound of a wolf howling in triumph, quickly joined by other approaching howls. A distant shotgun blast was followed by another and a third. *Wolves? Why now? Is Mr. Kerry really a* loup garou? *Has he now run with others frozen as an animal because I shot him? He shouldn't have been in my room. Fool man knew better, but he just had to try me, didn't he? And stole my sister's rock?*

My heart began to pound again when I checked my door latch. It was secure. *Now how in the name of the Good Lord Jesus did he do that? Is he a demon, too?*

There were no sounds outside in my own yard when I grabbed my robe, put the gun in my pocket, and slipped into my loose yard boots that I kept by the door.

As I had rushed down the stairs in the dark, I heard an almost mechanical but pumping sound like many gears and wheels grinding. That was followed by the high-pitched whistling steam engine and then a popping noise.

A crackle of heat energy and static filled the air as if lightning had struck nearby. It rolled in a wave that made me stagger on the steps just before I made my way out the front door. I knew I was lucky I had paused long enough to grab the lantern which remained lit at night for such emergencies.

When I looked out, I saw a pale day-blue haze shooting from the top of the stable, then wisping and vanishing. I heard Mabel shrieking in a startled cadence of terrified neighing as I rushed across the yard, convinced the men were either engaged in scientific experiments or magic or an odd mixture of both.

Dew from the late spring grass soaked my feet and drenched the hem of my gown, slowing me as it snagged on passing brambles. I entered—

"Mr. Easy–" I called, followed hesitantly by "Mr. Kerry–" even though I was concerned calling him might fetch something I really didn't want to see. Moving closer when I heard nothing, I held the light up and saw the bedding folded neatly, just the way it had been when I had given it to the men.

Gone? I stared at the open gate to the center of the stable. *Without taking me to see Caddie?* I shone the light around, feeling disheartened and hopeless, but then something on the ground glittered in the light. I swung the lamp to see it and then bent down. It was Caddie's quartz spear. *Why is this here?*

I remembered hearing Jerry go through his bag on the back porch earlier and hearing either he or Matt going to the riverbank while I had prepared the food. *Were they looking for more of these? Wonder why?* We used to collect them from the riverbank and from parts of the cave when we were children. *They're pretty when they're pure and smooth, but—*

I reached forward to touch the clear-looking rock but drew back my hand when I noticed it was hot. A gold filament wrapped near the base of the stone ran like fence wire to a point beneath another clear rock, similar in shape to it. I turned with the lamp and froze.

"There. There she is." I clearly heard a female voice speak.

"Caddie?" I turned again and stepped, looking up in the direction of the voice I knew was hers. There were eight spears set out around the spot where I stood in the shape of an eight-pointed star.

"I see her!" Caddie's voice squeaked, excited as a child seeing the first flakes of snow.

"Got her!" Mr. Kerry's voice descended above my head in a loud and demonic laugh "Now!" followed by a whumping noise and a whir as if he had thrown a mighty lever.

My vision turned sky blue, pink, and then white and I felt as if I had become full of bees. I was lifting and rising, thinning like smoke. Unable to hold the lamp, I dropped it.

"You let me go-o-o!" I screamed but heard my scream fade as if I had been snatched out of the sound of my own noise that had mysteriously turned back on itself.

"Aw, curse this! Really?" his voice growled in my ears just as I thought I had seen Mr. Kerry taking shape near me. "Hang on!" My first reaction was relief that he didn't seem badly wounded, but that was quickly replaced by a feeling of total disorientation. I stumbled and grabbed at anything upright in my blurry field of vision. Suddenly, everything reversed, and I was falling head downward. I saw the lantern I had dropped lying on the straw covered floor, oil leaking out. Evil-looking curls of red and orange flame were quickly sprouting into a growing blaze.

Matt's oddly furred and clawed hand grabbed at mine as he whispered ever so seductively in a tone I couldn't refuse:

"There, Sweet One, see it and pick it up. Put out the fire while I walk us back… on three…two…one…"

As I stared at it, the burning oil on the straw puffed out and the lantern magically righted itself. I grabbed it and lifted it and hung it on an upright support beam. I heard Mabel, no longer afraid, nickering gently in her stall and then felt as if I was floating backward to the moment when I first saw the star pattern made of quartz spears. When my eyes cleared, I was up in Mr. Kerry's strong arms being carried through the lower big bay of the old cave. I knew the place. It was where the underground river pooled. Until Caddie vanished, many children from the town would go exploring and collecting pretty bits of fallen stalactites and river stones.

This is where they say Caddie died, but something's not right—

"Mr. Kerry—" I groaned, still feeling quite ill "I'm not your 'Sweet One'. Just don't say things like that to me — ever." I gasped, noticing my surroundings had gone from black to pale. I heard Jerry's voice scolding Matt as he came nearer:

"What did you just do, Maatkare? Did you just re-hop her? On her first time? Did you want to kill her outright or just make her have a stroke and then beg on us to heal her? It is *not* the way you soften a woman up. You know better—"

"Hop?" I stammered, still woozy and starting to struggle my way out of Mr. Kerry's arms.

"Hopping." Jerry's concerned face entered my field of vision. He wore a strange helmet-like device that glittered with pale blue and prismatic gems and crystallized albino peacock feathers in a white gold base. He looked like a tintype I'd once seen of someone in an elaborate Mardi Gras mask.

I stumbled and tried to shake off the disorientation as I was set on my feet. Jerry removed the mask and solemnly touched places on my brow and neck. When he did, I felt balanced and unharmed but no less confused as he explained:

"There to here and back again through time and space –
via crystalline power – in this vessel or one like it. I don't expect
you to understand it at first, but with your intelligence I would
think you will soon enough."

"Where have you taken me? Where am I?" I looked at the
room, which seemed like a lovely and most fairy-like coach with
sumptuous pale blue velvet fainting couches and ottomans. The
walls swam and glittered with color.

"Maybe you should sit down." Jerry led me to the nearest
couch. It was too comfortable. I collapsed backward in relief.
Soon both men sat on another couch facing me.

"Through time and space? I'm not in Wolf's Landing, or
the caves?" I attempted to sit up; to look for some point of
entry. "I won't be held against my will." I cautioned them, my
hand silently grasping the gun in my pocket.

"Well, you are, and you aren't." Jerry ran his fingers
through his gold kissed hair, loosening it. "Let me try to explain,
Miss Hattie." He looked so earnestly into my eyes that I felt I
could trust him for at least the length of the explanation.

"You see, we were short one spear. They shatter from
time to time and become useless—so rather than trying to get to
Egypt for more Maatkare—Matt Kerry to you, took the one
from your room after I read its signature and purity. We built a
rudimentary sending cone, tested it and then, when you came to
the stable to see what caused the noise, lured you into stepping
into the pattern, so we could make the final tests." He reached
forward to hold my hand. "The dizziness you feel passes once
you get your hopping legs – they're like sea legs." then he gave a
dirty look at Mr. Kerry whose muscular chest looked as if
something was crawling under his skin.

"And, Mad'm—" Matt folded out his hand which
magically held my revolver. "Would you *please* stop using this on
every living thing that startles you. I appreciate a woman who

will protect herself without hesitating but save it for true danger." He handed it to me. "And by the way, those bullets don't hurt me. They just sting like a bastard until they work their way to the surface." he pouted, then pinched the spot on his upper chest which I had seen moving and extruded the mangled slug. "I believe this belongs to you?"

"You—" I started to say something but found absolutely nothing coming to my thoughts that made sense as I let him drop the slug in my cupped hand. "Let me guess, I needed silver bullets?" I grumbled and put the gun and slug back in my robe pocket, then shaded my eyes, overwhelmed.

Mr. Kerry gave a sidelong glance at me, smoothed the surface of his chest, and then re-buttoned his shirt. "I'm not a *loup garou* or a werewolf, by the way. I shift form, wolf/dog to man and back on whim, whenever I want to and for whatever reason."

"But—", still wondering about all the magic and growing increasingly interested in discovering how these men did these things and where exactly they had taken me. *In Wolf's Landing and yet not; transforms into a wolf but not, and Jerry —The helmet made him look almost like an angel without wings.*

"A bit ago," Matt continued, "I heard your thoughts about the cow and the noisy rooster that woke you. I wanted to fix part of your problem after you blasted me one and also get some fresh bird blood in my gut to speed up the healing process. Stringy old thing though. I should think you'd thank me – twice – no three times for going against my animal nature with a woman. "Truth be told, I saw your stable was starting to go up in flames because you dropped your lamp. I knew your fine old mare would be lost. I just reverse channeled you and took you back in time a little bit, so you could punch through, put it on the hook, and then set your horse free just in case—for all the thanks I'll get."

"Punch through? Back in time? Reverse…But these things are not scientifically possible. No one can go back in time –or–"

"Forward?" Jerry smiled, almost sheepishly "But we have."

"It's not—It has to be a trick of some kind and I aim to find out what it is." I was on my feet and marching toward a side chamber. *Time travel?* I remembered how the men had suddenly been out of jail and ahead of me on the road, the strange noises and odd lights, the gusting wave from the blast that did no damage to stable or windows, the seven quartz spears wrapped with gold wire plus Caddie's piece stolen from her dresser.

"Wait—" Jerry protested. "You can't go out there. You wouldn't understand---" his voice trailed because I wasn't about to let either of them stop me "— yet."

"Oh, you try me, sir." I bolted through the opening, then turned to see where I had been and froze. There, floating just above the water of the underground river was something that looked like a much smaller and almost fairy-like version of the Nautilus from "20,000 Leagues under the Sea" and "Mysterious Island" written by none other than Jules Verne.

"The Nautilus?" I repeated, dumbstruck—"from Jules Verne's stories? You read them, too, and built a little one?" I moved closer to see if I could touch the surface, then looked at the sheer gangplank filled with beautiful plantlike green patterns, as if it had been made of seaweed and glass.

"Jules Verne?" Jerry stepped in front of me, "Well I didn't read his stories, but we *did* meet in Paris at the salon several years ago. Once we were discussing the design of a combination airship and submersible for a story he wanted to write. I showed him this one—He liked the way it looked like a sea creature and then wrote about one big enough for a huge crew, so readers would believe it. We don't need that. It only takes one of us to run it, but two is helpful."

I made my way back in and sat numbly on the couch again.

"Jules Verne – His Nautilus from this?" I rasped, putting my head in my hand. "I have lost my mind."

"I told you, you wouldn't understand." Jerry sighed

"Land sakes, Hattie, does everything need explaining?" A woman in a flowing red and gold gown with long caramel-color hair emerged from a smaller forward room.

Caddie rushed over to me, arms stretched out to embrace me, but something didn't feel right when she sat beside me.

"Sometimes you just need to relax and let the knowledge flow through you from these wonderful men." Her smile and flirty "in love" looks made the men across from me smile.

That's Caddie – always looking to a man to bolster her thoughts.

"Not always." She answered as if she had heard me. I grew up Hattie." Caddie ventured. "I'm not the sad little country girl I once was. I was running away because of Jimmy Jay, but I wanted to see the place we played by the water once more. Then I slipped in the dark, fell and broke my leg in three places. I lay here for so long in the cold and then Djerah and Maatkare found me – brought me here and healed me." she beamed. "Now they're teaching me science, better than at that stuffy school where you went."

"Miss Kaethera why not show your sister how we run the ship while Maatkare and I finish up on the deep structure quartz and manganese we found." Jerry stood and went into the other room. He returned with his satchel. "We don't have much time. I heard on the crystal that your little stunt with the hen house woke some folks along Miss Hattie's road. There're already men going out to get some good wolf pelts. Soon they'll find her mare wandering and see her house is empty."

"Heard on the crystal? What are you talking about? You're not thinking of leaving—" I stammered. "I need to know more." I realized my chances for world travel and meeting with the likes of Jules Verne might be about to "hop" away. Then I thought of something else *She's leaving with them. It's not fair.*

I whirled to face Jerry and Matt, angry that they hadn't even offered to take me – or had they? *There was something he said about not understanding it at first, but with my intelligence I would soon enough.*

Caddie laughed and tugged me into the small compartment. "Just let the boys do their work, then. I'm sure we have plenty of catching up. Besides, I have to make sure everything's ready in here and then get you back."

What do you mean get me back? Who says I—— but the next sight left me even more open-mouthed. "Captain Nemo's organ? Really?" I gasped at the crystalline manuals and jewel-like draw knobs that filled the space below a window that looked out into the blackness of the cave. She didn't answer, having become focused on her assignment.

I sat beside her, watching as she checked the various levers and dials, switching the buttons and checking the indicators.

"So, you know how to work this, this - I guess it's like a boat?" I asked, keeping my eyes on every move and sequence of gestures.

"Djerah is teaching me. He doesn't need to do any of this, though. He just puts on this helmet and then thinks about where and when, but he's been doing this for years. I need to start with the mechanical ways. He says it's too dangerous."

"Let me see that." I reached for the helmet that lay on the top manual and looked inside it. *It really does look like a Mardi Gras mask in the front, all sparkly. He thought Matt shouldn't have done whatever he did to me either because it was too dangerous.* I popped it on my head and thought carefully as I could:

Take me home, morning of the next day to make the biscuits and gravy I promised.

I heard my sister screaming as the sight left my eyes and my world began to spin, but I concentrated as if this was the best lucid dream and I was directing everything about my reality. The pain was worse than any headache I had known and for the briefest of moments I thought I felt it burning my forehead. Caddie tugged, trying to take the helmet off. Then I lost sight of her.

I saw and slowly joined a speeded-up version of myself bustling around my kitchen, cooking breakfast and packing it. I went to the door when the men came by to bring Mabel back. They asked about the wolf attack and I affirmed nothing had happened.

Knowing they would be back, I saw myself writing a note that Caddie and her "husband" had returned from Europe and were taking me to Paris at once. The horrid pain in my head increased. I was nearly gasping as I added that Junebug the yard man should take care of Mabel while I was gone, tacked it on the door and then loaded fresh, hot biscuits and gravy in a basket along with marmalade, soft boiled eggs and a tin of coffee. *My head! I'll die.* And then: *Oh, but it was worth it. I had to just do it.* I tumbled forward into nothingness.

Hattie why? Caddie sobbed in the distance. *We warned you. Now you've killed yourself!*

"Wait. Here she comes—she did it! She's phasing in now and wait—Oh damn, what a woman! I can smell…" I heard Matt's voice and felt his arms around me again. This time they were more than welcome as he led me to the fainting couch and took my things.

"Biscuits and gravy, everyone." I stammered, and lay back, satisfied as Matt dug greedily through the basket and began to pass out breakfast.

"I'll steam us up some coffee and then–Paris," he winked and broke open a biscuit for me. They were the best batch I ever made, but not the last.

THE BEGINNING

Mobius

Thomas Woldering

Who holds an interview this early? I thought as I paced the hallway on the hundred and twenty-third floor of the Mobius Corporation headquarters. The halls really looked like something out of that old space odyssey movie; white, circular, and made from fiberglass. Both sides of the tube-like hallway had wide fiber-optic strips which slowly cycled through the rainbow embedded in them at waist level. *Do I just wait here? Let's get this started.*

I recalled what the Mobius recruiter, an older gentleman named Mr. Werner, had told me yesterday: 'Elise Desoto. Dr. Schiller requests you for an interview at Mobius at 6:30 in the morning tomorrow, December 21st, 2012 for the position of head physicist once you finish your research. Your student loans will be absorbed if you accept the position, and you will be paid five thousand dollars for showing up even if you do not accept.'

His offer was unbelievable. Anyone would accept it even if they just showed up and left, but it also made me incredibly suspicious. I wasn't worthy of that job… yet. I was working on something revolutionary which would make me the best candidate, but I had been very tight-lipped about it.

My invention and the subject of my research was more like Sci-Fi or magic than something you'd see in the real world. An instant, one-way portal to anywhere that I called a Translocator. It would usher in the next era of humanity. I invented it and I knew it worked, but I hadn't gone public because I couldn't explain why yet. *Has Mobius found out? How?*

They must know something if Doctor Rosalyn Schiller herself wants to interview me. She wasn't just <u>a</u> scientist or corporate leader, she was <u>the</u> scientist and corporate leader. She had been reading books and solving math problems before she could walk. Mobius, my school – New Babylon University, the whole city of New Babylon, and even the new state of Delmarva grew here around the farm where she was born in what used to be Delaware. She was that important. I felt a bit intimidated, but my curiosity about what they knew and my eagerness to work at a place like Mobius outweighed it.

I straightened my gray suit coat and skirt again, hoping she or someone from Mobius would come soon.

"Good morning, Elise."

A woman's voice came out of the walls around me. I was startled because the accent strip in the walls suddenly shifted colors with the modulation of her voice, like the output on a sound mixer. "Hello," I quickly responded, and then followed with: "Where are you?" I was instantly embarrassed by that. Confusion wasn't a good first impression.

The voice from the walls chuckled, then a set of doors at the end of the hall slid open with a whooshing sound. "Through here. I expected them to bring you right to my office," the woman explained.

I instantly felt worse. *That's definitely Doctor Schiller, and I'm looking like a fool. She must have cameras on me. How long has she been watching?* I worried more, but then I stopped myself. *It's okay. Just play it off like Auntie Rose said: 'It's not the mistake that matters, it's how you recover.'* I gathered my wits and headed for the open door. As I walked, I couldn't help but think about Dr. Schiller. *Why was she chuckling? She must be even more eccentric than the news says.*

The room I stepped into next was an enormous gallery with dozens of roped-off displays and a red carpet weaving a path around them on the black marble floor. It still had that faux-spaceship look to it, but scaled up to two stories. One wall was the glass-covered side of the building and looked out across the vast skyline of New Babylon. The center of the floor was taken up by a coin-filled fountain with a large metal rendering of the company logo, a mobius strip, suspended above it using an anti-gravity field.

Is this the observation deck? Where they take the tours? I had never bothered to come to Mobius to see it before; I wasn't a tourist.

On the far end of the gallery, I saw glass stairs that led up to a set of doors on an enormous frosted glass cube. The cube was suspended from the ceiling by thick cables. *Doctor Schiller's Office?* I thought. *She must really like talking to the public if she put it here.*

I stepped off briskly for the elevated office, but then I saw something old and gray hung in a glass display case. *A newspaper? That must be ancient.* I read the headline to myself quickly. "Albert Einstein debates physics with the Mobius Girls." *This must be talking about Doctor Schiller,* I realized. *How old was she then?* I looked for the date; 1952. *So, she was seven? I know she was smart very early, but that's amazing.*

The next display was a timeline. "1945, the Mobius Girls are born. 1948, US government forms the Mobius Project for Genius Girls to study hyper-intelligent girls born at the end of World War II. 1949, Mobius Girls brought together for the first time. 1958, Mobius Unlimited formed by Mr. Ross Schiller to take the inventions of the Mobius Girls into the private sector." *It's a good timeline, but I can't read the whole thing now.*

A much more interesting row of displays stood up the way, along the path to the office. *The first desktop personal computer from 1955, designed by the Mobius Project for Genius Girls.* I read as I walked past. *Computers got smaller so quickly. From whole rooms to desktops in just a few years, and all because of Mobius. Only the most powerful servers take up more than your pocket these days.* I kept heading down the row. *The first fiber-optic link-up from 1961 by*

Mobius Unlimited? That was how Mobius made its money – they invented and installed fiber-optic communications trunk lines across the country, only two years after inventing the internet. The next display was much larger and more stunning. *The first hover-car – 1967 – Mobius Corporation.* Their anti-gravity technology was one of their most famous inventions, and it played a big part in my project.

I looked up and shook my head. Just like that, I had fallen into the tourist trap. *Plenty of time to look at these later.* I rushed past the other displays: the first cellular phone from 1970, the first holo-projector from 1980, the first quantum computer chip from 1988, the plans for the first fusion reactor from 1996, force-fields, industrial air scrubbers, severe weather suppression, and more. Mobius had invented so much, but they had still never come across the idea of a Translocator. I smiled, thinking that it really deserved a place here. *I hope they see that too, it'd be amazing to work here.*

Then, I heard Doctor Schiller's voice. It was like it came from everywhere in the gallery.

"Elise Desoto. 23 years old. Daughter of Hikari Ito and Randolph Desoto. Half Japanese, Half American. Born in Japan, but raised here in New Babylon City, Delmarva. Your father left when you were quite young and you had a tough life growing up until you came to New Babylon. Still, you kept to your studies even with having to work the odd job for money. I believe you are working in a sandwich shop right now, yes? But you're also one of the top postgraduate physics students at New Babylon University. You're far ahead of others your age to already be working on a doctorate, and your work in dimensional physics is years ahead of anything else publicly available."

Okay, what? Have they really been spying on me? I couldn't believe how much she knew. I considered turning back. *No,*

Auntie Rose would never want me to pass up an opportunity like this, I approached the bottom of the glass steps. The doors to the office slid open.

"I never liked introductions, not that we need one." I heard a woman speaking from the top of the stairs, but the voice wasn't the same.

A different woman was standing in the doorway. She was Asian, with light skin and long straight hair like me. There was no way to mistake her for Doctor Schiller, whose fiery, red curls and round, green eyes were on the front of so many business magazines. Even though the woman at the top of the stairs had grayer hair and more wrinkles than when I last saw her, I instantly recognized her.

"Auntie Rose?" My voice shot up in surprise. I could hardly believe it. I had just been thinking of her, and there she was; my mom's friend Rose. I had always called her 'Auntie'. She had practically raised me while my mom was still working. We still e-mailed each other sometimes, but I hadn't seen her in person in at least twelve years. "What are you doing here?"

"Interviewing you. Well, not really. You're already hired, but I needed you to be here."

But... What? How? You? I stood there slack-jawed and tried to parse what she had said. The exciting thought 'Hired! She said hired!' rampaged through my head along with utter confusion, and a mix of relief and disbelief.

Auntie Rose laughed. It was the same sort of chuckle I'd heard from Doctor Schiller earlier. "I should take a picture of that. A fly could go right in there," she came down the stairs, tapped my jaw, and then took my hand.

"But you hate pictures," was all I could say as I wiped the dumb expression off my face.

She smiled again, calling me by my nickname. "You're looking right at me, Ellie, but you're not seeing it yet. It always does take a minute, but you're so clever. You'll get it."

"Huh?" I looked at her again. There was something strange about how she looked, but I couldn't put my finger on it. *Maybe it's just that I'm the same height as her now.* She was dressed formally, with an outfit that was identical to mine except for the blouse color. I had never seen her dressed like this. I always remembered her looking like she had fallen through several clothing racks at an outlet store; beaten-up jeans or skirts, fingerless gloves, and a mish-mash of different shirts, sweaters, and hats. I had to press her on it: "What's with the suit?"

"Well, this is how I dress at work. Looks like we shop at the same store. Come with me, though. I need to take you to the lab." She led me up the stairs.

"You work here?" I followed her through the office. It had everything a head executive's office would have, all made from glass and brushed nickel to match the walls. I managed to confirm it was Doctor Schiller's office by glancing at the nameplate on the desk as we rushed by. *Where's Doctor Schiller though?*

"Mobius has always been one of my top priorities. You were just a girl the last time I saw you. There was no need to talk about business." Auntie Rose told me as we approached a set of elevator doors in the back corner of the office.

That wasn't a good enough answer. "This is a lot more than business. You're important enough to be using a private elevator in Doctor Schiller's office. You never mentioned this even once, though. Mama never told me either, and she would have. You told us you were going to do relief work in the Middle East when you left."

She pressed the elevator button and the doors whooshed open. Then, looking at me matter-of-factly, she answered: "Well the Middle East isn't a desert anymore, is it?"

"No, it isn't… you're saying that you were on that team?" My eyes shot open wide. The terraforming of the Middle East was the first full-scale test of weather manipulation and rapid growth technology. The great redwood forests of Arabia now rivaled those that had existed for hundreds of years. It was mankind's greatest technological achievement.

"I was. Please, step in. I don't want to talk about that project right now – I want to talk about your research."

"What does Mobius know about my research? They seem to know everything about me," I asked her, wanting my suspicions relieved.

"I'm not asking for Mobius, I'm asking for me. I know you're a post-grad. I spent so much time teaching you years ago, I want to know what'll earn you a doctorate," she replied.

"Well, okay…" I hesitated again "…but I want the rest of this explained after I tell you."

"I'm sure it will all become clear soon enough," she pressed an elevator button labeled 'Project Mobius Lab'. We shot downward at a high-but-steady speed. "Go ahead."

"Well, it's been in my head forever. Remember when I was a kid and we'd hang up a curtain? How I pretended there were two totally different places on either side when I walked through it?"

"Yes, we did that a lot."

"Well, it's sort of like that. I could say more, but you wouldn't understand dimensional physics." I doubted.

Another chuckle. "You seem so certain. That doesn't matter, though. If you can't break it down into terms anyone can understand…"

"Then what's the use of having done the work? I know," I finished one of the phrases she had repeated to me so often that it was practically etched on my brain. "Okay, I'll try. It's a small project, just me and a few undergrads helping out, but it has so much potential. I'm building a Translocator. Like that curtain, you step onto the platform of our machine and step off… anywhere. Anywhere you can picture in your mind. You don't dematerialize, you're just suddenly elsewhere."

"Really? That sounds like fantasy, not physics. There's no way to travel instantly in the universe. It *would* be revolutionary if it were true, though," Auntie Rose sounded impressed. "Why do you think it can be done?"

I was glad she asked. I couldn't help going on about it, with how rare it was to find someone who was interested in the details. "Because it's not done in the universe. When we send something into the Translocator, it leaves the universe and comes back in at any point."

"Now that <u>IS</u> fantasy," she emphasized.

Shaking my head, I corrected her. "No, and you should know it if you're so high up in Mobius. It relies on your technology. I stumbled across it when I was toying with some of Mobius' anti-gravity emitters. I focused a bunch of them on a wood cube and part of it just disappeared — it left the universe."

Auntie Rose looked worried. "That's really dangerous, Ellie. You're intentionally making an anti-gravity storm," she told me. "Those maim people."

I shook my head. "I'm not done. I spent my first few postgrad years coming up with equations to read the storm and tune the emitters so that I could send entire objects out of the universe without being 'maimed'. My research now is on getting them to re-appear and how we can apply that."

"You mean you got something to re-appear after it was hit by an anti-gravity storm?" Auntie Rose sounded stunned and amazed.

I smiled proudly at her. "I did, and that's the strangest part – almost like magic. I could never get the receiving platform to work, but then one time in frustration I pictured the target re-appearing in front of me and it did! I know that sounds even more crazy, but it's repeatable. I've sent so many wood cubes up in the air, and sometimes they ended up down in the floor. We even sent one of my undergrad's pet hamsters across the room. It works! I've come up with lots of theories about how, but we need to observe what's outside the universe so we can make the receiving platform work. A person will have to go through to collect that data. Once the receiving platform works, imagine what we could do."

The elevator slowed to a stop, but the doors didn't open. "Oh, I can imagine," Auntie Rose said breathlessly, then gave me a very serious look. "If that's true, and that's a big 'if', who'd be going first, Ellie? It's such a risk."

"I'm going to go. I can't ask anyone else to. I'm not going to try to go across the world or something, just across the room. I know the material the best. I can make the needed observations so we can determine the science behind it and finish the receiving platform. The benefits are worth the risks – barely any need for cars, roads, boats, or even spaceships. It would help so many people, and that's all I've ever wanted to do."

"It's very selfless of you. It reminds me of well, me – when I was your age." She took out an old-style key and unlocked a keyhole next to the Project Mobius button. "So, would the Translocator look anything like this?"

The doors whooshed open, and shock hit me immediately. The room outside the elevator was massive, and the centerpiece of the room was a raised metal platform with thirteen metal arms reaching up from it. The arms were rough looking. They twisted and branched like they were knotty trees which had been turned to metal, but the centers of each arm became rod-like and bent in to point at the middle of the platform. Massive black cables snaked to the platform from the power supplies by the wall.

I felt betrayed and robbed. "This is my Translocator design! What's going on here? How did Mobius get this?" I exclaimed and took a few steps out of the elevator into the massive cement-walled room. It was full of massive supercomputers, control terminals, and other bits of tech. It lacked all the clean, finished features of the floors above except for the fiber-optic band at the center of the wall. There was also a large LED clock suspended from the ceiling, ticking away the seconds in Universal Coordinated Time.

I heard Auntie's heels tapping on the polished cement floor as she followed me out of the elevator. "I know what you're thinking. Mobius didn't take it from you. We've always had it," she told me.

I darted over to the machine and circled around it a few times, going over each detail I could lock my eyes onto. *Even down to the bolt patterns and cable connections. What's going on here?* It wasn't possible. "So, you were faking all that surprise then? God, what kind of trick is Mobius pulling? My design is here exactly, and it's just not being used? Why? What the hell is this?" I felt frenzied.

"Ellie, calm down," she tried to put a hand on my shoulder again, but I shrugged it away. She continued: "This machine has a very specific purpose. You need to go through this Translocator today. That's the way it has to be, a duty to the world, to science, and to the betterment of mankind." Her tone came across very solemn as she told me this. It wasn't what I was expecting at all.

I didn't feel frenzied anymore, just more confused. "What do you mean? Is Mobius spying on me? How did they get this? Have they traveled outside the universe and come back?" I insisted on knowing.

"Well, I have," she chuckled again, just like Doctor Schiller had over the intercom. "You're still not seeing it, Ellie. I'd better just point it out. Come over here with me," she beckoned me to follow and walked towards an old, wide mirror which was standing beside one of the terminals.

I froze as she motioned with her hand. *Her hand. How did I never notice that? Wait, she's not wearing gloves. She always used to wear gloves!* I thought.

Auntie Rose had a long, faded scar on the back of her right hand. I looked at the scar on the back of my right hand. *It's not just similar, it's the same.* A disorienting feeling of dread hit me.

"Come on. We're on a tight schedule."

I refused: "No." At the same time that the dread weighed on me, it felt like everything was falling into place as well. I studied her silently for a moment longer and the thought appeared in my head. *A mirror. No. It's not a mirror, it's reversed. That's why I didn't see it. It's like having a twin!* "Auntie, you look exactly like me – just older. You even have the scar Papa gave me."

"Are you going to come over here and look in this mirror with me?" she asked, grinning.

I walked forward with a jolt, quickly stepping over to join her. *She's entertained by this?* I wasn't ready for what I saw in the mirror then, not at all. As soon as I saw it, I looked away and covered my face in embarrassment. "Oh, you gotta be kidding me! What did you do to that mirror?"

She chuckled like Doctor Schiller had again, because that's who the mirror showed her to be. I saw a woman who looked like an older version of me, but the mirror showed an elderly White woman with red, curly hair.

"It's just a mirror. Inspect it if you like – break it even. I always encourage experimenting and observing," she spouted one of Mobius' taglines.

Your hair, I turned to her with that thought and reached into what I saw as her long black hair. *That's...* I couldn't believe what I saw. My hand was passing through what I saw as her hair like it was a ghost. I felt the curls instead. When I drew one of the curls out, it looked to my eyes like I was holding nothing. In the mirror, though, I saw the hair in my grasp. I thought of what sort of technology might be able to fake this, but came up empty. There was no invention that could do this. "That's how Mobius knows so much about me. You're Doctor Schiller!" I let go of her hair and stepped away cautiously from the weirdness in front of me. "How didn't I know?"

"I didn't make it easy for you. Wearing wigs and gloves, not using my last name, avoiding you in person once you were old enough to notice, avoiding reflective things, avoiding cameras – they show me as I really am too. At least Mama sees the same thing as you; that made it easier."

You said Mama? Why not call her Kari? That feeling of dread returned. I walked to one of the supercomputer rows and leaned on it for support a moment. I looked at the machine in the room, my invention, then back to her again. "You're me? Or I guess, I'm you?" I turned back to her. "That has to be it. You have the machine because I invented it, and you're saying I have to go through this machine today because you did. So, I'll end up as you?"

"That's a quick, smart deduction," Doctor Schiller gave me a surprised look. It's on the smarter end of what I've seen.

But, no it's not that simple. I am Doctor Rosalyn Schiller – but you can still call me Auntie, or just Rose if you want. What you see in the mirror is what's physically here, but what's in my head is what you see when you look at me. I was you when I stepped into that machine in my first, very different, 2012."

"Ah!" I exclaimed, stepping away from the computer and back to her. "So that's how they saw you as a child genius. It wasn't the birth of the atomic age, or new medicines, or any of those things they talk about in the history books. That's not really fair; it's like cheating on a test."

"I'd call it studying well," Doctor Schiller corrected.

"Fine, whatever," I didn't feel like pressing her on it. It really was cheating, though, and she wasn't any more gifted than me to start with. "So, it's obviously possible for a person to come back from outside the universe, but how were you born as a different baby in 1945?" I tried again, leaning in close.

"You ask more questions than I'm used to," she sighed.

"What are the answers?" I pushed.

"It was a long time ago, Ellie. I don't remember." Her admission astonished me. "One moment I was in 2012 with Doctor Werner running the machine while I went in to test, and the next moment I was being born."

I shook my head. It didn't make any sense. "Why did you build the machine again, then?"

"Because it has to be built. Who knows what would happen now if I didn't do it? It could destroy the universe if I let the loop end," she explained, sounding burdened from having to answer.

"No, that can't be right. This isn't a loop. If you're me, then Rosalyn Schiller was someone else the first time. You wouldn't have had an 'Auntie' that time around." It was obvious to me that a time loop made no sense. *Whiteboard. You gotta have one somewhere.* She did; it was off to the side of the

Translocator platform. I ran to it and picked up a marker. "Come on, let's figure this out."

Doctor Schiller's heels clicked on the cement floor again as she quickly joined me at the whiteboard. "Ellie, none of that matters. It's December 21st we…"

"So what? You're not saying you believe that junk prophecy about the Mayan calendar and the end of the world?" I was astonished. "It's being misinterpreted. No credible major religion puts a date on the end of the world."

"Religion has nothing to do with it, Ellie." She threw her hands up, sounding exasperated, then begrudgingly said: "I barely believe in anything religious with what I've been through. I'm a scientist first." She straightened her jacket and her tone turned more resolute. "I don't care about nutty prophecies. I just happened to go back on December 21st 2012 at 11:59:59 UTC. That's a little under fifteen minutes away, and you need to be imprinted and make your trip outside the universe before the time that I did," she insisted, glancing at a medical-looking chair nearby which was covered in sensors and other technology. "This isn't the attitude I expect from you."

"Attitude? What do you mean? I've always been curious."

"You should understand the significance of this duty and go through with it without questioning. The universe could depend on it."

"Well if it's that important, I guess I will." I could hardly believe what she was thrusting onto me. "But saying I have to go because you did still makes no sense," I shook my head. "We need to spend all our time up to when I have to step in there trying to figure out what went wrong. Just repeating this without fixing anything isn't the way to get a stable Translocator."

Doctor Schiller put her hand on her forehead and sighed. "This isn't a translocation experiment anymore. It's a system, and it's much bigger than you understand."

Just then, an old-looking landline phone on a desk near the whiteboard rang.

"Oh, good timing. Pick it up. Maybe this is the best way for you to find out," Doctor Schiller folded her arms now, waiting for me to answer the ring. "You have to go. You always go."

I stepped over and got it. "Hello?"

"Is that you, Ellie? It must be," a woman on the phone greeted me. "I remember that voice. This is President Hill. Are you ready to go through? We're all counting on you."

The President? President Jeanine Hill? Why is she... no! I stared at Auntie Rose as the rest of it dawned on me. "How many of us are there?" I asked into the phone and loudly enough that I knew Doctor Schiller could hear me too. *It's the Mobius Girls. Plural.*

"You're number Fifty. This doesn't sound right. Let me talk to Rose," the President of the United States ordered.

I handed the phone over and stepped away. *Fifty? Auntie sent forty-eight other copies of us back in time after she went? I'm just the latest in a long line? Why? What purpose could that serve?*

"No, it'll work out, Jeanie. No, it's not like number 23 again. Just a sort of curiosity and persistence I haven't seen before. I think she knows what's at stake now. No. As is, if I have to. We didn't imprint originally, but we did by your time. It's not strictly necessary. Okay. We'll see you in D.C. in '49."

I heard her talking and walked closer to the strange chair she had looked at when she mentioned imprinting. *So many cables to the head. Imprinting what? Information? That must be it! Auntie's going to pack my head full of information to carry back?* It only took a moment for me come up with a theory. *It's so they can have their latest inventions ready to be re-invented in the past, isn't it? That's why we had such a jump in science and technology after they were born. Forty-nine people all with heads full of designs and theories. They bring back more each time!*

Doctor Schiller hung the phone up. "Are you ready for imprinting now? I just promised the President we'd get you sent back even if we had to skip the imprint, but we can still get it done I think. Just take a seat and we'll start," she said, walking up behind me.

I turned around to face her. "Promised the President? You know that doesn't carry the same weight if I know she's just an earlier version of me. I can't believe this! Forty-eight times without even questioning what went wrong? What are we to you anyway? Vessels for information? That's why we're being 'imprinted', right? Am I going to carry back the designs for your latest rapid growth technology, so you can put a forest in the desert in 1980?"

"No," she shook her head vigorously, then stopped suddenly. "Well, yes I was going to imprint that, but you're so much more." She corrected herself, then continued. "She's the president, after all. All of us are important to the world. You could be a corporate leader, a cultural icon, a powerful politician – whatever you want. We are the people who move this world forward. Our technology has saved so many lives and the planet itself," she smiled proudly and continued. "We've prevented major historical disasters too. When I was you, there were two buildings in New York - the twin towers of the World Trade Center. They fell to a terrorist attack and plunged America into a long war on terror. As Rosalyn Schiller the first time, I convinced the government to take precautions. We averted the disaster. By the fifteenth time, terror groups never arose in the Middle East in the first place. The Mobius Girls prevent the deaths of millions by using what we know from the future-past.

Can you think of any disasters to prevent for next time? I could certainly name a few: the S.S. Imperius' crash on the Moon and the loss of the Atlantis submersible colony. That's what we do, and it's great."

"Auntie," I tried to stop her. I couldn't believe what I was hearing. *You're in control of the whole world and you fix any disaster – but what about me and Mama?*

She continued without recognizing I had spoken. "Now, you'll be disoriented when you get there, but it'll be around my birthday – August 6th 1945. Don't be scared if it's dark, you might still be in the womb for a few days or weeks. You'll have to keep quiet once you're born until it's reasonable for you to show your intelligence. That won't be too hard, though, your new body will be busy growing up. Get to know the family you end up in. You'll most likely be in the news for your genius about the same time that we all get into the news. The US government will find you shortly after they find me and then start up the Mobius project. We'll all be brought to Washington D.C. in 1949. Now, get in the chair and we'll get you imprinted."

I walked back to the white board and started writing out my thoughts on what might have gone wrong with the experiment. "If you think of something it comes back. It comes back in where you see it coming back. If you don't think of it, it's lost forever. We all end up in different bodies… but why would you not come back where you think you would?" I quietly recited to myself as I wrote.

"Ellie, are you even listening? Please, get in the chair." Doctor Schiller walked up close to me again.

I wanted to ignore her and keep trying to solve the problem. It galled me that she was presuming so much, and every moment I was getting more upset that Mama and me suffered so much while she was the most powerful woman in the world. I couldn't think of her like the respected scientist Doctor Schiller anymore. I couldn't even think of her as an 'Auntie'. I turned to face her. *This could go badly, but I can't let this go on.* "Rose, I'm not going."

She let out a short, absurd laugh. "What do you mean? Of course you're going. You *must* go. We can skip the imprinting if that has you concerned, but that would delay our plans to terraform Mars." Rose waited for me to reply, but I said nothing. Her tone incredulous, she continued. "I mean, why wouldn't you go? There must be some reason. None of us has ever even considered saying 'no'."

"What about 'Number 23'?" I called her out on what I'd just overheard her saying to the President.

"Elise number 23 is Doctor Yevette Sutter, the famous psychologist. She hesitated because she ended up a psychologist, not a scientist, when she was you. Some sort of fluke. She thought I was crazy until she saw the mirror. Even though she barely understood us, she knew we had to continue," Rose shut down the argument. "Why would you consider saying 'no'?"

"Because of what you did with me and Mama," I barked at her. *Talking at me like I'm stupid or crazy for saying 'no', I'll spell it out for you then!* I continued, my angry tone telegraphing exactly how I felt. "You deceived us for years, when you knew the sort of things that were going to happen. We still suffered so much." I choked up as some of the memories came back to me, but managed to keep my tears down. "I still have the scar from Papa on the back of my hand just like you. I've still had to support both me and Mama. Why haven't you stepped in?"

"What do you mean? I did. I helped you two come to New Babylon and get away from Papa," she sounded offended at the accusation.

"And Mama still has cancer! You could have done more, but instead you disappear except for emails. Then, you reveal who you are a half-hour before you ask me to become a new person in the past to support this system of yours! What kind of bullshit is that?"

"Now don't be vulgar," she quickly responded, but I could tell she was struggling to continue her response. "You don't understand. I have to make sure you go through what I did each time so you turn out the same. We had to make sure of that, especially after Elise 23. Don't worry about Mama, she'll be young again and live again…"

"And she'll be abused by Papa again and suffer cancer again too! For the fifty-first time!" I was practically screaming at her.

"Look, you need to calm down. You're not seeing this rationally. Please go." Rose restarted, requesting earnestly, then followed with: "Don't make this about you. Maybe in future cycles we can make Elise or Mama suffer less – but that's no reason to end all the improvements that we make. Besides, I told you stopping could be disastrous."

"No, it's not a loop," I interrupted her.

"Fine, it isn't," she admitted. "We are all linked, though. Our timelines happen within the one before," she thought about it for a moment then stuck her finger up like she'd just had a great idea. "Ah! It's more like one of those Russian nesting dolls and we keep making more, smaller dolls inside the larger one. If we suddenly crack them all open and jump back from the center to the outside, it would be too much of a shock for time to handle."

Though I was still angry, she had a point. I had made this about me, and there could be danger the way she described things. *If I have a problem with her, I can just have nothing to do with her after I go back,* I looked down and considered for a long moment. *I would be bound to live over and over again, though… but maybe it's a duty. I wouldn't want to sacrifice the universe for just me.*

Gosh, what's it been like for her to live fifty times? What about the first time she lived? She must have been so alone with no Auntie, I thought about it more. *Wait a minute, she said she had Doctor Werner helping her. Werner… Was that the same Mr. Werner who came to me with the offer?* The realization really shocked me. *He's not a scientist. Did she make it that way?*

I had been cooling down, but this realization reignited my anger. *She really changed his life. Has she changed it each time? That's so manipulative. How many people has she manipulated with what she knows? It's like she's…* A striking thought on the subject occurred, and at that moment I knew I needed to stop her.

I locked eyes with her again. "No. This isn't just about me. There's so much more than that."

Rose had worn a look of confidence before I spoke, but now she stumbled bleakly towards one of the terminals. I followed her.

"I need to sit down," she plopped down heavily in a chair and put a hand on her brow, leaning on the terminal desk. "None of us are ready for you to do this. We haven't made any plans for what to do with the world past 2012 – if we even survive you ending all this. At least go through and give us a cycle to make preparations and research what would happen." She appealed to me and offered her hand in friendship. "You want to figure out what went wrong? Fine, figure it out next time. It's a good compromise."

"No!" I stepped away from her hand and offer. "Don't you see how immoral it is to make the world go through this? We can't do it. This happens now. If you haven't prepared, then maybe that's the punishment due for… God, this Mobius strip you've turned time into." I couldn't believe I hadn't noticed that. "That's why you picked the name, isn't it?"

"It is," Rose said, a hint of offense in her tone as the desperate, pleading expression left her face. "And what do you mean punishment? Who are you to judge us for that or any of what we do? Who are you to punish us?" She looked to be getting as riled up as me. We really were alike. "We acted for the betterment of the world, and we have improved it. So many things were worse in my 2012. We had significant global warming, plastics pollution, water supplies tainted by fracking, lack of resources causing wars and famine – I could keep listing problems until we run out of time."

"Yeah, and the next time around there's a whole new set of problems to deal with. All that's really different is you've made yourselves more important and you've stripped everyone else in the world of their agency just like you did to Doctor Werner," I accused her.

"What? Don't you dare bring Doctor Werner into this," she stood back up angrily, raising her voice at me. "I've made sure his life is one of complete privilege and comfort every time!"

I knew I'd hit a nerve. I still continued with: "but he's not a doctor. He's not my supervisor," I stood my ground.

"What kind of stupidity is that?" Rose belted out with disdain. "Of course, he isn't. We can't have him inventing the machine first with someone else."

She's just admitting it. He's a pet, and she doesn't see it! I was astounded. "See? What if he wanted to be one? That's the decision he would have made without you interfering. You've devalued his life, just like you've devalued everyone's lives! No matter what things go wrong, you just go on making more technology and reset it all again. They live, but their lives don't matter in the end."

"And? Why should anything from the last cycle matter? It un-happens when we go back," she yelled finally.

I walked back to the white board, then turned to face Rose again. She was quaking in anger. *I guess she must have been closer to Doctor Werner than I knew. I've gotta defuse this before I give her a heart attack.* I continued more calmly. "No, it doesn't. You remember it, so it happened. Look, I don't want to argue about this. I don't have to explain myself to you either. I wanted to, but if we're just going to have a screaming match then I'm just going to leave."

"You think you have that option?" Rose cynically dismissed, then sat down again at the supercomputer terminal beside her. She keyed in some commands quickly.

"Warmup initiated," a computerized voice called out from speakers along the wall. It startled me so much that I nearly jumped into the whiteboard. The machine beside me hummed to life, dimming the lights for a moment with the start-up. Magnificent blue wisps of light started to dance in the center of the platform as the anti-gravity emitters on the arms powered up in order. I felt a slight unease in my stomach from gravity being manipulated so powerfully close by me. The stripe on the wall started cycling through blue shades, giving the whole room an odd glow.

I darted to the other side of the white board, putting more distance between myself and the Translocator. *What's she thinking?!* I faced her, then glanced behind myself for a second to make sure I wasn't backing toward any other machines.

Rose started walking toward me slowly and menacingly. "You're going, whether you like it or not. Don't make me push you."

"You'd really do that? You'd throw me out of the universe?" I was stunned, but then a thought occurred to me. *Oh, but that's it, isn't it? That's why we couldn't come back into the universe where we wanted! But why August 6th 1945? Oh! Hiroshima Day! But that means...*

Breakthroughs came to me most often when I was under pressure, and a big one had just hit now. Thoughts and notions were bombarding me so quickly. I had just figured out why we weren't coming back how we expected, and some of the possibilities in my head had shocking implications. *I need more time. I need time to sort this out and make her understand what's happening here, but she's about to grab me and throw me on the platform.* I paused and thought about that for an instant. *Wait, why am I even worried? You're sixty-seven.* I dashed away quickly and climbed up on top of one of the supercomputers, breaking a few handles on the casing on the way up. "Good luck, Rose."

"Get down from there!" she yelled, quickly walking up to the edge of the computer.

"No. I can stay as long as I want up here. You probably can't call security down here to get me down. You wouldn't give anyone but us access to this room."

She looked at her holophone watch for a moment, then lowered it again. I knew I was right about security.

"Damnit!" She tried to jump and reach up for me, but could barely get her arm over the top of the computer. Neither of us was very tall. "Damnit! Damnit, why are you doing this?" she stormed away. "You must do this. We all did this! It just has to be." Pointing up at the clock, she continued. "You see that clock up there? 1155 – We have less than five minutes!"

"No, I need a moment to think," I told her while I tried to sort out all of the ideas which had just come to me. *If I just try to explain it straight through, she'll just shut me out. How do I get this across? Wait, she's like me – I'll just trick her into asking the questions.*

"Elise Desoto, you get down here!" she demanded again like a cross mother, but stopped short of more yelling.

"It's Hiroshima Day," I told her resolutely, leaving it at that.

"What?" She looked to the Translocator and then back to me, confused.

"August 6th 1945. You and all the rest of us go back on the day Hiroshima was bombed."

Rose pointed at the floor and commanded. "Stop wasting my time with things you know that I know. Get down here now!"

"No, I'm not done," I continued forcefully. "We all come back there because that bomb obliterated so many people within seconds – it sent them out of the universe and we got sucked in. It's the only place it could happen!"

Rose shook her head and paced again, then pointed up at me, accusing. "You'd see the universe end for your personal crusade and it's not even well-reasoned! You've brought things back in elsewhere yourself, or did you conveniently forget that?"

I grinned. *I knew I could egg her on into asking that.* "That's the easiest part of all this. You can't bring yourself back into the universe where you want because you're not in the universe anymore!"

"What?" she took a step back and asked.

"When we brought everything back, we were still here and we'd gone forward in time when we brought it back – no issues." I paused a moment to punctuate it, then took off again. "Once we're outside, only someone else could have brought us back. No one did, so we got sucked back in at the same time so many other people were blasted out."

Rose stood silently, then shook her head in disbelief. "It's a sound theory. Are you done pushing us to the brink now? Come down and get on the Translocator, please. You've proven your point, Ellie."

I smirked. "That's not possible now. You know the truth, and you'll be incapable of putting me out of your mind now. I'll never be able to be sent back, so give it up!"

"Shit!" she stormed away, then banged her fist so hard against one of the computers that she started cradling it when she drew it back. "You had to do that, didn't you?" she turned back to me. "Why? Even if things don't un-happen, everyone out there still gets to make decisions. We haven't destroyed free will and agency."

"In the big picture, you have. You've taken out consequence and legacy along with it," I said, but stopped short of another round of arguing. "Fine. I didn't want to go this far, but what if I could prove more? What if I could prove you've been killing people directly, too? Just snuffing their souls out like candles?"

"Then I'd call you a religious nut like you tried to call me," Rose snapped back, still cradling her hand.

I started on her. "Proof in fact. Forty-nine times the consciousness of one person has been transported from one body into another that was about to be born. Call it a soul, a mental imprint, or whatever you want – it is a person. Human bodies are not born without consciousness of their own. Those bodies existed before the original August 6th 1945 and had their own. Therefore, you personally obliterated the original Rose Schiller and stole her body. You didn't know what would happen that time, but you did for the forty-eight times afterwards. You wilfully disposed of the minds that belonged in those bodies."

Going pale, Rose stammered, "No. No, even if I did all the other things you said – robbed the world of agency, consequence, legacy… even if I manipulated everyone… I've never murdered anyone. I help people!"

"Only those lucky enough to get a place in your world. How many more souls never got a chance to come into the world because you changed things and they were never born? Thousands? Millions?" I stepped down on her harder.

Rose crumpled down into her chair by the terminal and started sobbing. That's... well, I mean... I never thought..." she mumbled out more shocked phrases.

I had crushed her, and it didn't feel good. *I'm sorry, Rose. I had to stop this,* I thought. I climbed down from the top of the computer carefully.

As I reached the floor, the center of the platform flashed as the air around the center glowed a translucent blue. It shifted and wavered unnervingly. "Warmup completed. Aperture established," the computer read out in a cold, electronic voice. "You may proceed into the aperture."

Rose looked up at me, her face red and soaked. "Do you think there's forgiveness for what I've done?"

I sat down on the floor in front of her and the terminal. "I forgive you. You're just like me in the end. All you wanted to do was help people, and now that you understand what you've been doing you immediately agree that we have to stop."

"Yes, we do," Rose sniffed away her tears and dried her eyes. "I don't know what to do, Ellie. I'm not ready for this. It could all be over when that clock hits noon."

"I have faith that we'll get through it," I looked up and told her. "I don't mean religious faith either. I believe that if the universe is big and crazy enough that something as nonsensical as a soul jumping back in time into a baby can happen, then it will survive us. You were like that once – a young woman willing to step into a portal that would put her outside the universe just to take some readings. Be like that again."

"You're right," she sighed. "You know, you're more like me than any of the others have been before. I remember being as stubborn as you," Rose tried to smile, but she glanced up at the clock and her expression quivered and shifted into an uncertain frown. "Twenty-five seconds. Ellie, I'm scared," she admitted. "Not just of the world ending, but of what to do if it doesn't end."

"Then come down here. We'll face whatever's coming together," I offered.

Rose slid down from the chair and pushed herself up close to me.

I put my arms around her. "Only a few seconds now."

I looked up as Rose held onto me. The clock above the machine lazily ticked on to 11:59:58, 11:59:59, and then 12:00:00. It was 12:00:00 UTC. For the first time in over three thousand years, a new second became a part of history.

I saw a bright flash of white light from the platform. It hurt. I shut my eyes, but I could still see a yellow-red hue from behind my eyelids. It didn't go away. I heard Rose start to scream, but then everything went silent and faded away. I tried to call out 'hello', but nothing came out. I couldn't feel air on my skin, Rose's grasp, or the ground under my feet. *A void? Am I floating?*

Then, the most terrible feeling settled on me. *Falling. I feel like I'm falling,* I thought. Even without feeling a physical sensation, I had the distinct impression I was going down. *Was she right? Have I just destroyed time and the universe with it? No. It can't be. Whatever's happening, I still am. I exist. My thoughts are here.*

I couldn't tell how long the falling lasted, even my sense of time had slipped away. It didn't last forever, though, something caught me. It felt like the rushed catch of a drop ride at an amusement park. An instant later, I felt the ground, the terminal desk behind me, and Rose's grasp. I was breathing.

Smoke? I smelled and coughed. I still couldn't see anything except straight purple.

"Rose? Are you still there?" I asked, forgetting I was holding onto her.

"Yes," she took a few breaths. "I think so. I can't see. Did we survive? I was falling. Falling forever…"

"But something caught you. I felt it too."

"Are we still in the lab?" Rose coughed a few times too.

"I think so, I can feel the terminal," I reached up. "My sight's coming back, barely. It's really dark in here." I felt around on my wrist and lit up my holophone's flashlight. Shakily standing, I looked around as Rose held my other hand. "Oh," I remarked. "The Translocator melted."

"What?" Rose held her holophone up. "Call Maintenance." A few rings followed. "Yes, this is Doctor Schiller. Priority one, I need emergency lights and ventilation in the Project Mobius Lab," she coughed from the smoke again. "Yes, we felt it too. That's why it's priority one."

A moment later, dim white lights came on in the high ceiling of the lab and powerful fans began to suck out the smoke. The color strips on the wall started to cycle up, but they sparked and shut off again.

Rose scrambled up along the side of the desk, then carefully stepped closer to the pile of cooling metal and burnt-out circuitry that had been the Translocator. It sprayed sparks. "Manual Disconnect," she looked around quickly and stumbled over to an enormous switch on the wall by the elevator. "Ellie, help me pull this lever."

I joined her at the wall. The enormous lever was hooked into four gargantuan cables that ran to the Translocator. We pulled down on the level together and it forced the four cables out of their sockets. The sparking stopped and the lights came back to full brightness.

Then, I noticed it. "Rose, you're you! I can see you like everyone else does." I told her. I no longer saw her as an older copy of me.

"I don't? Are you serious?" Rose held her hands then lowered them sheepishly. "Well, I wouldn't see a difference anyway. You do, though?"

"It must mean everything's back to normal. We aren't linked like we were," I theorized as we walked back to the demolished platform.

"But what happened? Why did we feel like we fell? What caught us?" she spouted off questions.

"We don't look alike, but you sure sound as curious as me now," I smiled at her.

Rose blushed and slowed down. "The maintenance chief told me he and his crew felt the falling too, and I can't think of anyone more unrelated. Maybe the whole world felt it too?"

"That's gonna keep the conspiracy nuts going for a while," I joked.

Rose laughed as well, then sighed. "I don't even know how we'll explain this to the other girls, much less the public." She shook her head, overwhelmed, then surveyed the platform. "Ruined. That doesn't make any sense. These are just anti-gravity emitters."

You're right on that, I considered it too. "The circuitry would have blown before getting hot enough to melt metal. Logs?"

Rose was already moving to check them the moment I said it. "It needs to be rebooted," she waited. After reading the screen a moment, she sat back and rubbed her eyes. "I just… No. No, I can't. No more today."

I came over and looked closely at the screen. It was filled with lines of texts in various languages. About halfway down the screen, I saw one in English: 'Exploit Forbidden. Vulnerability removed. Repair completed. Do not attempt again.'

"Is this what I think it is?" she asked. I noticed her hands quaking.

I steadied them with mine. "I think it's clear, but we just can't accept it."

She shook her head and looked back at the screen again, typing a few more keystrokes. "Everything's gone except this screen. The programs, the equations..."

"I'll bet my prototypes are melted and my computers back at NBU are flushed too. Whatever caught us, fixed things, and did this is beyond us and beyond this universe."

She looked at me with a humbled look. "God?"

"If you want it to be. It doesn't have to be religious," I reminded her.

"Wow, I just really can't do this day anymore," she dragged her palms down her face. "No one will ever believe us."

"And they don't need to. I don't think this ever needs to go beyond the Mobius Girls. Let this mean whatever it means to everyone else. This world is theirs again now." I explained how I saw it.

Rose looked back at me with some pride, but I could tell she was still concerned. "Well I hope whatever fixed all this is as forgiving and open about this as you."

I smiled and pinched her arm. "Hey, it's not the mistake that matters, it's how you recover. We're still here, so we've been given a reprieve."

She chuckled again, then sighed in relief. "I think today has been all about you giving my own advice back to me." She shut off the terminal and looked to me again. "What'll we even do now? This is totally uncharted for me."

"You're still Doctor Schiller, CEO of Mobius. You can still do so much. You just have the same stake in the world as everyone else now," I encouraged her.

"You're right again. Such a problem solver," she got up with an optimistic smile on her face. I'll move Mobius forward now. I'll make things we never had the time to develop before, stop having to worry about re-inventing. It'll be a new start for us!" she looked up with such a triumphant expression. "So, what'll you do?" she looked back to me.

I smiled at her and stood up, straightening my suit jacket and skirt. "Well, my dissertation is out the window for now and I can't exactly afford to start over. Is that job offer still good for a post-grad?"

Rose laughed again. "Welcome to the new Mobius, Ellie," she took my hand and we walked to the elevator to face the new world together.

THE END

Lyana Rikmon, Warrior of Donothor
Benjamin Towe & Nils Visser

Suregood Forest

Much of the southwest extremity of the Kingdom of Donothor was covered by dense woodlands called the Suregood Forest. The forest to the north of the great River Luumic was mostly uncharted territory, though a few Gray Elves had settled there. They were not an uncommon sight south of the river, where they visited settlements like Knottington to trade with the farmers, vintners, woodsmen, and tradesmen who called Suregood Forest their home. Although the woods folk tended to keep to themselves, they weren't entirely isolated, as the main road from Fort Luumic to Tindal passed through the forest.

It was on this road that our tale begins. There had been trouble of late. Unexplained disappearances, rumours of Magick and strange creatures lurking in the depths of the woods, preying on wood folk trying to earn a living. Fear was rife, trade was affected. The mayor of Knottington drafted a letter to King Eomore Aivendar to request assistance, and asked the town's sheriff, Lyana Rikmon, to personally deliver the letter to the king in Lyndyn.

The sheriff hadn't ridden all that far when she encountered a heavily armed party of cloaked travellers on the road. Halting her steed, she eyed them warily. They were strangers and in these troubled times it paid to be careful.

There were over a dozen of them, and they in turn had stopped their horses to take stock of the single rider. They saw an attractive woman of about thirty years old, with dark hair that flowed down her back, and piercing blue-gray eyes. She was of average height with a well-conditioned muscular frame. Her clothes were unremarkable, common even, though she wore leather armor and carried a short sword, elfish bow, and well-stocked quiver. Although greatly outnumbered, the woman remained calm and confident; her fearless manner suggesting that she knew how to use her weapons.

Lyana assessed the party with quick efficiency. Though much was concealed by their cloaks, and some wore their hoods up, she could see that the group was diverse. It included two dwarves and a young red-haired female elf. What she could see of the party's garments, armour, and weapons suggested quality. Whoever these people were, they looked like they meant business.

Lyana presented the crest of the Aivendars, symbolic of an emissary carrying official business to the king. She stated in a loud and clear voice, "I am Lyana Rikmon, the sheriff of Knottington. I bear a message for the king of Donothor from the mayor of Knottington. Give me passage!"

A wiry man in a dark cloak at the head of the group asked, "What tidings do you carry to King Eomore?"

Lyana answered, "I owe you no answer, stranger. This group… are you wanted by the crown? Are you highwaymen? Know that I carry no treasure. If you force me to tarry, there will be great consequences!"

Lyana grasped the hilt of her sheathed sword with her right hand and drew the blade with blazing speed.

The wiry man said, "Stay your hand. You address the King's party."

One of the men at the rear of the group rode forward, slipping off his hood. He was followed by another, who likewise slipped off her hood. Lyana had seen their images often enough. She gasped, sheathed her blade, dismounted, and bowed to one knee.

"My Lord King, I did not intend insult." Made nervous by the sudden, unexpected exalted company, Lyana rambled on.

"Why are you here? Clairvoyance? I know of the powers of our queen. I am graced by your presence, my Lady Queen."

King Eomore said, "Arise. I know of the service of your family to Donothor, Lyana Rikmon. What tidings do you bring?"

Lyana answered, "Mayor Braxton Blowhard sends greetings and seeks the aid of the Rangers of Donothor." She took the mayor's letter from her saddlebag. "This epistle details recent ill events in the Suregood Forest. I suspect it's the work of Big Jon Loxly and his robbing hoods."

"What do you know of Loxly?" One of the other men in the group came forward, the same wiry man who had spoken first.

King Eomore said, "I present my son, Ranger Captain Prince Vanni. He bears Exeter, the Blade of Truth."

Lyana bowed to Prince Vanni, overwhelmed by the proximity of even more illustrious company. "We know his band of murky men lurk deep in the forest, my Lord Prince. Most of his deeds are mere mischief. But recent time has seen more dastardly deeds. I think his perpetrations have escalated."

"Hand me the letter." After Lyana had done so, the king said, "We come here on a different mission, but I will hear your request. Not here though. We will follow you to Knottington. Lead the way, Sheriff."

"Yes, my Lord King," Lyana said, and smartly remounted her horse.

Her mind swirled with a thousand questions. As sheriff, it was Lyana's duty to enforce the laws of the kingdom in the name of King Eomore. The Rikmon family had filled the position of sheriff of Knottington for four generations, Lyana preceded by her father, grandfather, and great-grandfather. Like all the inhabitants of Knottington, Lyana was steadfastly loyal to the crown of Donothor, but she had never expected to be leading the king, queen, their son, and retinue towards her home town.

Their arrival in Knottington was greeted by excited confusion and some panic. There had been no forewarning. No chance to sweep the streets, hoists banners and garlands, don fine clothes, or prepare a welcome for the royal party.

Mayor Blowhard had hoped that Lyana would return within the month, with a party of rangers and perhaps a spell caster or two. He was usually a stoic and calm fellow, but upon understanding that Lyana had returned on the very day she had left in the company of king, queen, and prince, he changed into a nervous wreck before their very eyes. Fretting, pacing to and fro, issuing orders even as he offered profuse and endless apologies to his royal guests.

The Town Hall was made available to the royal party, its meeting chamber quickly swept, the central table cleared of rolled parchments and leather-bound ledgers, and refreshments brought in. Prince Vanni excused himself, and soon thereafter could be seen departing Knottington in the company of his lieutenant, dwarf ranger Deron, and the other rangers in the king's party, all of whom wore their red dungeon battle dress.

After King Eomore and Queen Cara had taken their seats, the others followed suit. The mayor and sheriff were formally introduced to the king's retinue. The red-haired elf was named as Erinnia, the second dwarf as Brute Leigh, a legendary warrior whose name was known throughout the kingdom. Completing the party were Half-Draith Cyttia Uberroth, and the Queen's brother, Cade Nightshade.

King Eomore laid the mayor's letter, as of yet unopened, on the table.

"I would read it, Mayor Blowhard. But since we are here, perhaps it would be easier for you to tell me of your troubles personally."

The mayor, still flabbergasted, swallowed, nodded, then added a hasty "Yes, my Lord King."

Blowhard proceeded to speak of the local folk and travellers who had gone missing in Suregood Forest. Of ominous signs. Foul things left hanging in trees. The shadows of strange creatures which may or may not have been seen by eyewitnesses. The increasing fear that threatened to paralyse the economy of Knottington, largely reliant on the woods for its income as it was.

"Lyana Rikmon is a capable sheriff, My Lord King, more than able to deal with robbers, thieves, ne'er-do-wells, and beasts of the forest. But I fear there is an evil behind this which is beyond our ken. It was my hope that you could send a party of rangers, accompanied by spell casters, to help rid us of whatever foul presences poison our humble town and woodlands."

King Eomore and Queen Cara exchanged a meaningful glance. Deeming herself unobserved, Lyana allowed herself a grimace.

"You doubt the mayor's assessment, Sheriff?" Cade Nightshade asked.

All eyes turned to Lyana, who felt distinctively uncomfortable at receiving so much attention. She paused, trying to formulate her feelings. Her work required her to be pragmatic, to focus on facts, not gossip or old-wives' tales. She believed that which she could perceive with her own eyes far more than the unseen.

"The sheriff is convinced that much of this is the work of Big Jon Loxly and his murky men," the mayor supplied.

"The man is a rogue and a nuisance, My Lords and Ladies," Lyana defended herself. "Forever skirting the edge between lawful and lawless behaviour. Loxly and his robbing hoods have often resorted to trickery and deception…"

"Making life difficult for the sheriff?" Brute Leigh chuckled into his beard.

Lyana shrugged. It was true. She could deal with truly evil men and women, for they were on the wrong side of the law she was sworn to uphold, and she dealt with them accordingly. It was harder for her to understand a scoundrel like Big Jon Loxly, who thumbed his nose at the law when he chose to, and had outsmarted her at times, the memories of which still stung her pride. "I've put out a reward for his capture, so that he can be questioned. But Loxly and his men often help out those in trouble. The rogues are much beloved by most folk because of that."

The king and queen exchanged another glance, this time with bemused expressions on their faces.

"He may be a rogue," Cade Nightshade said. "But a clever one." He tapped the side of his forehead. "A thinker, and a more than capable fighter too, as I understand it."

"But the law," Lyana protested. "The king's own law!"

"The exploits of Loxly and his robbing hoods have reached as far as Lyndyn, my dear sheriff," Queen Cara explained.

"They sing ballads about him in the taverns." Brute Leigh grinned. "Would you like to hear one?"

"We digress," King Eomore said. "Much as I would like to be of assistance to you, Mayor Blowhard, I fear that you are not the only one to make report of ill tidings. Similar tales have reached my ears from all corners of Donothor."

Queen Cara nodded sadly. "Tell me, have you heard of Tigarn Nocerre?"

Lyana frowned. "The assassin, my Lady Queen? Is he involved? In Suregood Forest?"

"Indirectly," Cade Nightshade answered.

"Who is this Tigarn?" Mayor Blowhard asked.

"Tigarn Nocerre," Cyttia Uberroth spoke up for the first time. "Poses a great danger. He hates Magick. A sorceress humiliated him as a youth, and he has dedicated his life to the destruction of all things Magick. His efforts culminated in the creation of *Death of Magick,* a sword he has employed to end the life of many a sorcerer."

"As a consequence of which," Cade Nightshade said. "There are gaps in our defences against primordial evil."

Erinnia began to speak, with a melodious voice and in a manner that suggested she was half-absent, her mouth describing what her eyes saw elsewhere. "The sorcerers fall one by one. Their vacant places are sensed. Things are stirring all over the kingdom. Lesser creatures of darkness with raging appetites. Twisted souls indulging in long-yearned-for depravities. Their reach is limited–"

"But fatal nonetheless," Queen Cara interjected mournfully.

Erinnia continued as if she hadn't heard the queen. "Worse, far worse, is the rousing of the greater creatures of darkness. Ancient, malevolent beings with insidious ambitions. Reaching out in all directions with their senses, tasting opportunities, exploring possibilities…"

Lyana felt a shiver traverse her spine. These weren't old wives' tales.

Cade Nightshade began to speak. "Erinnia speaks of–"

King Eomore raised a hand to silence his brother-in-law. "The situation is precarious. The troubles you report around Knottington are but a small part of it."

"I had no idea, no idea at all that it was so dire," Mayor Blowhard said.

"This is only the start of it," Erinnia intoned. "The evil ones are still gathering their strength, probing for weaknesses, plotting and planning. It will be a dark day for Donothor when their full power is unleashed."

"So we have to fight them now!" Lyana cried out.

"That's the spirit!" Brute Leigh laughed heartily. "You were right, my Queen, about this one."

Queen Cara smiled at the dwarf, then turned to Lyana. "That is what must be done. First and foremost, the *Death of Magick* must be found before Tigarn Nocerre murders more sorcerers with the sword. Then," she shivered, "we must subdue the greatest evils afore their plans can be hatched."

"I suppose it won't be easy to find Tigarn," Lyana said.

"Indeed," Cyttia Uberroth said. "He has hidden the *Death of Magick* through the power of a True Wish. Much has been done though, by this very party, along with the help of High Priestess Knarra of the Fane of the Setting Sun, and Archmage Roscoe of Briar Garden."

"We now know where Tigarn can be found," King Eomore said. "By means of a Locating Potion and Locating Stone–"

"Which we located!" Brute Leigh guffawed.

The king continued: "–and a ritual in the Room of Knowledge at the Fane of the Setting Sun, using the Chalice of Mystery…"

Lyana hissed. "The Chalice of Mystery! I thought…the demon Uyrg created it!"

"Its use is not advisable." Cyttia Uberroth nodded. "It's extremely dangerous…and seductive. The demon Uyrg saw to that."

"Which is why," Erinnia spoke. "It has been secured in the Room of Knowledge for the past seven hundred years. Bound by the most powerful Magick at our disposal."

"We had no choice this time," King Eomore explained. "Tigarn Nocerre must be stopped. *Death of Magick* must be taken from him. The Chalice of Mystery revealed the location of the sword. The assassin keeps it in the Dungeon of Infernos."

Lyana's head was spinning as she tried to make sense of it all. "There's one thing I don't understand, what part does your visit to Knottington play in all of this?"

"Two things," Cade Nightshade answered. "First there was the small matter of locating a Gate Key to the Dungeon of Infernos, its hiding place also revealed by the Chalice."

"Small matter?" Brute Leigh snorted. "If you call battling Dark Elves and Black Dragons a 'small' matter. Not to mention that headless Dullahan. And that horrible screaming Banshee!"

"You conducted yourself in an exemplary manner, Master Leigh," King Eomore said. "For which you have our gratitude. We obtained the Gate Key and are now on our way back to the Fane of the Setting Sun, from whence a party will set out to the Dungeon of Infernos."

"And the second reason?" Lyana asked.

Queen Cara answered, "We have enough spell casters, but are in need of more fighters. Good ones. We were hoping you, Sheriff Rikmon, would join us."

"Me?" Lyana was flabbergasted. "But…surely there are many famed fighters in the kingdom?"

"It is true that Donothor is blessed with splendid paladins," King Eomore said. "However, we have already lost some to the evils unleashed by Tigarn Nocerre. And in many places, that evil has spread to a much greater extent than here in Knottington. We've had to despatch many fighters and spell casters to those places to try and turn the tide of darkness."

"All for nought," Erinnia said. "If Nocerre and the *Death of Magick* aren't taken out of the game. Soon."

"My Lord King, my Lady Queen," Lyana said. "I'm honoured, truly. But my duties here…" She looked at Mayor Blowhard.

He said, "It seems to me that if you await events here in Knottington, you may well find yourself and your deputies facing a tidal wave of evil…on your own. We will have to manage without you for a while, Sheriff. It won't be easy, but…"

The king spoke to the mayor. "Rest assured that Lyndyn will send you a small party of rangers and a spell caster to keep Knottington safe for as long as possible." He looked at Lyana. "The journey will be hazardous, Sheriff Rikmon, and you would be placed in great danger. It is for that reason that I am not commanding you to join us, but making a request instead."

Lyana made to speak, but Queen Cara raised her hand. "Do not answer us now, Lyana Rikmon. Sleep on it this night and deliver us your answer in the morning." She looked at Mayor Blowhard. "We have come from far after facing considerable dangers and are in need of rest. Could we impose on you—"

"And food! A warm meal." Brute Leigh rubbed his stomach.

"I will have a meal prepared, and the guest chambers, your Majesties," the mayor said. "Though I fear both rooms and fare, the best we have to offer, may seem crude and rustic to—"

"Ha!" Brute Leigh exclaimed. "We slept by the roadside last night, and before that in flea-ridden hovels, caves, and shepherd's huts. I for one, am sure that I'll eat like a prince and sleep like a king!"

King Eomore smiled. "I sleep like a king every night, Master Leigh, and can assure you it's no hard task."

Nervous laughter met his statement, but eased the tension and sense of doom.

Somewhat to her surprise, Lyana slept soundly that night. She had expected to spend the night tossing and turning. Not because she was in search of an answer, since there wasn't a hair on her head that considered declining the king's request. However, there was a lot to digest. She was a good fighter, her father had taught her well, but in no way as renowned as many in the kingdom. Lyana had been to Lyndyn a few times, but she had not competed in the large tournaments there. Instead, she had prevailed in more local competitions in Kanath, Three Forks, Tindal, Prille and Fort Luumic. She had even won a fencing event at the dwarf citadel of Hillesdale. The quickness of her right hand hid the fact that she was left-handed, and her ability to transfer her sword from one hand to the other allowed her to surprise competitors. She had no doubt though, that facing opponents in a rule-bound tournament was something entirely different from foes without scruples intent on killing her.

The next morning found her in the meeting chamber again. The great table had been moved aside. Two high-backed chairs had been placed at one end, occupied by King Eomore and Queen Cara. The other members of their party stood to either side of the makeshift thrones. Notable citizens of Knottington, including the mayor, lined the side of the room.

"Sheriff Rikmon of Knottington," Cade Nightshade announced her arrival formally.

"Approach," the king commanded.

Lyana walked closer until she was in the centre of the room, facing the thrones. She bowed. "My Lord King. My Lady Queen. If it pleases you, I have come to offer you my sword."

Their reaction wasn't what Lyana had expected. Both King Eomore and Queen Cara turned their heads sideways, to Erinnia, who had taken a step forward. She looked intently at Lyana, who returned the look, not quite understanding...but then she noticed the elf's eyes, oh those eyes. They seemed to be swirling with colors, sparkling with silver and gold. It seemed to Lyana that the eyes looked straight through her, no, into her.

She felt vulnerable and exposed, as if she was standing there naked, all secrets and flaws revealed. When it became almost too much to bear, Erinnia looked away, and Lyana felt relief wash through her, as well as a strange emptiness.

The elf gave her a brief glance, her eyes normal again, and a small apologetic smile on her lips. Then she spoke to the king and queen. "My Lord, My Lady, her heart is pure, her courage formidable, and her loyalty unquestionable."

Before the king and queen could respond, the chamber door burst open to reveal Prince Vanni and his rangers – short and tall – stride into the room along with another man. Lyana's mouth dropped open when she recognised Big Jon Loxly's impudent grin. Strolling into Knottington town hall, into the presence of the king and queen of Donothor as if it were no great matter to him. As if there wasn't a price on his head. He was even carrying his weapons: a bearded battle axe, long oak staff, and longbow.

Instinctively, Lyana's hand sought her sword, ready to pull it out of her scabbard and apprehend the rogue.

"Once again, I command you to stay your hand, Sheriff Rikmon," Prince Vanni ordered. He indicated his own sword. "Exeter, the Blade of Truth, has vouched for this man."

Forgetting that it wasn't her place to question a prince, Lyana asked, "How did you manage to find Loxly?"

It wasn't a strange question to ask, considering that she had been trying for years to locate the scoundrel, and she was sure she knew Suregood Forest a great deal better than the prince, ranger as he might be.

Prince Vanni didn't seem the least bit concerned with Lyana's trespass. He just smiled and admitted, "I didn't, truth be told. But I figured that Loxly would find me!"

"'Tis true," Loxly thundered contentedly. "There's little in Suregood Forest that escapes my notice."

Lyana bristled; the man's arrogance seemed to know no bounds.

"Exeter has spoken?" King Eomore inquired of Prince Vanni.

"Indeed." The Prince answered. "As we thought, Loxly is true of heart."

"And you have spoken to him about our predicament." Queen Cara asked

"He has, Your Majesty," Loxly performed a clumsy bow. "The prince also told me that this one here," he gave Lyana a sour look, "has tried to tell you I'm guilty of recent foul and evil deeds in Suregood Forest."

He looked at the king and queen. "I have lost men to these unspeakable evils. Good men. Men I considered brothers. To think that…"

"We doubt it not, Big Jon Loxly," Cade Nightshade interceded. "But can you honestly say you have never, ever given the sheriff reason to seek your hand behind mischief in the woods?"

Loxly grinned sheepishly. "Well, if you put it that way…"

"We tarry," King Eomore declared. "The both of you have been found worthy to join our quest. We have the sheriff's answer. What about you, Big Jon Loxly. Will you pledge your services to the royal house of Aivendar?"

Lyana and Loxly stared at each other, aghast. They spoke simultaneously.

"He…"

"She…"

"By my axe!" Brute Leigh thundered. "The lives of every man, woman, and child in Donothor are at stake. Surely you two can drop your petty rivalries in the face of much greater danger? If all goes well, you will return to Knottington where you can spend the rest of your lives trying to outsmart the other."

"I would have put it more diplomatically," Prince Vanni said thoughtfully. "But Master Leigh is right. Can you put aside your differences for the duration? They are but minor compared to the shadows that threaten to overwhelm our kingdom."

Lyana felt ashamed. Loxly stared at the floor.

"I've pledged my sword," Lyana spoke. "And stand by my promise."

"And you have my axe," Loxly nodded.

"Good, I'm glad that's settled." Cade Nightshade nodded approvingly.

"And my bow!" Loxly added.

Lyana sighed.

"Very well…" Prince Vanni said.

Loxly wasn't finished though. "And my quarter staff! Three for the price of one." He flashed Lyana a grin and she rolled her eyes in response.

Thus it came to be that the Sheriff of Knottington and Big Jon Loxly of Suregood Forest joined the quest.

Fane of the Setting Sun

They left Knottington that same day. It was a less glorious departure than Lyana had imagined because of Loxly's presence. His inclusion seemed to diminish the honour she had initially felt at being invited. To be put on an equal footing with the rogue dented her pride.

Loxly wasted no time in unleashing his charm on the party, riding first next to one, then next to the other. Joking, laughing, and bantering as if he had known them all his life. One by one, they fell for his charisma, driving Lyana into a sullen silence. She had never really been much enamoured by social interaction if it served no practical purpose, driven instead by the motivation to fulfil her responsibilities to the best of her ability.

In all fairness, Loxly sought to make peace, riding next to her for a while, gossiping about mutual acquaintances back in Knottington, trying to get her to smile.

"I'll fight at your side, Loxly," Lyana told him curtly. "Because the king and queen command it. But that is the extent of it."

His face fell, reminding her of a scolded puppy and Lyana immediately felt guilty, but there was no chance to make amends because he ceded to her wishes straight away.

"I didn't mean to impose," he mumbled. "My sincere apologies."

He rode off to find more amiable company, and soon thereafter his mood picked up again as he was relating an anecdote to Brute Leigh.

To Lyana's relief time for social chit-chat grew shorter. Erinnia had been right. Creatures which normally concealed themselves far away from humans had become emboldened. They stalked the party, keeping everyone on their guard, and many grew audacious enough to dare an attack. Wailers, baxcats, leicats, adherers, shape-changers, worts and more, there seemed to be no end to them. Both Lyana and Loxly were able to prove their worth with sword, axe, bow, and quarterstaff as they helped fend off the attacks.

Their first stop was the dwarf citadel of Hillesdale. Lyana was pleasantly surprised to find the dwarves there remembered her well, and the citadel's armorers presented her with a splendid suit of chain mail armor. It was pleasant to sleep safely behind the thick walls of the keep and not set a watch for a restless night.

Their next stop was Briar Garden, where they were received by Archmage Roscoe. The Archmage had been badly injured in the quest to gain the Gate Key, and despite having access to some of the best healers in the kingdom, it would be months yet before he would be back on his feet. It was a dire reminder of the dangers that awaited them at Infernos. Roscoe supplied an incessant stream of advice and invited the spell casters in the party to replenish their spell components from his ample supplies.

After two days of respite at Briar Garden, the group travelled on to the Fane of the Setting Sun. Lyana had never been there and was much impressed by the fortified temple complex, which offered views every bit as splendid as its name suggested. High Priestess Knarra, ageless and wise beyond mortal comprehension, received them with high honours. Knottington seemed far away to Lyana, who felt a little bit lost amidst the splendour of the Fane.

Queen Cara and High Priestess Knarra took Lyana aside and requested that she follow them through countless halls and corridors, until they reached a stout, ironbound door.

"The Room of Knowledge," Queen Cara said.

The High Priestess produced a key and unlocked the door. Lyana stepped inside with some trepidation. Once inside, she barely registered the room, her sight drawn immediately to an arched recess in the far wall. The niche contained an ornate chalice.

"The Chalice of Mystery," Lyana spoke, hardly daring to believe she was looking at an object of which so many stories were told. "I thought it was kept contained and sealed?"

"Oh, but it is, dear child," Knarra said. "The seals are not visible to most, but you'd find out soon enough if you were so foolish as to try and touch the Chalice."

...Lyana...

"I can hear it call my name," Lyana exclaimed in alarm.

"That doesn't surprise me," Knarra nodded. "The Chalice has sensed your presence. Stay here long enough–"

"Which we shan't," Queen Cara said quickly.

Knarra continued, "–and it will be more than whispers reaching out to you. You'll hallucinate, see visions. The Chalice will offer you glimpses of great power, wealth, and Magick. Make sweet promises, that all these can be yours, if you would free it from the Magick bounds we set upon it and take it far away."

Lyana did indeed feel the urge to approach the Chalice, to make it hers. Nothing seemed to matter in the world besides possessing such a marvellous thing and commanding the power within. She fought the compelling need with all her will-power.

"Good girl," Knarra said. "You are strong indeed, for someone naïve to Magick."

Queen Cara explained, "The Chalice of Mystery was created by the demon Uyrg, who endowed it with its powers. Anyone who succumbed to the Chalice's seduction would soon find themselves bereft of their free will, their mind enslaved, and the remainder of their existence in servitude to the will of Uyrg."

"Come, let's away from here, Lyana," Knarra said. "You have passed this test well, but there is no reason to expose you to the Chalice's malice for any longer than absolutely necessary."

Lyana, still struggling to resist the allure of the Chalice, nodded gratefully. The high priestess had said that she was naïve to Magick, which was true enough. She recalled the intrusive sensations when Erinnia had seemed to look right into her soul back in Knottington, and now the alluring magnetism of the Chalice. Reasons enough to avoid Magick if possible, Lyana reasoned. She felt lost in this strange new world, diminutive and small, half-wishing she was chasing outlaws through Suregood Forest where she knew what was what.

"There are matters to discuss," Queen Cara told her, as Knarra locked the door after they left the Room of Knowledge. "We didn't tell you everything in Knottington, as we didn't know who would be listening in on us."

Lyana had suspected as much. She followed the queen and high priestess down a corridor but looked around when she perceived footsteps behind them. Turning around, she glimpsed Prince Vanni, Cade Nightshade, and Loxly approaching the door of the Room of Knowledge. Lyana supposed that Loxly would be tested as she had been. Big Jon looked up and caught her eye. To her surprise, Lyana felt relief at seeing a familiar face in this strange and imposing place. Something that belonged to home. Something familiar. Before she could restrain herself, she gave Big Jon an encouraging smile. Just a small one, which Loxly immediately ruined by responding with an exaggerated look of comical surprise.

Fine. I hope you fail the test. Lyana huffed and turned away, hurrying to catch up with the queen and high priestess.

They didn't go far, entering a small chamber. A fire burned merrily in a small hearth. Facing it were some couches and chairs. Erinnia and Cyttia Uberroth were waiting for them.

"You passed," Erinnia, usually aloof, beamed a smile at Lyana.

"Is the room secure?" Knarra asked.

Cyttia said, "Almost as secure as the Room of Knowledge. We can talk freely."

"Good, thank you," Queen Cara said. "Lyana, have a seat."

When they were all seated, Queen Cara began to speak again. "There are things you must know, Lyana, and I do apologise that we haven't been able to divulge all this before. Please understand, that your free choice in these matters is of the utmost importance. Should you so desire, I will release you from your vow if…"

Lyana shook her head. "I made an oath, My Lady Queen. A Rikmon never–"

"Hear us out first, child," Knarra said.

"My apologies," Lyana quickly said. "I will listen."

"First of all," Cyttia began. "There is the matter of the Dungeon of Infernos, but I must tell you now, that Infernos is only one part of the quest."

"You expressed surprise," Queen Cara said. "Back in Knottington, that we had chosen you when indeed many warriors would have gladly volunteered. It is true that many are needed elsewhere, but there is another reason for our choice of both you and Loxly."

"*Death of Magick* may only be handled by one naïve to Magick." Knarra said. "And yet one with a mind strong enough to retain free will. Most of our party, or other possible contenders, have been touched, blessed, or tainted by Magick. You and Loxly–"

"But," Lyana interceded. "Erinnia read my mind, my heart, and just now…the Chalice…"

"Absolute necessity, kept to a minimum," Cyttia said.

"And we will need to keep it that way," Queen Cara said. "To all intents and purposes, the two of you still qualify."

"Two of us," Lyana murmured, still feeling resentment at Loxly's inclusion.

"'Tis harsh," Knarra spoke. "But the fact of the matter is that it's likely than one of you will fall ere we find the *Death of Magick*. We will do our best to keep you safe, but a guarantee can never be given."

Erinnia explained. "There is only one way to keep you untainted by Magick in the Dungeon of Infernos. But it's perilous."

Queen Cara said. "Archmage Roscoe has given us a rune scroll. Its dweomer creates an anti-Magick shell, or reflecting dome. The anti-Magick shell is impenetrable to Magick and will deflect spells. But that would include our Healing Magick and Protective Magick. We would not be able to protect you with spells."

Cyttia added, "You would be vulnerable to any creature that breaches the shell. If so much as a small goblin with a dagger enters the shell, it poses a danger. Normal weapons can penetrate the shell, you would only be safe from Magick."

"But it would be within range of my blade!" Lyana declared with far more confidence than she felt. "I am loyal to Donothor, and if I'm chosen to bear the *Death of Magick* for my king and queen, I will do so, willingly and gladly."

Queen Cara smiled. "Your courage becomes you, Sheriff Rikmon. Yet I fear we ask of you to place yourself in even greater danger if you agree to this."

Greater danger? Lyana was under the impression there could hardly be anything more dangerous than entering Infernos unprotected from all non-Magickal threats.

"I have observed the Chalice of Mystery for many years," Knarra explained. "Oftentimes it has been dormant, sometimes for so many decades that it seemed bereft of all powers, though I suspect that was a deception to trick the unwary. At other times it's been active, struggling against the Magick that binds it. But of late, it has been unusually lively."

"Which can only mean one thing," Erinnia spoke. "One of the greater evils roused by Tigarn Nocerre is none other than the Demon Uyrg. Obtaining the *Death of Magick* will halt the further spread of foulness, and all but a few of the lesser creatures of evil will scurry back to their hiding places. But Uyrg…now that we have his full attention he won't be discouraged that easily."

A cold shiver crept along Lyana's spine.

Queen Cara said, "As you may imagine, many have tried to vanquish the demon over the centuries. To no avail, tis easier said than done. Yet possession of the *Death of Magick*… Tigarn may well have done us a great favour, achieving the opposite of what he intended if we can thwart him. It is a unique opportunity, one which we must make use of!"

"But," Knarra said gravely. "The *Death of Magick* will only serve one master. If either you or Loxly obtain the blade, it's you who must slay the demon."

Lyana took a deep breath. She opted to try some of Loxly's humor. "So all I have to do, is go into Infernos with scant protection, grab a sword, and then march off to chop a demon into bits. I can go home after that?"

The queen and high priestess laughed heartily. Erinnia frowned, and Cyttia looked worried.

"Fear not," Lyana told the latter two. "I'm not underestimating the dangers."

"We ask much of you," Queen Cara confessed. "Too much, I'm afraid."

"Yet is shall be done," Lyana declared bravely. "When do we start?"

As it was, they started straight away. Knarra produced the rune scroll gifted to the quest by Archmage Roscoe. She muttered the elusive old elfish phrases of the incantation. At the same time, Cyttia crumbled Shypoke eggshell fragments over Lyana's head, whilst Erinnia placed a magnetic stone against Lyana's forehead. When it was done, deep blue light, and then an iridescent glow bathed the sheriff of Knottington to signify she was now protected from all Magick, good and evil.

After they had parted company for the day, Lyana sought solitude to mull things over. There was much to think about. She was brave and courageous, but not foolishly so, and the prospect of imminent danger, pain, and death was not a thing to be casual about. Climbing up the winding stair of a defensive tower, she strolled along the battlements, her mood amplified by the glorious hues of the setting sun over the magnificent vistas the Fane offered a view of.

She discerned Loxly leaning against the parapet. Like her, a blue glow surrounded him. So, he too had offered to risk all to save the kingdom. She wasn't sure what to do. He had been true to his word since she had asked him to leave her alone, and avoided her company as discreetly as possible, for which she was grateful. Most men she knew had difficulty understanding such a request, seeing it as encouragement to double their efforts instead, eager to prove that she had misunderstood what splendid blokes they really were. It seemed wrong to her, to reward his respect by intruding on his privacy, for surely he too had come to ponder on things. However, it seemed far more wrong to turn her back on him now. For better or worse, they were both committed to the same cause, and would soon set off to face the gravest dangers they had ever known. Perhaps, a small voice suggested, they had always been on the same side, seeking to protect the inhabitants of Suregood Forest in their own ways.

Lyana dismissed that last thought, not wanting to contemplate it too deeply. She approached Big Jon. He must have sensed her but didn't turn his head to look at her until she paused by his side. Gone was the mischief on his face, the ne'er-care-about-nought impudence. Instead, he looked deadly serious.

"Tis no small thing." Was all he said.

Lyana nodded, and echoed his words. "Tis no small thing."

They said no other words, but stood there for another hour, watching the sun sink behind the horizon in silence. To her surprise, Lyana drew comfort from his presence. There was, perhaps, much to speak about, yet it remained unspoken. Nevertheless, when they parted after twilight set in, Lyana felt that they parted as friends.

The Dungeon of Infernos

Nineteen intrepid adventurers left the Fane of the Setting Sun the next day. Ten were rangers in their red dungeon battle dress, led by the dwarf ranger Deron. Four were warriors: Prince Vanni, Brute Leigh, Lyana Rikmon, and Big Jon Loxly. Three were spellcasters: High Priestess Knarra, Cyttia Uberroth, and Erinnia. The remaining two, leaders of the party and well equipped to cast spells and fight as warriors, were Queen Cara and Cade Nightshade.

King Eomore had reluctantly taken leave of them at the Fane. His task was to return to Lyndyn. As normalcy unravelled, the citizens of Donothor would need their king to look to for assurance and comfort. Moreover, someone would need to co-ordinate the information streaming to the capital from all corners of the kingdom and despatch small groups of warriors and spell casters to deal with the greatest threats. Last-but-not-least, the army would need to be gathered, because the expectation was that at some point a great many creatures of evil would unite and mount a co-ordinated attack.

The journey to Infernos took two weeks and was fraught with danger and marked by many assaults. Although both Lyana and Loxly fought as well as the others, Lyana could not help but notice that Deron had clearly spelled out to his rangers that the two from Suregood Forest must be defended at all costs. She knew the reasoning but could not help but feel guilt as three of the brave rangers fell before they reached the gate of Infernos.

Battles, traps, and riddles abounded upon their entry into Infernos. The first room contained only a slow-moving zombie. The creature persisted in its slow attacks until Knarra ended its timeless suffering with a simple fire spell.

Soon after, they encountered heretofore unknown beasts. One such beast rose from the surface of a mirror. The hobgoblin-sized monster was seven feet tall. The purple beast had one eye, two horns, wings, bandy legs, pointed ears, sharp fangs, and forearms with talons. Lyana's shell not only deflected the beast's Banishment Spell, but also reflected it, sending the creature whence it came.

When a Succubus appeared, all the males but Loxly dropped their weapons, failing to resist the charm of the most feminine of demons. The Succubus attacked Lyana, firing a Ray of Enfeeblement at her. Once again, reflection followed deflection, and the Succubus was thrust backwards. Cyttia leapt through the air and landed both her Drelvish boots squarely into the demon's chest. The force of the blow knocked the already weakened demon to the floor. Erinnia ineffectively attacked the demon with a Fire Seed. Knarra's Lightning Bolt Spell produced little effect. The she-demon struggled to its feet, but fell again when Cyttia struck it with a shuriken. Brilliant orange ichors spilled from the wound and burst into flame upon hitting the stone floor. Knarra cast Protection from Fire. Both Lyana and Loxly loosed an arrow at the Succubus, but both arrows ignited into flame when they struck the demon, reduced to ash in seconds.

The Succubus screeched and unleashed a Spray of Color against its active opponents, the stunned males still bewildered and no threat. Red light struck Queen Cara and produced the effect of a chilling and excruciatingly painful Cold spell. Blue light hit Erinnia and the Magick Missile ripped a wound in the young elf's chest. She collapsed, bleeding profusely. Orange light struck Knarra and a gust of wind knocked the priestess backward, slamming her against the wall, snapping several ribs. Green light bathed Cyttia, who benefited from natural Draith resistance to Magick, but nevertheless doubled over clutching her stomach.

The violet light hurled at Big Jon and yellow ray aimed at Lyana were both reflected. Yellow and violet hues danced around the she-demon. The Succubus kicked and screamed in agony, as it was both vaporised and devoured by its own spells.

The males came out of their daze, looking in surprised confusion and alarm at their comrades strewn about, battered and bleeding.

Big Jon approached Lyana, worry on his face. "You alright?"

"Yes," Lyana answered, touched by his concern. "You?"

"Aye, don't know how. That was a close call."

Deron ordered his rangers to stand guard, whilst Cade tended Knarra so that her greater healing skills could be employed as the two of them tended the others. Lyana had never seen the effects of healing spells, and was astounded by their efficiency, even though their full recovery took several hours. She noted the worry on Prince Vanni's face as he observed Lyana and Big Jon, reminding her that neither she nor Loxly could count on Healing Magick, should they be hurt.

The party resumed their descent into Infernos, fighting many skirmishes and losing one of the rangers before they reached the 12th level of the dungeon. Once there, a decrepit creature approached them. It was barely more than rotten clothing draped over bones.

Cade frowned. "That looks just like the zombie we found in the first room of the dungeon."

Brute Leigh scowled, "After everything we've been through, we are to fight another zombie?"

The Blade of Truth rasped in its metallic voice: "Powerful enemy!"

The creature was not a zombie. It was a Lich!

The Lich pointed its bony fingers toward Lyana and uttered guttural sounds. An apparition floated from its fingertips. The terrifying purveyor of the Death Spell wafted to Lyana, surrounded her, failed to steal her soul, and reflected back to the Lich. Nothing happened. He was already dead. The apparition faded harmlessly.

Prince Vanni and Brute Leigh directed Lyana and Loxly to the rear, where the remaining six rangers formed a protective circle around them. The spell casters unleashed a torrent of spells at the Lich. Flame and Fire Spells, Magick Missiles…Magick bathed the Lich but didn't seem to hurt it at all.

Queen Cara, Prince Vanni, Brute Leigh, and Cade advanced on the creature, their weapons drawn. The Lich moved phenomenally quickly, stunning and knocking over the warriors. It then struck Erinnia and bent down to give her a soul-stealing kiss, swiping at Knarra and Cyttia who tried to intervene, hurling them back until they struck the dungeon walls with loud thuds.

"HEY!" Lyana shouted at the Lich, to distract it from Erinnia. Both she and Big Jon drew their bows and loosed arrows at the creature. They both hit but the arrows had no effect other than achieving the Lich's attention. The undead fiend abandoned Erinnia and charged the remaining members of the party. The rangers stood no chance, knocked aside effortlessly. Lyana drew her sword. The Lich reached out to her, pushing its foul arm through the anti-Magick shell.

Intense heat struck Lyana as the Lich's outstretched arm burst into flames and burned away rapidly. The Lich screeched in pain and fury. Understanding, Big Jon used his axe to hook and draw the Lich's other arm into his anti-Magick shell, and it too burst into flame, singing Loxly's eyebrows and hair.

The Lich staggered backwards, armless. It was set upon by Prince Vanni and Bruce Leigh, back on their feet and hacking and stabbing frantically with sword and axe, even as Knarra touched the Lich's shoulder with her staff, setting the creature ablaze until nothing remained but smouldering ashes.

An opening appeared in the far wall of the room, but the party ignored it, as once again there were plenty of wounds that required urgent attention. Cure Disease and Neutralize Poison Spells abounded, and they exhausted their supply of Tar Heel ointments.

Death of Magick

When all the wounds had been treated, focus turned on the revealed secret doorway.

Knarra said, "The opening leads to the Blue Room, the thirteenth level of Infernos. It's there that we'll find the *Death of Magick*."

"Good," growled Brute Leigh. "The sooner we're back at the Fane, the sooner we can get a decent hot meal and proper ale to wash it down with."

"Wait!" Queen Cara commanded. She looked at Lyana and Big John. "Do you recall the Chalice of Mystery? Calling your names?"

The two from Suregood Forest nodded.

"You will hear the sword calling in much the same manner," Queen Cara continued. "It will try to lure you to do its bidding. It will seek to destroy the rest of us. You resisted the Chalice, but that was just a short exposure."

"I thought we were protected from Magick?" Big Jon asked.

"The anti-Magick shell protects you from all spells cast at you," Knarra said. "But it won't keep sweet whispers out of your head, the spell that causes that is directed at the sword, not at you."

"You are here out of your own free will," Queen Cara said. "*Death of Magick* will attempt to extinguish that free will and make you its own play thing."

"Sheriff of Knottington has been trying that for years," Big Jon quipped. "To no avail."

Lyana began to frown at him, but when she saw his grin and semi-apologetic shrug, she smirked back at him. "Just you wait, Big Jon Loxly. Just you wait."

"You two done flirting?" Brute Leigh asked. "I'm hungry. I want roast boar."

"Flirting?!" Lyana exclaimed. "Why I..."

"Later," Prince Vanni said. "We've got work to do." He picked up his burning torch, and made his way towards the opening, Exeter at the ready in his other hand. "Warriors on me. Spell casters behind. Rangers to protect Rikmon and Loxly at the rear."

They entered a short corridor that led to a stairwell. As they started descending Lyana could hear a soft, beguiling female voice.

...Lyana...Lyana...come to me...

"I can hear *Death of Magick* calling," she reported.

"Me too," Big Jon added.

"Resist!" Exeter's scraping voice ordered. "RESIST!"

They came to a room that formed a perfect square. It had no other visible doors or gates, nor furnishings apart from an altar of blue stone at the far end of the room. The room was carved out of the same blue stone, polished so smoothly that the flames from their torches were reflected by floor, walls, and ceiling. A vorpal blade rested on the altar, its four-foot blade gleaming ominously. Arcane runes were etched on the weapon's hilt. Next to it lay a scabbard, filigreed gold patterned across blue velvet. The spell casters uneasily gazed upon the weapon that had been used to slay countless sorcerers.

"There're no creatures here," Cade stated the obvious.

…come to me…pick me up…wield me…

"Be ready!" Knarra warned. "Other than either Rikmon or Loxly, no one is to touch the sword."

Cyttia said, "That's elfish lettering. The runes read 'Death of Magick' and 'I am the end of Magick'.

…wield me…come to me Lyana Rikmon…

The sword seemed to flicker into life, sparkling blue tendrils running up and down the blade, purple hues radiating from the weapon.

"Erinnia!" Queen Cara said urgently. "What's happening?"

The elf closed her eyes, focusing intently. "It's Tigarn Nocerre! I can see him…he's in a cellar I think…in Lyndyn! But he's preparing a Return Spell."

"So that's how he retrieves *Death of Magick* when he needs the blade," Prince Vanni said.

…come to me Lyana Rikmon…

"The sword is still calling out to me," Lyana said, feeling its magnetic draw grow stronger.

"I no longer hear it," Big Jon said, sounding disappointed.

…come to me Lyana Rikmon…come to me Lyana Rikmon…

"It thinks…it thinks," Exeter rasped. "It thinks Lyana has the weaker will because she's a woman."

"Does it now?" Lyana asked furiously. "We'll see about that, won't we?"

"Loxly, don't touch the sword, it'll kill you now," Cittia said.

"Tigarn will be here any moment now!" Erinnia warned.

…COME TO ME LYANA RIKMON…

"Tigarn mustn't get hold of the sword!" Knarra urged. "If he does, he'll be nigh unbeatable."

The purple glow around *Death of Magick* began to expand.

"Lyana!" Queen Cara shouted. "Now!"

…YES! NOW! COME TO ME …

The party divided to let Lyana through as she paced towards the altar. More sparks, in the corner this time, more purple hues emitted from an invisible source.

"Tigarn is coming!" Erinnia called out.

Lyana's hand closed around the grip of *Death of Magick*. She felt a sharp shock shoot through her arm into the rest of her body, gritted her teeth, and raised the sword in the air.

"NOOOO!" A stranger's voice wailed.

Death of Magick turned, twisted, buckling wildly in Lyana's hand. She had to exert all her strength. Not to subject the sword to her will, but to prevent it pulling her off her feet, dragging her towards the Magick users.

…OBEY MY WILL…

"NEVER!" Lyana screamed defiantly, bracing herself as the sword jerked to the left, then to the right.

The others saw her body heave this way, then that, in a bizarre dance illuminated by both the anti-Magick shell's blue glow and the purple shimmer of the sword.

Tigarn Nocerre had fully materialised now, scrambling about on all fours in what seemed like a blind panic. For someone who had caused so much damage and fear, he was wretched little man, dressed in the simple robe of a scribe, face filthy, lacklustre brown mop of hair uncombed.

"Tigarn!" Brute Leigh snarled, clutching his axe with both hands.

"Have mercy!" Tigarn crawled towards the group. "I'm unarmed! I'm powerless! Have mercy!"

"It's true," Erinnia said. "All his power is in the sword."

"Still, he must be contained!" Knarra raised her staff, the end of which began to glow...

...MAGICK! KILL THE FILTHY SPELL CASTERS! KILL! KILL!...

Death of Magick lunged towards Knarra, dragging Lyana behind it.

"NO MAGICK!" Exeter screeched. *"NO MAGICK!"*

"Knarra! Stop!" Cittia shouted at the high priestess. "Magick triggers and empowers the sword."

Knarra desisted immediately, allowing Lyana to wrestle the sword back in a semblance of control.

...OBEY ME!

With surprising speed, Tigarn turned from a frightened, scurrying creature into a determined projectile, hurling towards Lyana. He drew a wicked looking dagger from the folds of his robe.

"Don't let him penetrate her Anti-Magick shell!" Prince Vanni shouted.

Instinctively, the spell casters made to cast, but were stopped by Queen Cara's outcry. "No Magick!"

Big Jon shoved the end of his quarterstaff between Tigarn's moving legs, causing the little man to trip and land on the floor. Snarling, Tigarn scrambled up and launched himself at Loxly.

Lyana perceived the events around the dome of blue and purple light in which she wrestled with *Death of Magick* as if time outside of her shell had slowed down. She saw Big Jon drop his staff and reach for his axe, saw the flicker of Tigarn's dagger, saw Prince Vanni and Brute Leigh rush forward, clutching their weapons…and knew they were too late…the dagger would pierce eye, slide through into brain…

Roaring with fury, Lyana's hands tightened around *Death of Magick's* hilt, and with one final effort, she subdued the sword to her will, bringing it down in a swinging arc that cleaved right through Tigarn's middle. The two parts of his body flopped onto the floor in a fountain of blood, the dagger clattering away harmlessly.

…now kill the rest…

The sword had ceased its physical struggle, and its words no longer deafened Lyana, yet it continued hissing. Grabbing the scabbard from the altar, Lyana slid the sword in, relieved to find that shut it up. The purple glow started to fade.

She looked at the others, who were staring at her. "I've got it." Lyana said, rather needlessly.

Queen Cara was the first to speak, "Excellent, superb. I am…"

She was interrupted by Erinnia, who suddenly clutched her head in her hands.

Exclamations of concern by her fellows were silenced by Knarra. "Give her space! Let her speak!"

"In the Lachinor," Erinnia intoned. "Thousands of fell creatures have flocked to the banners of Uyrg. His legions threaten Kanath in the south, and the Fane of the Setting Sun. Goblins, hobgoblins, ogres, troglodytes, lizard men, black dragons, renegade Dark Elves, giants, riff-raff from Rancide…a tide of darkness…"

"The king must be told," Prince Vanni said.

"He knows, he knows," Erinnia replied. "Dwarves march from Hillesdale. The king's host marches from Lyndyn. Draith Lord Calaiz is already at the Fane. Prince Vannelei leads the Gray Elves."

"These are ill tidings," Cade spoke. "By the time we reach the Fane…"

"This room," Prince Vanni said. "Tigarn used it to transport…if it facilitates…"

"The Phantom Servant spell?" Cittia ventured.

Cade frowned. "We need an exact location. Erinnia, can you see where Uyrg is? Is he with his legions? Or skulking in the Lair of Xollos still?"

Erinnia closed her eyes, her expression one of intense concentration. Then she shook her head. "He's shielded himself."

"The Lair of Xollos is huge," Cade said. "Without an exact destination, the Phantom Servant spell could have us materialise in a pool of lava, or within rock, to be crushed to death instantly."

"Also," Big Jon added. "Doesn't Magick trigger the sword?" He glanced at Lyana, who was attaching the sheathed sword to her belt.

"Not when it's in the scabbard," Cade said. "But we still don't know…"

"Unless," Queen Cara declared. "We have something of Uyrg, to function as a scent for the Phantom Servant."

Cade shrugged. "It'd have to be an essential part of him."

Queen Cara smiled. "Knarra?"

The High Priestess nodded. "I have such an item." She patted her satchel.

"But…" Cade looked puzzled.

"Forgive me, brother," Queen Cara said. "But the less people who knew, the better the chance that it'd escape Uyrg's notice."

"You've brought the…" Lyana began to exclaim.

"Hush," Knarra said. "Do not speak its name until we're ready."

"Listen carefully, all of you," Queen Cara commanded. "We haven't much time. The Phantom Servant will take us directly into the presence of the demon. We'll be disorientated, hopefully that will be countered by Uyrg's initial surprise at our apparition. We can't go with weapons drawn, all must be secured."

She looked at Lyana and Big Jon. "We'll have to lift the Anti-Magick shell protection, otherwise you can't go with us. Loxly, your part is played, you need not go. Lyana, without your presence, it would be…"

"I will uphold my oath, my Lady Queen," Lyana said, knowing that the *Death of Magick* was vital.

"The sheriff saved my life just now," Big Jon grumbled. He scowled at Lyana. "Do you have any idea what that's going to do to my reputation back in Suregood Forest? Bested by the sheriff? Me?!"

"I've got a fairly good idea." Lyana grinned. She was beginning to enjoy word-sparring with Big Jon. "I will pay a bard to compose a ballad and have it sung in every tavern along the Luumic."

"Do you see my peril, My Lady Queen?" Big Jon asked. "I would level the field by returning the favour if I can. I would stay by Lyana's side."

"Granted," the queen said. "Lyana, you must keep *Death of Magick* sheathed until the right moment. When you draw the sword, we won't be able to cast spells."

Lyana recalled the extra strength lent to the sword by Knarra's attempt to start casting a spell. If all of them were casting at once, she wouldn't be able to control *Death of Magick*, and it would invariably lead to Lyana assaulting her companions. "Yes, My Lady Queen."

"That still leaves any spells cast by Uyrg," Knarra looked at Lyana intently.

"I understand," Lyana said. "I will be on my guard, the sword is mine to control."

"Good," Brute Leigh pronounced. "My kind of sheriff. Now, is there any chance of stopping at the Fane's kitchens on the way to Lair of Xollos? I hate fighting on an empty stomach. It makes me grumpy."

Lair of Xollos

The Anti-Magick spells were lifted, after which the spell casters gathered around the altar to prepare the Phantom Servant.

The warriors and rangers checked their weapons.

Big Jon came to stand before Lyana. "Erm," he said.

"Erm, what?"

"I come to beg a favour," Big Jon said, reddening.

"Favour?"

"Like at a tournament." Big Jon shrugged. "Except I haven't got a lance, but I got my quarterstaff."

Lyana was flabbergasted when she realised the implication of his words. At tournaments, the male contestants would beg favours from ladies, tying ribbons or scarves to their lances as a public statement of their romantic interests.

She looked down at herself. Covered with dirt and grime from their journey. Splattered with Tigarn's blood. Smelling of sweat.

"I'm a bit short on fancy ribbons, today, Loxly. And this isn't a tournament."

He looked genuinely disappointed. *Bloody hell, Big Jon,* Lyana thought. *I'm interested. But is this really the time for it?*

It occurred to her that their remaining time might well be extremely limited. She glanced at the altar, where it seemed that spell preparations were reaching their end. *How long does it take to do this apparition thing? And then? It could be over in a manner of minutes. Everything. The end.*

"Maybe this will do?" She asked and reached out to pull his face towards her. Their first kiss was short, perhaps because they both drew away, startled by it. The second one was longer. Much longer.

"I hate to break it up," Prince Vanni called out to them. "But you're in danger of an imminent inappropriate comment by a grumpy dwarf."

Brute Leigh snorted and was about to respond when Knarra called them all over to the altar. They surrounded it and watched as Knarra took a smooth box from her satchel and placed it on the altar's blue stone surface. The surface of the box was made from prismatic dragon scales, glittering in the torch light, but the box appeared to be a solid object, with no sign of a lid or other means to open it.

"Ready?" Knarra looked around and waited until she had a sign of affirmation from everyone. After that, she swept her hand over the box. "Lylysis!"

The prismatic dragon scales shimmered brightly but then lost their cohesion. The box disintegrated into its separate components, scintillating on the table, revealing the Chalice of Mystery.

Unsealed, it began to call out to all members of the party – louder and louder to overcome the incantations of the Phantom Servant uttered in unison by the spell casters. Louder and louder…a fierce pain stung Lyana's head…the blue room spinning round and round…a blinding light…

…she hit the floor rolling, hurled out of centrifugal spin. Her arms and legs collided with those of others, until everyone came to a halt, dazed, half-blinded. The Chalice of Mystery, clattering over the ground, was the last to stop rolling.

Lyana heard ominous laughter, in deep bass tones. She blinked, started scrambling up.

"KNARRA!" a voice boomed. "My old adversary. You've come to return my chalice to me. How very considerate of you."

Lyana overcame her nausea and dizziness to take in her new surroundings. They were in an immense, dimly lit cavern. Water dripped from a myriad of stalactites above, and stalagmites formed a surreal miniature landscape on the cavern's floor. Mauve vapors hung in the air, and the Archdemon Uyrg came walking out of a particularly thick patch of it. The vile creature had opted for a flaming presence and its weapons of choice were a huge sword and a blazing cat o' nine tails. Red and orange scales of fire dragons and salamanders composed its armor.

"You have chosen poorly, Knarra. You should have brought a thousand sorcerers and as many warriors!"

Knarra didn't reply. She was looking around to see all the companions regain their focus. She gestured silent commands at them.

"This sorry lot is the best Donothor has to offer?" Uyrg goaded her. "Mere women? Puny dwarves? Scruffy outlaws?"

The warriors and rangers fanned out to the flanks. The spell casters gathered in a loose group in the centre, strengthened by Queen Cara and Cade.

Lyana stayed behind them. Big Jon, at her side, complained, "who's it calling scruffy?"

Knarra looked at Lyana, who nodded. *Keep Death of Magick sheathed…until the right moment.*

"I will kill all of you as slowly and painfully as possible," Uyrg promised.

Knarra spoke at last, but she aimed her words at her companions. "This conversation is boring. Kill it!"

A barrage of spells were unleashed at Uyrg. The warriors rushed out to form a broad circle around the demon as it responded with spells of its own. The air between the spell casters and the demon hissed and fizzled with bright colours, flashes, and negations.

Though *Death of Magick* remained silent, Lyana could sense its increasing restlessness. She closed her hand around the sword's grip, just in case it broke loose from the containment of the scabbard.

The warriors rushed in from all sides, but Uyrg was quick as lightning, countering spells hurled at him, casting his own, while at the same time using sword and cat o' nine tails to parry incoming blows and strike back.

A ranger stumbled backwards, clutching the stump of his sword-arm. Deron fell, his life's blood pouring out of gaping wounds. Cyttia was hurled backwards, alive but incapacitated.

Uyrg lashed out at the air above with the cat o' nine tails, its burning strands cutting through even the thickest stalactites as a hot knife cuts through butter, causing deadly missiles of pointy rock to rain down.

"They won't last long!" Loxly shouted in alarm.

He's right. Though their companions were still putting up an epic fight, Lyana could feel their efforts flagging. Hurt, tired, a desperate determination to at least fight to the death. Hope was slipping away. Uyrg was too powerful.

Death of Magick rattled in its scabbard, driven to madness by the Magick laden air. How it yearned to be unleashed. Lyana glanced down at the sword. Would she be able to control it this time? The sword fed on its hatred for Magick, stronger in the vicinity of spell casters, bloodthirsty when Magick was used. In the current circumstances it would be screaming for a feeding frenzy that would shame a pride of hungry Cheethras.

"Lyana!" Big Jon shouted.

Uyrg had cast a Temporal Stasis Spell at the spell casters. Queen Cara, Cade, Knarra, and Erinnia went down. The spell's wave rolled over the inert bodies, right towards the two from Suregood Forest.

Big Jon grabbed Lyana and pushed her, shoving her forcefully behind a bulky stalagmite where she was shielded from the blast. Big Jon was still half exposed and came crashing down, heaving and coughing.

The demon boomed laughter as it turned on the remaining warriors.

It was nearly over now

Lyana clutched the hilt of *Death of Magick*. The spell casters were down; there was no need to co-ordinate her attack on the demon with them. She only had to land one blow on the vile creature.

"…you're a good fighter…" Big Jon uttered between gasps for breath. "…but not against Uyrg…too powerful…"

"I'm not," Lyana conceded, but rose to her feet nonetheless. "But I've an idea. Jon, if I stay beserk, knock me out, bind me with elf ropes, or just kill me. Protect the spell casters."

"Stay beserk? Lyana!"

"Protect the spell casters," Lyana insisted. "Even from me." She looked down at him, gave him a quick smile, then stepped out of the shelter of the stalagmite.

Uyrg was fighting both Prince Vanni and Brute Leigh, driving them steadily backwards, away from the prone spell casters. The demon clearly had the upper hand.

Lyana strode past the spell casters. Her eye found the place where the Chalice of Mystery had rolled to a halt, and she kicked it towards the fighting, further away from her stricken companions. She was taking a gamble, that *Death of Magick* would focus on the nearest source of Magick, or else the most powerful or threatening source. If she was right, Uyrg's superb brute strength was about to become his biggest weakness.

She gave the cup another kick. The further away from Queen Cara and the rest, the better.

"HEY!" She hollered at Uyrg who was lashing out at Prince Vanni and Brute Leigh with his flaming cat o' nine tails. "YOU PUTRID BAG OF FAECES!"

The demon turned her way, its eyes fiery malevolence, a snarl on its hideous face.

Lyana came to a stop, the chalice by her feet. She drew *Death of Magick* from the scabbard. The sword's screams filled her head instantly, louder than before.

…STOP RESISTING. **OBEY ME!**

"YES!" Lyana cried out. "I'm yours to command. I will obey!"

She lost instant control of her body, the sword's will and determination rushing into her, controlling her, directing her. Only a part of her passive mind remained hers, incapable of anything other than observation…and feeling pain shoot through her body as she grew a foot taller, her muscles bulging, her agility enhanced, and speed multiplied.

Lyana and *Death of Magick* were as one now, striking at the Chalice of Mystery with a serpent's speed. The artefact shrieked as its metal was torn and twisted, rent asunder.

Uyrg howled his rage, but when the Chalice' last whimper ceased, he shrieked with invisible pain. That drew *Death of Magick's* attention. The sword directed Lyana towards the demon.

"YOU'RE AS GOOD AS DEAD!" Uyrg bellowed at Lyana.

Worse. I might be trapped in my mind for as long as the sword allows my body to live.

The demon swung its huge sword at Lyana. She countered with *Death of Magick*. The blades met in a deafening metallic twang and explosion of sparks. Uyrg's blade glowed red hot for a moment, then disintegrated into ashes.

The expression on its face was priceless, but *Death of Magick* had no interest in such distraction. Even as Uyrg stood observing its empty sword hand, Lyana rushed the demon, seeking the cat o' nine tails and promptly destroying it.

…KILL THE MAGICK…KILL THE MAGICK…

The sword was ecstatic. Yearned for more. This is what it had been forged for. In the hands of an experienced sword fighter, rather than its wretched little creator, there were no limits to its power. All Magick would die…all of it.

Uyrg stared into Lyana's eyes, saw the battle rage and bloodlust in them. For the first time in its millennia of existence, the demon understood the meaning of fear. The demon took a backwards step. Prince Vanni and Brute Leigh rushed to Lyana's side, getting as close as they dared to the dome of purple hues that surrounded her.

Death of Magick directed Lyana forwards, lunging at Uyrg. The demon anticipated the move and swung a mighty arm to smite the attacking warrior. Quick as lightning, Lyana rolled onto the ground so the demon's arm passed only through air. She jumped up and thrust *Death of Magick* at the demon's exposed stomach.

The sword, like it's creator, suffered from overestimation. It could destroy all Magick but wasn't immune to Magick itself. Lyana drove the sword into Uyrg until the cross guard slapped against the creature's leathery flesh. The demon ululated in pain, to which were added agonized screeches from *Death of Magick* itself. The purple hues enveloped the demon, icy blue tendrils of lightning shooting out from the wound. Lyana received a shock that was so intense she had to let go of the hilt and was thrown backwards ten feet.

Foul black smoke started to pour from the demon's wounds, then from its nostrils, mouth, ears. Its eyes imploded, the gaping sockets too funnelling the sulphurous smoke. The whole foul mess began to collapse, melt and smoulder, until at long last nothing remained but a puddle of vile goo. Uyrg was gone for good. So was *Death of Magick*. It was over.

Lyana was wracked by pains when her body receded to its former size. Prince Vanni and Brute Leigh helped her up.

"Best sheriff ever," the dwarf declared. Prince Vanni said nothing, but Lyana could see respect in his eyes. When she stood, he bowed his head to her.

The spell casters were getting to their feet, bleeding and battered, still affected by the spell so they stumbled around like drunks evicted from a tavern.

Lyana was pleased they were alive but walked past them. To her relief Jon was getting to his feet as well, disorientated, but in one piece.

She folded her arms around him, and he returned the embrace. She said "I apprehend you, in the name of the law…"

"Gladly," he responded.

Lyana laughed. She'd had her bellyful of magic swords, mysterious chalices, and foul demons. All she wanted was to return to Knottington, with Big Jon Loxly her captive, as she was his. That was the sort of thing the bards should be composing ballads about.

THE END

Sacrificed to the Dragon

Johan Klein Haneveld

Lupita N'doko, special envoy of the Renewed Federation of Human Nations, felt like she was suffocating. Something sharp and rigid pressed against her throat. When she tried to breathe in she heard an unpleasant hiss, like air escaping from a rusty valve. Moreover, she was unable to fill her lungs, leaving her gasping. All her eyes could see was a blue sky and a bright light that impressed red spectral images on her retinas. She was on her knees. Panic overwhelmed her rational capacities. She writhed and twisted, trying to raise her hands to her throat. However, her wrists scraped painfully against metal and her fingers clawed ineffectively at nothing at all.

In desperation Lupita threw her head backwards. Warm, dry air filled her lungs but now the rigid object that had constricted her throat cut into her neck. She tried to move her head sideways, to the left and right, but she couldn't escape its grasp. She tried to tear her body loose, but something unyielding constrained her and all she managed to achieve was to almost cut off her breath again.

Lupita shut her eyes. She swallowed the gluey slime that had gathered at the back of her throat and waited until the flood of fear subsided to a manageable level. Turning her face away from the hot sun, she brought her breathing under control, focused her eyes as best as she could, and tried to assess her situation.

She could see that her left wrist was encircled by a broad steel band that was welded to a metal rod. It ran past behind her neck to meet her right wrist, similarly bound. Her arms were held upward so rigidly that her sinews and muscles hurt. Lupita glanced behind her as far as the steel pain around her neck allowed. It seemed that the band around her neck was attached to the same rod the wrist restraints were. A short chain was also attached to the rod and led to a stout stake. She tugged the rod forward, but no matter how hard she tried to budge the stake, it had been sunk so deep into the ground that it didn't give way even a little bit.

Lupita was relieved that her legs hadn't been constrained, but the chained rod prevented her from scrambling upright. She realized that her official diplomat's outfit had been stripped off her, replaced by a tatty loincloth. There was a worse shock when she perceived that she had lost her dense curly hair. Her scalp itched as if recently and roughly shaven. Sheer humiliation coursed through her and brought tears to her eyes.

She had failed in her mission, an important one. The planets which had belonged to the Federation of Human Nations before the Great War were to be invited back into the fold. Even if they had lost their technological advances and had fallen back to a medieval level of civilization, or lower still. The core planets of the Renewed Federation were determined to raise the fallen planets back on a par with the others at any cost. Lupita had been one of the envoys sent out to bear the good news.

Her initial welcome on this backwater planet had been a warm one. The local king had listened to her proposals nodding enthusiastically all the while. He had ordered a feast. Bizarre six-legged animals had been roasted on a spit and served with dishes of purple vegetables. A strong-bodied wine had been offered to her, one that had left a feisty aftertaste which burned in her throat. Lupita had only taken a few sips of it, but that had been enough to make her dizzy. With hindsight, she should have taken more care, because she couldn't recall anything that had happened after that.

Lupita blinked furiously, both to shed her eyes of the tears that had welled up and the blurriness that hazed her long-distance focus. Behind her was a steep incline of red sand and pale yellow sun-bleached grassy polls. A broad landscape stretched out in front of her, a parched horizon blending into the heat of the burning sky, ghostly mirages of non-existent water pools shimmering here and there in the vast wasteland. There were no signs of human habitation. Low ridges of sand and a few forlorn copses of trees formed the only landmarks. The only sign of life out there were vulturesque circling dots high up in the sky.

To Lupita's right were three more stakes. Two nearly naked men and a woman were chained to them, their wrists manacled to iron rods at head-height, just as Lupita was constrained. The man who was closest to Lupita, was slouched forward. The iron neck band dug deep into his throat. Pink foam was oozing out of his mouth and Lupita could see no sign of breathing.

Turning her head to the left, carefully to avoid the choking grasp of her neck band, she could see three more stakes. All of them were occupied by human misery. Closest by was a young woman, on her knees like Lupita. Her facial features revealed beauty still, with high cheekbones and a pointed chin. Her scalp had been roughly shorn. Like the other staked prisoners, a red 'V' had been daubed on her forehead, the point of the letter just above her nose, the letter's arms smeared out over her eyebrows. Her lips were cracked and her pale skin was turning a bright pink, like a prawn in boiling water. The woman's eyes were clear though, and she was regarding Lupita warily.

"You're not from here," she said. "That's why you are the central offering. The dragon is given the best of the best."

Lupita could understand the archaic form of Eurenglish without effort. Not all of her accessories had been taken away from her. Her weapons had been built into her gloves, and her communication unit into her belt. She'd lost both of those.

There was more intimate technology though, like the translation device inserted behind her left ear.

The emergency communication module!

She turned her dry tongue in her mouth, to press it against her upper right wisdom tooth. Green lights flickered across her vision. Lupita wasted no time sending a distress call, although she wasn't optimistic about its effectiveness. Her ship was far away, out of detection range from the planet's optical instruments, and the signal from the emergency communication module was weak, it would have trouble traveling beyond the atmosphere.

Lupita twisted her tongue to the left and pressed twice against her lower wisdom tooth. A red dot started blinking in the corner of her vision. If worst came to worst, she had a final card to play, but that wouldn't help her escape the merciless grip of the iron that bound her. Not alive, anyway.

Sighing, she turned to the girl who had spoken to her. "What did you say? Offering? A dragon?"

"You're really from some place far away." The girl spoke slower this time, articulating carefully as if addressing a village idiot.

Lupita wondered if her translation device had been imprecise, maybe in the intonation.

"Everyone knows about the dragon." The young woman shook her raised arms, rattling the chain attached to the rod, probably to emphasize her words rather than to free herself. "Everyone knows about the sacrifices as well."

"Well, nobody told me about it," Lupita said.

"Why would they?" The woman looked scornful. "It's known, I said. There isn't a person on the planet who doesn't know."

The young woman looked to her other side, where a man was kneeling, the red V on his forehead, his right hand twisted at a strange angle as it dangled from his wrist restraint. "Isn't that right?" She asked him.

His eyes were wide and he shivered. His voice was a soft croak. "The dragon will devour us."

"It's not known where I'm from," Lupita said. "I conducted an in-depth ecological analysis from my ship before I flew my shuttle down to the surface. The composition of the population of grazing stocks shows no indication of large predators. Certainly not a flying and fire-breathing one. If our definition of 'dragon' is the same, such a creature would leave tracks, signs of its passing…"

"Huh? What are you on about?" The young woman looked at Lupita as if she had gone mad. "Can you not see the tracks?" Indicating her head, she asked: "What about those?"

Lupita had to stretch her neck as best she could to see what the young woman meant. Four deep indentations worn into the ground. A black circle in their midst. The sand there seemed to have been molten into glass, something that could only be achieved by immensely high temperatures.

"The dragon has been coming here for centuries," the young woman said, without a trace of emotion in her voice. "Since the days of my grandparents' grandparents."

A quick calculation told Lupita that this didn't equate centuries. She decided not to comment on it because the communication between them was strenuous enough already. It was clear to her though, that this monster had started appearing roughly around the time that the connection with the old Federation had been broken.

Lupita swallowed, her throat was parched and ached. "People have seen this dragon with their own eyes?"

"Only from a distance. It flies on wings of the wind, has bright, burning eyes, and scorches anybody who comes too close. It's armoured with impenetrable scales and its claws cleave the hardest granite without effort."

That sounds like a dragon alright.

"It's an animal?" Lupita asked. "Can it speak? What does it want?"

The young woman nodded left and right at her wrist restraints. "Why do you think we are here? Every year seven sacrifices are chosen. Young men and women, in the prime of their lives. They…we are affixed here at the edge of the plains and abandoned. Then the dragon comes. Nothing is left of them…us the next day. Nothing."

Lupita couldn't resist a fearful shiver. "And if the offer isn't made?"

"Then all our people must pay a price. Did you not see the traces of fire in the city? The half-destroyed tower at the castle?"

"My father saw it up close," the wide-eyed man next to the young woman whispered hoarsely. "The monster came flying over the hills, borne on black clouds, and then fell upon the city. Its claws scooped up scores of men and women to toss them aside like broken toys, its breath…"

The man stalled for a moment, his eyes glazing over. "Whole neighbourhoods were set alight. The soldiers peppered the creature with arrows and spears from the castle walls but that didn't help. The dragon cleansed the battlements with its fiery breath. After that it attacked the main tower with its claws. There was nothing that could be done to stop it. Nothing…"

The young woman interrupted. "Since then we have paid our dues. Like all other peoples on this world."

"But now it's your turn," Lupita said.

The young woman looked down at the ground. "My sacrifice will keep my family safe for another year. And many other families."

Lupita tried to shift on her knees, to ease the pressure of the iron band pressing against her throat. She turned her eyes to the sky. It was so bright that it was almost impossible to look at. The sinking sun seemed enlarged, as if trying to fill the whole of her vision. "When will the dragon come? Do you know?"

"You're just full of questions, aren't you?" The young woman said, but she did answer after a few moments, perhaps grateful for the distraction. "It won't be long now. The soldiers said that it always arrives before sunset…in fact…"

The young woman paled, her mouth fell open. The man next to her began to scream. He twisted and writhed, fighting his restraints as if hoping for a last-minute reprieve that would allow a miraculous escape, but the iron that bound him held fast and the stake he was chained to didn't budge. The other intended sacrifices screamed or cried, all but the lifeless young man.

Lupita felt her heart pounding away like a runaway machine. She could see what had driven terror into the others. A black dot, like a bird of prey gliding on a thermal. This one wasn't circling though. It was headed towards the staked offers in a straight line. It left trails of white smoke behind it. There was an almighty bang so loud that it reverberated around Lupita's skull. The human offerings at the stakes became silent as they watched the monster approach, accompanied by a distant, growling rumble.

How much time? A few minutes at most.

Lupita tapped her top right wisdom tooth with her tongue. There was no response to her distress signal. Even if she had managed to make contact, her ship would have never made it here in time.

The growl swelled into a growing roar. Lupita made a decision. She turned to the young woman.

"We do have stories about dragons, where I come from. Old ones, originated on Earth itself."

"You do?" The woman asked, without taking her eyes off the growing dark form of the monstrosity roaring towards them.

"Yes, we do." Lupita spoke calmly, almost casually. "They dominated mankind, like your dragon. They demanded that kings surrender their most beautiful daughters, and Lords their most faithful retainers. Knights who set out to combat the dragons were burned and torn asunder. Eventually though, they disappeared, living on only in fairy tales."

The creature had now come so close that Lupita could see its wings, flashing in the sun's rays. She had to speak louder now, to be heard over the beast's roar.

"The age of the dragons came to an end when gunpowder was invented. An explosive mix. A single keg enough to blast apart a wall. It exploded when it came into contact with fire. So what did people do? They baited the dragons with giant puppets, decoys with kegs of gunpowder sown into them. They tied bundles of it to sheep, a fire arrow at the ready when the dragons came to feed. Some people sacrificed themselves in suicide attacks. Every time a dragon fed on gunpowder it was torn to shreds. Before long there were none left."

"A fine story," the young woman said. "But of no use to us."

"You're wrong," Lupita said, with calm confidence.

The dragon had reached them and came to a shuddering halt. It hovered above its previous tracks for a few moments, howling fiercely and blowing up great clouds of red dust from the ground. Lupita had seen enough of it to confirm her suspicions though.

The terrifying creature that now landed with a loud thud wasn't a dragon at all. It was a spaceship. One with wings to carry it through an atmosphere, and an array of weaponry poking out of its nose cone. A door slid open. Men dressed in a motley assortment of spacesuits emerged. Their visors were screened, and they carried handheld laser weapons.

One of them saw Lupita and pointed at her. He started walking toward her, followed by two others who slung their laser weapons over their shoulders.

Lupita sagged against her restraints, giving the impression that she was weak and beat, her spirit deflated. She pressed the tip of her tongue against her lower left wisdom tooth. The little red light in the corner of her vision blinked patiently. She activated it, so that the weapon was primed, ready to be triggered at the next touch. It was tiny, concealed in a single tooth, but Lupita knew its destructive potential was vast, its explosive radius wide.

The young woman had been wrong, ancient fairy tales could be instructive. All Lupita had to do was wait for the right moment to destroy the dragon from within.

THE END

Nicole Falling: A Southwest Horror Story
Greg Alldredge

Nicole woke to the steady purring rumble of the cherry stock '68 Mustang Convertible. The tires made a steady thud-dump, thud-dump, thud-dump, like a heartbeat as she drove. She took a quick glance at her mutt sleeping on the floor, the bag on the passenger seat, and the rearview mirror to look for any pursuers. Satisfied she wasn't being followed, she pulled her eyes back to the mesmerizing flash of the amber lines on the road's surface racing past the car.

"Where the hell are we?" she muttered to the sleeping dog. The heartbeat sound of the tires coupled with the hypnotic nature of the passing flares of yellow tried to drag her back into a trance-like state. She shook her head, attempting to clear her thoughts.

"I still can't believe his woke ass called me a dirty *slant* to my face..." Anger worked well to wake her up. She hadn't fought her way to America for that racist crap.

Her eyes glanced in the rearview mirror again. The glow of the city had disappeared. Her mind raced. *Damn... must be out of it... Need some rest. I left the city. Ditched the asshat in the dust... two days ago? Must've blacked out... Last thing I remember was dusk and the circling vultures. How long ago?*

"Damn clock!" The clock in the dash pointed straight up and down. It might have been saying either six AM or PM, but either way, the sun should be up. It was pitch-black outside, and she was certain now the clock was broken.

She reached for her bag, glancing over long enough to unzip it slightly. Inside lay piles of twenties wrapped and neatly stacked. Reaching in, she felt around the stolen Beretta until she pulled her cell out. The phone had no signal and still read six PM. "Damn!"

She flung the cell back in the bag and reached for the tuning knob on the classic radio. Twisting it, the selector glided over the various frequencies, finding only static. "Damn, and double damn! I must be way out in the sticks."

She rolled her head, attempting to crack her neck and failed, then looked out the windshield up at the night sky. The Milky Way blazed overhead, the lack of light pollution evident by the number of stars visible. There was no glow of civilization on the horizon. Upon checking the gas gauge, it showed three-quarters of a tank. Nicole figured enough for 250 miles. Of course, she had no idea where she was or how long until the next station, though she had a feeling she traveled south.

There must be a storm following behind, no light, no stars. The night was black as a lawyer's heart. The sagebrush flashed by, washed in the glow of the headlights. The calm of the desert outside was an inverse reflection of the storm of thoughts inside Nicole's head.

§ § §

Maria hustled down the single aisle of the diner, built into an old train carriage, carrying a glass pot full of freshly brewed coffee. As she approached the couple seated in the end booth, their hushed tones ceased. A genuine smile crossed her lips as she held the coffee up for the pair. The woman looked emotional, like she'd been crying. "Would you two like a refill?" She looked over the couple. The balding man with gray at the temples, a worn suit a few years out of style. Across from him was a raven-haired woman, dressed like a twenty-something but obviously long past her thirties. The older woman turned her head to hide her mascara, which had run, giving her the visage of a gothic creature waiting to steal a child's soul.

The balding man motioned to fill both cups then went back to watching out the window. Down the hill and across the road, an eighteen-wheeler was being unloaded in a truck stop parking lot.

Maria left the couple. She thought, He is such an asshole for making her cry.

§ § §

Eric was whispering his disdain for people before the waitress walked up. "Will you look at those wetbacks working in the heat? I bet they stole those jobs from hardworking Americans."

"Eric!" Candi hissed. "How can you tell if they are undocumented? You can't even see them in the dark." She hated the bald man and everything he stood for.

"I can tell, just like I can tell what that half-breed waitress is like and that spear-chucker of a cook. Should ship them all—" He stopped talking as the woman walked up with the coffee. He motioned for coffee, then turned his head to hide his contempt.

§ § §

Maria walked back behind the bar to serve coffee to the heavyset woman with the crewcut and plaid shirt. At least, Maria thought she was a woman. With the name of Sam, Maria wasn't too sure. She'd been in the joint a few times, but they never really chatted.

Sam nodded and accepted the coffee. After Maria poured, Sam reached her hand out, placing it over Maria's on the coffee pot. Stopping Maria in her tracks, the older woman shot her a knowing glance and motioned with her head to the couple in the corner. A wordless conversation went on between the two, ending with a raised eyebrow from Sam and Maria rolling her eyes. Both acknowledged the jackass sitting at the far end of the restaurant.

§ § §

In the kitchen, Cookie was unaware of the little drama taking place in the seating area out front. The old black cook pulled the ticket for Sam's order and set the steaming platter of pancakes on the stainless steel shelf of the window opening, ringing the bell to draw Maria's attention. "Short stack is up!" Cookie barked with the voice of a drill sergeant.

At the same time, the bell on the front door cheerfully announced the arrival of a plump blonde woman, red-faced and out of breath.

Maria called out, "Hey there, Jessie."

"Sorry I am late, dear; a storm is blowing in from the north. It looks darker than usual out tonight." Jessie's eyes lingered on the locked display case filled with custom-made knives. "Sell one?"

"Sure did, the nice Bowie." Maria beamed. "Money's in the till."

§ § §

Speeding down the highway through the flat desert, Nicole saw lights approaching, which she soon identified as a truck stop on the left of the road and a diner of sorts on the other.

Max, the mutt, who had been asleep the whole time, woke with a jolt. The mutt whimpered.

"What's a matter, girl?" Nicole always felt better with animals than with humans.

Max rose and clambered into the passenger seat. Nicole slowed the car as she cast a worried look at her four-legged friend. Max looked back at the rear window, uttering a low menacing growl, the hair on the dog's neck and back standing rigidly upwards. Max started barking.

"Sshhh," Nicole tried in vain to quiet the dog. The barking became more frenzied. Drops of dog spittle sprayed the back of the car.

Nicole peered into the rearview mirror. She saw nothing behind her. Only the black of the approaching storm. "Shush, girl, it's just a storm." Nicole tried to calm the dog, and her own nerves, as the hair on the back of her neck began to stand on end. "Must be an electric storm." Whatever it was, they were both on edge as they approached the truck stop and diner.

As the convertible passed the truck being unloaded, she heard a clunk under the hood, and the warning lights flashed wildly. All power was lost, and the car rolled to a slow halt.

Max was now going wild. Nicole smelled the fear from the dog, which only increased her own apprehension, even if she had no idea what there was to dread. She felt it in her bones, a dark primal horror, as if stalked by an unrelenting creature hell-bent on destruction. Not a person easily scared, this shook her to the core.

The Mustang stopped at the bottom of the slope the diner sat upon. She opened the door, and before she fully exited the car, Max was out and running back the way they had come, growling, barking, and urinating as she went.

"Damn it!" Nicole grabbed the bag containing her cell, money, and pistol. "Max, get back here," she shouted after the dog.

As soon as Nicole got out of the car, the lights from the truck stop and the diner went out. She was plunged into darkness, the only source of light was faint starlight to the south. Everything to her north seemed swallowed up by unnatural darkness.

Torn between the safety for her dog and the safety of the cafe, she took three timid steps to the rear of the car, trying to spot Max. She walked into a wall of stench. Certain items have a distinctive smell. Materials like rotten eggs, cabbage, or decomposing flesh are easy to remember, like the human body is hardwired to recall such stenches and recoil. This was worse. One step into the smell, Nicole projectile vomited. That was when she heard Max, first growling like she was fighting something in the blackness, next a yelp as if hurt, finally she went deathly silent.

Nicole noticed her world was noiseless. No wind, no rain, no sound of humanity. She realized how alone she truly was. Holding the bag to her stomach while trying hard not to throw up again, she fumbled for her gun.

She felt her bladder weakening. Terror left the taste of bile in her mouth. Frozen with primal inaction until she beheld the neon of the diner flash back on, the hum of an emergency generator in the distance. The tubes wrapping around the outside flickered to life. Nicole ran towards the perceived safety up the hill.

§ § §

When the lights blinked out in the diner, there were yelps, more surprise than fear.

"Dammit!" Cookie had been chopping carrots. "Maria! Jessie! Someone bring a flashlight and a clean towel. I added some protein to the veggies."

Not entirely sure what Cookie meant, Maria scrambled for a flashlight in a drawer.

"You see to Cookie," Jessie said. "I'll get the generator started."

Jessie made her way down the hall to the back door as Maria switched on the flashlight and used it to locate a clean towel.

"What the hell is going on with the lights? What kind of shithole is this?" the balding man in the corner hollered.

"Sit your ass down and keep calm," Sam snapped at him. "Staff are dealing with the situation."

"Honey, calm down," the woman in the corner told her unpleasant companion. "Please, Eric. I'm sure they'll have the lights back on in a second."

Arriving in the kitchen, Maria gasped when the flashlight revealed Cookie looking pale, holding up a bloodied hand. The index fingertip had been severed altogether. The red of the blood seemed darker running down his dark skin.

She grabbed the first aid kit and helped Cookie to a small prep table at the back, where she made him sit down.

Jessie must have managed to find her way to the back door and the emergency start switch for the generator. Maria heard the soft purr of the propane-powered motor hum to life.

The lights flickered back on. Maria took a deep breath when she saw the amount of blood in the kitchen. The missing fingertip lay in the middle of a pool of Cookie's blood on the floor. Maria gagged, and struggled not to throw up.

Jessie returned, calling out into the kitchen, "I think that storm that's brewing knocked out the power. I'll check the news." Shortly afterward she announced, "No reception."

Jessie poked her head through the stainless steel door. "Holy crap! Cookie, I thought you'd just nicked yourself."

To Maria's relief, Jessie helped to bind a tight bandage around Cookie's mutilated finger, and also found some painkillers. Cookie was clearly in pain.

They had just finished when the front door bell announced the arrival of a newcomer.

Nicole approached the door at a dead run and observed a rather ordinary looking scene unfold in front of her. People in a diner, drinking coffee, perhaps waiting for their meals.

Her level of dread shrank the farther she retreated from her dead car. She still smelled the stench in her nose and internally prayed that it did not cover her body.

Slowing to a walk as she approached the door, she tucked her pistol into the back of her pants and covered the grip with her shirt. The last thing she wanted was to draw attention to herself. Nicole wanted this night to be over so she could continue her journey, running away from the past.

The bell tinkled as she opened the door. The noise above her head startled her, but she pushed through her jitters and she stepped into the diner. Nicole picked the booth closest to the door so she could keep an eye on it and the patrons. Making herself as small as possible while moving to her chosen perch, she slid the bag containing the money in first, then rested the pistol between the bench and her back. It gave her a comforting feeling. She observed those in the cafe as they watched her.

It's all so maddeningly normal. Surreal. How many days has it been since I left the asshat back in San Francisco? What day is it? Where am I? How real is all of this?

Nicole was shaken from her reverie by a plump waitress who approached with a pot and cup. Her name badge said JESSIE.

"What can I get you, hun?" Jessie asked.

"Can I have a cup of black coffee?" Nicole thought for a moment before adding, "What time is it?"

Jessie looked over her shoulder at the large clock displaying the time over the kitchen pass-through. "Well isn't that strange?

The clock stopped at midnight when we lost power. So it must be shortly after midnight. Odd how it stopped right at midnight, isn't it?" The older woman shrugged.

"Is that the only thing strange that has happened?"

"Now, honey, this is the night shift, something strange is always happenin'." Jessie turned to leave, and Nicole looked out the window next to her.

She couldn't see her car at the bottom of the slope. It had been swallowed up by the darkness that spread around the pool of light of the diner. The diner's window lights and neon advertising spread as far as the cars parked out front, there ceasing abruptly as if it had an unnatural sharp edge.

§ § §

Eric watched the newcomer enter. "That damn slant looks stoned out of her gourd."

Candi timidly shook her head before picking up her coffee cup. "Do you have to be an asshole all the time?"

"I just call them as I see 'em. Most people can't handle my brutal honesty."

"No, most people can't handle your blatant racism."

"I can't help it if *those* people can't compete with me."

Not sure what to say to such a stupid comment, Candi quietly sipped her coffee.

§ § §

Sam, who had been listening to the not-so-hushed conversation, gritted her teeth and spoke to herself softly under her breath, "Don't get involved, it's not your fight."

§ § §

Jessie went to the sink behind the counter to fill the coffee pot. When she turned on the spigot, there was a loud clatter, followed by a hiss of air rushing out of the faucet. A smell of nauseating decay filled the diner.

The patrons and employees began choking and coughing, trying to fight the gag reflex overpowering everyone. Before Jessie managed to shut the spigot off, blood-tinted water began to fill the coffee pot.

Shocked, Jessie let out a scream. Her natural reflex was to release the pot, which was quickly filling with gore. The dropped pot shattered in the sink. The foul liquid sprayed Jessie in the face and covered her white shirt. Still screaming, she stumbled back until the bar stopped her retreat. The crimson-colored water continued to flow, the intensity of the spray increasing as if propelled by an unseen force. The sanguine fluid sprayed up the spotless stainless steel, down the white walls, and out onto the white tiled floor.

Maria came rushing out of the kitchen to see what was happening. Ignoring the foul spray, she and Jessie fumbled with the faucet handles.

"What the hell is going on?" Cookie shouted from the kitchen.

"Ummm, not sure!" Jessie shouted back.

"Problem with the well, I think," Maria called out. "The water is as red as blood!"

"None of the Old Testament crap! What's happening?" Cookie responded.

The two waitresses secured the faucet at last, and the vile spray ceased. Maria grabbed a towel and gave it to Jessie, whose front was soaked in red gore. Maria had been splattered as well, but not nearly as bad.

Cookie emerged from the kitchen, looking around at the mess behind the counter, and on the walls, with bewilderment.

He nursed his bandaged hand and looked pale. "Well, holy crap! Would you look at this?"

Eric had had enough. Throwing a ten-dollar bill on the table, he shorted the tab. "Let's get the hell out of here. I can't take this smell any longer."

Candi, still overcome by the stench, wrestled back her gag reflex and was quick to nod, sliding out of the booth and falling in three steps behind Eric.

"I left the money on the table," he called out to no one in particular as he passed the mayhem behind the counter.

Nicole thought she saw movement outside – just out of the corner of her eye but gone instantly – but she was sure she had seen something moving.

The balding man and the woman trailing him were about to pass her, on their way out the door… to whatever was waiting outside.

"You can't leave!" Nicole blurted out at them, panic rising in her.

"Say what?" the bald man asked, disdain on his face.

Nicole jumped up, blocking the way. "You can't open the door. Something is out there!"

"I know what's out there, lady. My car, that's what's out there." He turned to his companion. "I was wrong, not stoned but batshit crazy. Probably a foreigner."

Desperate, Nicole drew her pistol and aimed it at the obnoxious man. "Nobody is opening this door."

The balding man quickly stepped behind his companion. The woman, who looked like she had been crying, tried to defuse the situation. "Honey, I don't know what you think is outside, but we don't see anything."

The staff behind the counter had been distracted by the mess but now became aware of the situation and took in the scene by the door warily. So did the woman trucker on her stool by the counter. Nicole could see her tense up.

"There's something wrong outside," Nicole raised her voice, so all could hear. "There's something out there, something bad."

She turned to the trio behind the counter, the gun's barrel following her view. "Give me your keys. We need to lock the door."

The waitresses and cook, his hand bandaged, raised their hands in the air. The cook called out, "We ain't got much money in the till, but you can have it. Just lower that gun."

Exasperated, Nicole replied, "I'm not trying to rob you. I'm trying to save your asses. Now give me the damn keys!"

The cook looked at Nicole warily. "Right. I got the keys on my belt. I'm going to reach down and get them… slowly, okay?"

He reached for the keychain that dangled from his belt, detached it, and held the keys out. "It's the big platinum one."

Nicole motioned with the gun. "Everyone, go sit down on the stools."

She took the keys and motioned at the balding man and his companion. "You two, sit down." She turned to the cook and the waitresses. "You stay behind the counter, keep your hands up in the air where I can see them." It took everything she had to keep from shaking.

Everyone did as they were told. Nicole was especially wary of the cook. She'd noted how muscular his arms were and the tattoo on his right forearm: an eagle, globe, and anchor, her guess — a former marine.

Once the cook was behind the counter, Nicole quickly turned to lock the door, after which she stuffed the keys in her front pocket. The screaming tension in her head subsided somewhat. The diner felt safer, only having to deal with a bunch of strangers, hostages she held at gunpoint.

Nicole started a nervous grin, trying to hide her fear, but was startled by the ear-piercing screech of a smoke alarm in the kitchen. By the grace of the gods, she didn't pull the trigger by accident.

The cook made to move, stopped, looked at her, and said urgently, "I had something on the griddle. I gotta deal with this unless you want a fire."

Numbly, she shook her head. The cook had disappeared into the kitchen before she realized she'd have to leave either him or the rest out of her sight.

There'll be chef's knives in the kitchen.

That settled it for Nicole. She followed the cook into the kitchen.

§ § §

Maria and the others stared at the kitchen door as it swung closed in momentary disbelief. The woman with the gun was gone, but how long before she was back?

Eyes started searching. The way out was locked. Throwing a chair out of a window might be an...

Eyes widened. The pool of light around the diner was unnatural, the cars out front were left, but the rest of the world was swallowed whole by the eerie ink-black darkness.

Even more unsettling were the thousands of horned lizards which had migrated into the section of ground between the café and the wall of darkness. The horny toads made the ground appear as a mass of spikes, undulating over one another, seeking to keep out of that strange darkness, clawing each other to remain on top of the horde.

§ § §

Meanwhile, in the kitchen, Cookie was attempting to extinguish the small grease fire that had cropped up on the griddle.

Nicole grabbed a broom and jabbed it at the smoke alarm with the handle. To no avail. She cursed. It was taking too long. She should have been keeping her eye on the cook. If he was ex-military, this was precisely the situation he might have been waiting for.

She reversed the broom and took a step forward to angrily swipe the smoke alarm with the broom's head.

Panic struck as her feet started to slide away from beneath her. Nicole registered blood on the kitchen floor, a lot of blood.

"What the...!"

She couldn't stop her forward motion. Slipping and sliding as she was, the broom missed the smoke detector altogether. The head splashed hard into the near-boiling oil of the deep fat fryer, right next to the cook who was beating a fire of smoldering black lumps on the stovetop.

The broom's head displaced a great deal of the oil, fountaining out and cascading over the cook. The oil scalded his flesh, creating instantaneous blisters. Flash-fried like a pork rind. The cook tried to shield his face, so his arms took the brunt of the searing spray.

Bloodcurdling screams emerged from his mouth as he was literally deep-fried alive.

Nicole dropped the broom – its head ignited, now blazing – and stood frozen, struck by the horror of it. The others crowded in from the diner just as the spilled oil was ignited by the smoldering mess. The fire spread almost instantly, swallowing up most of the cook's upper body. He flailed about, a sheet of flame stumbling blindly on two legs.

The cook stopped screaming, and shortly afterward, his body collapsed.

Nicole watched as the waitress named Jessie raced to a corner and pulled the handle of a device labeled emergency halon fire suppression system. The smoke alarm, still shrieking, was joined by the hiss of high-pressure halon being released from ceiling nozzles.

Nicole stepped backward until her back was pressed against the wall as the opaque firefighting gas filled the space.

Most of the others fled the kitchen, apart from the Jessie woman and the trucker woman.

As the suspended particles of the firefighting agent began to settle and the flames died down, they all stared in horror at the cook. His ebony skin had cracked, charcoal black with blood red flesh showing through in places. His blistered and burned face was barely recognizable as human.

It was too much for Jessie. She fled the kitchen, hand over her mouth, gagging.

§ § §

Jessie rushed down the hall into the small staff toilet space, her bulky frame nearly filling the sink area. She spat the bile that had worked its way into her mouth in the sink. Her mind elsewhere, she turned on the faucet to the cold water and was met with a steady stream of bloodred gloppy water.

She had the presence of mind to shut it off before she was covered again. Gripping the sides of the sink and considering her face in the ancient mirror, she took stock of her running mascara, thinking, *What else could possibly go wrong?* That's when she heard buzzing, and a fat bumble bee landed on her left hand.

§ § §

The trucker looked away from the hideous remnants of the cook, taking in the sight of Nicole pressed against the wall, her hand still gripping the gun, knuckles white.

What the hell was going on? Nicole thought.

"You killed him?" the trucker asked.

Nicole shook her head. "It… it was an accident, the oil…" How could she explain she wasn't a murderer?

The trucker ignored the grease and blood that covered the floor. For a moment, Nicole thought she might make a lunge for the gun.

A scream echoed down the hall outside the kitchen… from the backdoor area. The panicked cry for help was quickly followed by pounding on a door like someone got locked out.

Someone might have tried… Nicole thought… *outside!*

She quickly glanced around, jittery, hands still shaking. The Latina server watched through the serving window.

Nicole hustled herself out of the kitchen.

The old barfly dragged her bald man into the hall. They blocked Nicole's exit. A quick wave of the gun and they backed out of her way.

Right now, she needed to distance herself from the butch woman with the crewcut.

A few steps brought her to the end of the hall and two doors, one clearly to the outside and barred, one labeled STAFF.

The voice had to be the server, Jessie. She was the only one missing.

Nicole turned the knob but could not force the STAFF door open. Jessie's bulk was pushing desperately, trying to escape. The screaming from inside grew higher pitched, the pounding more intense. Nicole tried to tell her to stop pushing so they might release her.

More hands pushed against the door, overpowering the force that fought them.

As soon as the door cracked open, a flurry of bees flowed out of the crack.

The bald man shouted, "I'm allergic to bees! My EpiPen is in the car!" and sprinted to the front door, urgently trying to escape.

"Eric, you asshole!" someone shouted.

The Latina waitress came armed with a rolled newspaper. The struggling on the far side of the door subsided, and three pairs of hands forced the dead weight of Jessie's body back with the door, enough to open it. The swarm of bees had disappeared. The floor was covered with them dying, and a few stragglers attacked the three women as they took stock of Jessie's inflamed body. They found no visible inch of her bare skin not covered by a welt. Her fingernails were missing, embedded in the door during her panicked attempt to escape the pain.

"She's not dead," Nicole's words slipped out in astonishment. "Help me get her out of here."

Nicole examined Jessie's arm and noticed that each welt had a stinger embedded with part of the bee attached. She did her best to scrape the stingers out of Jessie's arm before grabbing hold of it. The butch woman grabbed her other arm, the whole time glaring at Nicole. The younger server held the door. They half-carried, half-dragged Jessie out of the bathroom and into the eating area, unceremoniously dropping her body on the floor once they were clear of the kitchen. The three women slumped in various positions next to her. They carefully began removing stingers from her wounds as Jessie labored to breathe.

The bald asshole retreated to the far end of the train car. He used a lifted bar towel as an impromptu shield. "Just keep her the hell away from me. One bee sting and I will die without my EpiPen."

"You are all big talk, Eric. You are afraid of bees, peanuts, and everything else you're allergic to. You talk all that crap; you aren't worth being with any longer. You're a coward," his female companion shouted over her shoulder.

"Candi…" Eric paused.

Nicole figured he needed to think of a comeback.

Eric finally shot back, "Candi, you're nothing but a little slut I picked up out of a bar. You can kiss my ass."

"Will you two shut the hell up before I shoot both of you? Don't you see what's going on?" Nicole threatened them both with her pistol.

"I see that you're holding us hostage! I see we're going to die in this dump if you don't let us out of here, cunt!" Eric growled as best he could while cowering behind the bar towel.

Her words came in a feral snarl, "My name is Nicole…" She tried to keep her anger in check; some words just set her hair on fire.

Nicole did a quick calculation. She estimated Eric's chances of survival outside at zero. She also figured she would kill him before too much longer, which gave him a limited life expectancy. "You know what, I just met you, *Eric*, and I already hate you." She hauled herself off the floor and made her way with the keys to the front door. "If you want out of here so damn bad, I'm no longer going to stop you." She turned the key, checked to make sure the door was unlocked and went back to work on Jessie. "Get the hell out of here if you want to before I shoot you," she finished.

§ § §

Eric inched his way toward the door, peeking out the front window. He witnessed the growing mass of horny toads fighting to escape the dark. Beyond the back bumpers of the cars, there was nothing, only darkness. The lizards attacked each other, the dead and dying lay under those still fighting. Reptile blood everywhere.

He did a quick survey of the scene inside, paying attention to the four women treating Jessie for anaphylactic shock. He did his own quick calculation. He decided his odds were better inside, and he moved back to his spot and a half-finished cup of coffee. Despondent, he pulled out his phone, checking for a signal.

§ § §

"Do you have a landline?" Sam stood back and closed her phone, unable to find a signal.

The woman with the gun, Nicole, kept Jessie between the two.

Maria pointed down the hall towards the back door that was barred from the inside. "There's an old payphone at the end of the hall."

The way the bees came from. "Sam… are you sure it's safe?"

Sam paused. Maria thought, *In horror movies, people who separate from the group always die.* The trucker headed toward the phone.

While Maria worked on plucking out the stingers from Jessie's face, she said, "I can't believe Cookie is gone. He could be a real pompous ass, but to make it through the war without a scratch and to die here in this Podunk little wayside is… pathetic." Maria whispered, "What happened?"

Nicole stammered the answer, "I… it was an accident. I slipped on the… grease."

Maria shook her head. The best way for her to survive this mess was to make friendly, maybe she would be the last one to be shot.

Her captor continued, "I saw his tattoo. Marines, right? Where did he serve?"

Disheartened but still alive, Sam returned. "I couldn't get a dial tone."

"Afghanistan, I think. He never talked about his time in-country. The only thing he would say was he would never take another human life. Once he got to know you, I'm sure he would've told you all about his pacifism." Maria paused. "He told everyone…"

Maria kept a wary eye on Sam, who said, "My Arney was in the first Gulf War. He would never talk about his experiences. He had some terrible dreams though."

Maria asked, "You were married?" Doing little to hide the surprise in her voice.

Sam gave a sad chuckle. "For thirty-five years before cancer took him away three years ago. Let me guess, because of the haircut and the shirt you guessed I was a lesbian?"

Nicole watched Sam.

Maria looked down, ashamed, and shook her head, focusing on removing stingers to hide the embarrassment.

"You suck at lying. No, I prefer men over women. I dress like this because… Well if it wasn't bad enough to lose my husband three years ago, two years ago, I needed a double mastectomy. They lopped both the girls off. Since his death, I haven't found the urge to get close to a man. Dressing like this tends to keep the hounds at bay," Sam explained.

As they removed the stingers from Jessie's body, her labored breathing continued, and her eyes fluttered as if dreaming.

"So, tell me, what are you running from that made you sneak in here to hide?" Sam asked Nicole.

Maria paused her work on Jessie, her eyes shifted between the two women.

"I'm running from some asshole in Frisco. Been on the road for three days… I think it has been three days. Where are we?" Nicole asked.

"New Mexico. This little place has no name. It's a crossroads between Albuquerque and Roswell. Nothing around but a few ranches, the truck stop, and this little hole-in-the-wall. The truck stop!" Maria jumped to her feet. "Maybe someone there can help!"

Nicole shook her head. "I don't think so. It went dark before I came in. I never saw a light or heard any noise from it."

"You were afraid when you first came through that door. What is outside that caused you so much fear?" Maria asked.

Nicole glanced up from the floor. "If I told you, I don't think you would believe me."

Sam grunted. "At the moment, I'm willing to believe you, but you have to give us something, tell us something about what scared you outside."

Nicole looked down and tried to fix Jessie's hair around the swollen bee-stung face. "At first, I would say there is nothing outside. My dog, Max, sensed something in the nothing and went after it. I heard Max die. Whatever's in the dark killed her. I went to help, but I could smell death. I felt death surround me in that darkness. As far as I know, there is nothing in that dark but death."

Peering out the window into the nothingness, Maria asked, "How can I not see a thing? Normally on a cloudy, moonless night, you can still see something. I can't see anything past the cars. I can't even see the glow from the highway lines. The lights usually light the parking lot to the road."

Sam grunted and struggled to gain her feet from the floor. She joined Maria, examining the nothingness out the window. "I have been driving a truck for over twenty years. I have never seen the night look like this. We should be able to see something past the ends of the cars, even if it was a mere reflection. In fog, the moisture will glow with the lights, not soak it up."

§ § §

"Would you hens shut the hell up? I need to think up a way out of here!" Eric just couldn't keep his mouth shut.

Candi rose from the floor and walked down to Eric's booth.

Eric had a habit of speaking too loudly. "What do you want, slut? I bet you wish you were still spreading your legs in that bar I picked you up in."

She looked him over, deciding what to do, then left him without a word. Candi strolled to her purse sitting on the bar, glanced back at Eric, and held his gaze for a moment. She took a cigarette and a lighter out of her purse and turned away. With her back to him, she lit her cigarette.

"I know there's no smoking in here, but I can't take it anymore." She took a deep drag on the cancer stick to help steady her resolve.

Maria turned from the window and walked over to Candi and asked in a hushed voice, "You seem like such a nice person. How did you end up with such a dick?"

"Funny you should choose those words to describe him. He is hung like a horse. Too bad he has the brain of a jackass." Candi smiled and winked at Maria. "Honey, can you find me a clean can of Coke?"

Maria, still the waitress, walked back behind the counter and grabbed a clean glass filled with ice and a can of Coke.

Handing them both to Candi, she went to watch Nicole and Jessie.

Candi took the glass, opened the can, and poured half of its contents into the glass. She took a flask out of her purse and added a couple of shots to the glass and can, adding something to the can from a small packet she retrieved from her bra. She took a drink out of the glass. Leaving it on the bar, she sashayed down the aisle and placed the can in front of Eric.

"I knew you couldn't say no to this." Eric grabbed his crotch under the table, making a suggestive motion with his right hand. The little drama was interrupted by a sudden scream near the front door.

Both their attention was pulled to the entrance where they spied a very colorful red and yellow flash slithering along the floor. Nicole and Sam scrambled onto the closest benches away from the coiled snake, while Maria jumped on the counter, all attempting to put some distance between themselves and the red, black, and yellow snake.

Nicole pulled the pistol out of her belt and aimed it at the snake now resting on Jessie's leg.

Before she pulled the trigger, Maria shouted, "Don't shoot, it's not poisonous!"

Sam and Nicole both shot Maria an incredulous look, but Nicole held her fire. Candi's attention was grabbed by a flash of blue and red reflecting off the back wall. She turned to survey out the front window in time to spot the flashing blue and red tree atop the dark green of a New Mexico State police car that had just pulled up.

The trooper jumped out of the car, rushed to the front door, and flung it open in time to witness the snake rear back and show off its bright red, black, and yellow stripes.

He backed out of the door, slamming it shut. He reversed course, running to the cruiser, and the shotgun nestled in the front gun rack. As he reached the rear bumpers of the parked cars, all the lights on the squad car died, plunging the trooper into the all-encompassing darkness.

The snake slithered off, looking for a less populated section to hide in. The people inside waited for the trooper to return, but now they couldn't even see his car in the tar black outside.

Eric reached down and drank from the doctored soda can Candi had offered. He fashioned a way to sit with his feet off the ground and his butt on the back of the booth.

Maria eventually broke the silence. "He's coming back, isn't he? He has to come back!"

Sam offered a weak, "Honey, if he is capable of coming back, I'm sure he will."

"Why didn't you let me kill the snake?" Nicole asked Maria.

"Because it isn't poisonous." Maria began a short little nursery rhyme to explain,

"Red touch yellow, kills a fellow

Red touch black, venom lack

Yellow touches red, soon you'll be dead

Red touches black, a friend of Jack."

She'd almost sang the damned thing. "It was red touching black, that means it was a king snake. My dad used to keep snakes. He made me memorize that."

"I'm not sure what color it was, but if I see it again, and I can find a clean shot, it's dead," Nicole said.

"You probably won't see it again. It had to be as scared as we are to come in here with us around. Snakes don't really like people," Maria added.

Sam spent the whole time watching and waiting for the trooper to return. "I don't know how much more of this I can take."

Candi sat across from Eric. She cracked an evil grin when the wheezing started.

From the door, they heard Eric cough. The three of them turned in his general direction to observe his face beginning to swell. As his hands reached up to feel his face, they could see his fingers growing to the size of bratwursts.

"Holy mother of God, what's wrong with him?" Sam asked.

All Eric did was wheeze and struggle to breathe, his face and throat swollen.

Candi offered, "He's allergic to everything, one of his many weaknesses."

§ § §

Eric began clawing at his throat, unable to breathe. He needed the EpiPen from his car. With time running out, he had to decide which he feared more: the unknown outside, the snake hiding in the restaurant, the crazy Asian woman with a pistol, or suffocation from his allergic reaction.

His eyes swollen shut, he did his best to slide off the bench back and stagger, feeling his way, in the direction of the front door. He hesitated for a moment before pushing through and heading towards the baby blue Cadillac taking up two spaces at the far end of the diner's parking lot. He fell five feet from the driver's door, his body continuing to swell.

"I guess it was too far for him to make it." Candi turned from watching Eric's struggle to reach his car and headed back to the bar where her soda glass awaited her.

Nicole watched her take a deep drink before the older woman opened her purse and pulled Eric's EpiPen out and set it on the counter. "Would you look at that?"

Here I'm trying to save them, and... She couldn't finish the thought. If that trooper came in, Nicole's life would be over. The money, the gun, the death... it would all land at her feet.

Anything that happened in this joint was my fault... and this bitch just murdered that man.

Nicole didn't shed a tear for Eric. But the callousness Candi showed at his death surprised even her.

Sam shifted her gaze between the three other survivors. "I don't think we're all going to make it out of this."

"I don't even know what the hell this is," Maria said.

"This all seems vaguely familiar like I've read about something like this or maybe seen it in a movie. I don't know, it could be hell, I just don't know," Nicole rambled as she went back and sat down next to her forgotten bag of money. Pistol on the table, she stared at it, considering her options.

"I'm not even sure what that asshole had an allergic reaction to. I mean he was sitting in the back away from everything and everyone." Sam inspected the path back to where Eric had been sitting while she spoke.

"I don't know. I do know the world is better without his racist, misogynistic ass taking up air from the rest of us." Candi continued to drink.

"It seems so weird for him to die in such a mundane manner. Cookie's death and Jessie's accident seem almost supernatural," Sam continued.

"There was nothing supernatural about it. Cookie died in a kitchen accident. Jessie stumbled into a bee swarm," Maria countered, her voice remarkably calm.

"A bee swarm, in a bathroom, in a diner, in the middle of the desert. Like that's not strange?" Candi asked.

Did she just chuckle? Nicole questioned her reality in silence.

"I'm not a religious person, but what about the blood that covered you?" Sam asked Maria.

"It's not blood. They have started fracking very close to here, and I think it is screwing with our well water. I know there's a lot of iron oxide in the ground here. That's why we have terra-cotta clay, and our caliche is red."

"Candi, what did he mean when he said, he should've left you back in that bar?" Sam asked as she reached Eric's vacant seat.

"Do I have to spell it out for you?" Candi swiveled on the stool to watch Sam. "All right, if you need it spelled out, I am a wanton woman, a streetwalker, or if you prefer, a whore."

Sam reached for Eric's half empty Coke can and brought it up close to her face. "And yet you stayed with him?"

"I told you he was hung like a horse."

Sam sniffed at the oval opening in the Coke can. "Do you normally like peanut butter with your Jack and Coke?"

"Eric was an asshole." Candi remained indifferent.

"And you're a murderer," Sam declared.

With that, Candi broke her glass on the table and launched herself down the aisle towards her accuser.

Sam moved to defend as Candi's small frame plowed into her. The fight was swift and brutal. Sam tried to protect herself with raised arms, but Candi slashed unmercifully at the older woman's arms and body, until finding Sam's exposed neck. She swiped with the broken glass, severing her left carotid artery. Sam's vital fluid painted the glass behind her in a pulsating stream as she slumped to the floor.

The lights began to flicker and dim as if the generator was dying. Nicole stood and took four steps to better cover the two women fighting. Her vision narrowed as she watched the fight anxiously, pistol shifting aim between the two of them

Candi finished killing Sam, turned. Nicole leveled the pistol at her center mass. It was impossible to miss at such a close range. Nicole squeezed off two quick shots. Two crimson blossoms rose to coat Candi's white skintight shirt with blood. She fell back on top of Sam's body.

Focused so intently on the carnage at the far end of the cafe, Nicole never noticed Maria's movements. She turned to find herself face to face with the other survivor. Feeling pain, pressure, and a tug, as the Arkansas Toothpick, more of a small sword than a hunting knife, tore through her flesh. The double-edged blade slipped between her ribs and pierced her racing heart. *The damned knives in the case.*

Maria took the pistol from Nicole's hand as she collapsed to the floor. With her dying eyes, Nicole watched Maria walk off with her bag of money and gun down the darkened hall to the barred back door.

Nicole hissed through blood-stained teeth, "Good luck getting out of here, bitch."

The lights in the diner went out. Nicole closed her eyes for the final time.

THE END

Sleeping Dragon

Marc vun Kannon

If the Holy Grail really was buried somewhere inside Glastonbury Tor, Sarah Mack couldn't feel it. She didn't expect to, but it would have been so cool if she could.

The Night of Echoes, when the magic had come back to the world, was only sixteen years in the past, nearly all of her life. Some geezer in the States, right there where it happened, had worked a spell almost immediately, they said. Before the magic had spread, before anybody else in the world even could. Now he was the Grandmaster of the Wizard's Union. She used to think he was a lucky bastard.

Years later, when the magic was strong enough, the creatures started coming back, and she stopped thinking he was so lucky. One of her earliest memories was watching a pixie invasion of Buckingham Palace on the telly, laughing. Mr. Tom told her to shut it, and together they watched as the wizards expelled the little flying buggers from the Palace and set up a shield to keep them out.

That worked, for a while, but over time larger creatures would appear, and they'd have to redo the shield. Yesterday a griffin the size of a four-banger was seen running up the A1, unable to fly. And if the magic wasn't strong enough yet to get a griffin off the ground, you could bet it wasn't strong enough to wake up the Grail. If it was even there.

So it was a good thing she wasn't there for the Grail.

§ § §

Sarah stood in a place where she was barely able to see the base of the ruined tower at the top of the Tor, catching her breath, apparently taking in the magnificent view. On the inside she was wishing she knew even one spell to turn herself into a medium-sized dog, so she could have taken one of the pet trolleys up. It was a lot easier to climb this hill now than it had been when she was younger, but that didn't mean she liked it.

Staring out over the patchwork of land, she closed her eyes, opening up her other senses to input that only she could perceive. Even mediums couldn't actually *see* the spirits they sensed about them, but with her magic harnessed to that other sense, she could. Mr. Tom couldn't see this way, but he seemed to know something about how it felt, and once again she wondered where he'd come from. Why and how had he taken her under his wing, 'taken' being the operative word. She had to have parents somewhere, right?

Not that it mattered. Magic never bred true. Her parents wouldn't have known what to do with her anyway. Probably.

The Wizard's Union would, of course, but they'd take as much as they gave, if not more. The Union was just a front, that's what Mr. Tom said, a way to control the wizards so that they wouldn't feel like they were being controlled. Each night in front of the telly was another lesson in their kind of oppression, not bad, just…stuffy.

Sarah didn't do stuffy. Or like being limited. Mr. Tom always said limits were things to beat.

She cast her perceptions far wider than she normally could, drawing on the strength, the faith of the people passing by her, on their way to the tower. God knew they'd be useless by the time they got all the way up there, and she'd be lucky to cast farther than she could see. Before it came back, the magic had been gone for five centuries, and the Tor had been depleted, if not emptied, of whatever power it held. All that wonderful faith and spiritual energy the other pilgrims carried leeched into the ground with every step, wasted.

She turned her head, looking away from the fields and

farms and all the life there, towards the town, seeking something that wasn't *quite* alive. Mr. Tom said it was there, but Mr. Tom could be a bit of a nutter sometimes. Like sending her out now, when he'd specifically warned her off picking pockets this trip. He was always sending her out to cut a few, said it was good practice, using her hands without letting anyone see. He'd even let her keep most of the take. Now was the busy tourist season 'round these parts, and here she was keeping them to herself.

Someone stopped, near her but not close, dragging on her normal senses, never mind the other ones. A man, a patient one, to hang about like he was doing. "Oi," she said, without opening her eyes, "Can't you see I'm communin' over here?"

"As am I," he snapped back. "Like I do every week this time of year, but today you're standing in my patch."

She barked out a laugh. "They must have taken the sign with your name down. I'd go back and complain if I was you." She turned her attention to the lower end of High Street, away from all the crowds she could feel on the high side. Good luck on her finding Mr. Tom's needle in that haystack, especially when she had a straight hanging about.

"Nah, I'm big," he said dismissively. "I can share."

Perhaps it was her annoyance, boosting her occult senses just that little bit more, but she suddenly sensed an answering prickle in her awareness. It didn't taste alive, Mr. Tom had that right, more like something that was delicious once but now it'd gone off. She spat the sensation out of her mind. "Well, I can't, so you can have it," she said, walking back down against the flow, opening her eyes and closing the other sense. She knew what she was looking for now. She'd be able to find it again later.

§ § §

Much later, the crowds on the High Street had moved away from the stores, museums, and curio shops, to the hotels, restaurants and bars that were, fortunately for Sarah, not on the High Street. Not this part of it, anyway. Most of the girls down here walked the streets for a different reason entirely, not that Sarah would ever have been mistaken for one of them. Have to see her to mistake her, and between her clothes and her hidden talents, no one saw her.

That gagging feel of the not-quite-right didn't grow or fade with distance, more's the pity, so she knew where it was, even if she didn't exactly *know* where it was. Or even what it was. Maybe a zombie like all those TV shows, wouldn't that be a kick, but it didn't seem to be moving, either. With no changes in intensity to go by, she had to triangulate. She found herself circling one building in particular, a shop that called itself a 'shoppe', and she would have burgled it for that alone.

The 'shoppe' had a 'yarde' in back, with a 'shedde', no idea what for, and no interest either, since the smell she followed was inside the main building. The door was wired, of course, but so was she, in a manner of speaking, and when her wires spoke to the door's wires they stayed quite mum about her opening the door.

The door opened onto a storeroom, which would presumably open onto the store floor itself. Dangerous places, storerooms. She had a spell for night vision, very useful in her line of work but hard to come by, since it *was* very useful in her line of work and the Wizard's Union didn't want that sort of thing on their watch.

With spell-enhanced senses she navigated her way to the other door, neatly avoiding a jumble of stuff just piled right by. The door opened behind the counter, with its register open and no till in the drawer. Out of habit she wondered where it would be in a third-rate dump like this one, but she wasn't there for that, not tonight.

She stepped out from behind the counter onto the recently swept floor. The store wasn't very large, mostly items for sale on the sides and back, with some other things in the front, meant to lure the rubes into the store in the first place. The stinky doofer was down there, even now not as clear to her sight as it should have been. Nor could her senses tell her where the floor creaked and where it didn't, so the short walk down to the front was slow and careful.

It was a sword, as she expected, from seeing the shape silhouetted against the front window. It was old and rusty, sticking out of a chunk of some kind of solidified muck. She rapped on the block, and found it harder than she expected. Looking down on the table, she found a hand-lettered sign that read, *Excalibur?*

Yeah, right. Some sword lost in a bog somewhere, most like. Those things were getting stepped on all the time. Still, a good bit for the season, probably stays in the shed out back the rest of the year.

She looked the thing over, hands instead of eyes, and eventually found the bloody thing that had been giving her a headache all night. Something stuck on the block. She used a small knife to pry it lose, and held it in her hands, a little blob of something gross. A union of things that oughtn't go together, like zombified flesh.

Those things don't just happen.

The good thing was, that since they didn't just happen, it wasn't hard to make them *un*happen. She closed her hand and focused power, enough that whatever had been mixed could separate itself again, like dynamite but without the explosion. Something popped, the feeling in her head going away as something else trickled out from her fingers. Then she focused more power, because it was gross and she didn't want to wait until she could wash her hands.

As she brushed the dust off, she took a better look at the sword. *Why this?* Standing next to it, she gripped the hilt and pulled, but it didn't come out of the block and make her rightwise Queen of whatever Bog it came from. Probably everyone tried that, or wanted to, but the store shouldn't allow it. It might pull the sword apart after a bit, it looked like the only things holding the rust together were the spiderwebs. She flicked her fingers but they were grime-free.

So much for the direct approach.

The problem was, as Mr. Tom often said, the direct approach was usually the proper approach. Magic was best when used in that manner, not trying to make things happen as shouldn't. Even the honest magicians knew that, and the dishonest ones even more so. Men you could cheat all day long. The Universe knew better.

Not to mention that anything that could break up the stone might also break the sword in it. Be a bit daft to try, then, and it would violate at least two of Mr. Tom's rules of magic as applied to thievery: don't attract attention to yourself, and don't make a mess.

On the other hand, the sword was a sword, the block was not. Swords are made, they have a purpose, and that purpose isn't being stuck in great hard blocks. They are meant…to be held.

Sarah turned her back on the block, reached across her body and wrapped her fingers around the hilt, not like she was trying to pull on it but like she was planning to draw it. She thought about all those programmes she'd seen, men going off to war, no, not men, *people* going off to war. Human beings who'd made the sword, who used the sword, who needed to pull the sword out of confinement right bloody now…

She fed power, tinged with as much martial spirit as she

could work up, into the sword and pulled. It slid. About a centimeter, and then it stopped again.

She tugged again, but the sword was having none of it. *What the hell?*

"I thought it would be you," said a voice, somewhat familiar, and Sarah froze in surprise, unwarned by her hidden senses. "I could almost feel your scheming, up above. What are you doing here, still in my patch?"

Sarah let go of the hilt, turning slightly to get the man in view, but otherwise made no moves that could be taken as threatening. "That's my boss' business," she said, her tone implying that his business was no one else's business. She gathered power. She was a thief, not a fighter, but Mr. Tom had made sure she knew how to fight.

"I doubt that," said the man. "'Training day', my arse. If he'd wanted that sword I could'a stole it for him when I put that tag on it, now couldn't I?" He advanced on her, looming larger, blocking her exit. "You know what I'm thinking? I'm thinking that your Mr. Tom knows more than he's lettin' on about that there sword and he doesn't want to share. I'm thinking maybe I should cut him out of *my* business."

The man pulled open his coat, and pulled out a knife. "Don't worry, girl," he said, as if he cared. "You'll live. You can go back and tell your boss how I feel about people pelfing on my patch, whilst I find out what's so special about that sword." He stepped forward, slashing.

Sarah turned away, to protect her hands, a wizard's weapons. Her hand ran up against the sword's hilt, and her fingers curled around it a second time. The man's knife cut her shoulder but that was all, and the force of his cut pulled him around a little too far.

Sarah pulled on the hilt, the pain and her fear adding power to move the block, intending to knock him down and get away. The sword pulled out of the block, and instead of whacking him on the back with a great heavy club she found herself slashing at his neck with panicked strength. He fell, leaking.

Swords are meant to be held, but they're held in order to be used, and they're used to kill.

She'd just killed a man.

She stared at the body, panting, half-expecting the guy to leap up as if it was just a ploy, but she could feel the life fading with her hidden senses. He didn't move, but the sword did. It quivered in her hand, and she looked down. The blade was some dark color, but the edge was a bright line in the gloom of the store. As she watched, patches of darkness fell off the blade, like chips of night, revealing gleaming silver underneath. The metal shivered, aware of her.

Waking up. Getting in a good stretch.

Her hidden senses screamed at her, and she tore her gaze away from the blade. The sword was practically glowing but the shop had disappeared into gloom, a darkness with weight and heft, a darkness she could sense. Behind her the light still came through the windows, muted and dull, not vibrant like the sword's light, or the shop's darkness.

She held up the sword, a light against the darkness, but the blade twisted in her hands, coming back at her, and she shrugged her shoulders and ducked her head, causing it to miss her. The darkness spoke to her, via her hidden senses, a voice inside her head, bright with anger.

That is not for you

The sword came up again, and she twisted awkwardly, grabbing the hilt with both hands. "Bloody hell!" she shouted, ducking again. She would have fallen, had not the sword passed over her head and pulled her up as it passed.

Above her head, the boards creaked. "Who's there?" she

heard a muffled voice say.

The sword paused. Sarah turned her head, and saw the block on its pedestal. Before the sword came around again she spun and aimed it point-first into the stone that had been its home and hopefully would be again. *Stay there and rust!*

The sword sank into the block as if it was soft cheese. The hilt quivered in Sarah's hands, and she pulled them off hurriedly, before she could accidentally pull it out again. The gleam paled as she gathered power into her hands, her own light against the dark, but as the sword's glow faded so did the shadow. The blade was just ordinary metal again, shining in the streetlight. Her hidden senses also calmed, the darkness gone from the room.

Stairs creaked, and Sarah released her grip on power. Whoever he was, he didn't deserve what it would do to him if she let it loose now, and she knew who did. She looked to her exit, but she'd lost her night-vision spell and didn't have a flashlight. She pounced on the front door, pulled it open, and flew into the night, the alarm clanging uselessly behind her.

Mr. Tom had some explaining to do.

§ § §

Back in the shop, the owner came to the bottom of the steps, flipped the switch for the lights, and got a good look at the room, the dead man and the gleaming silver sword. "What's all this?"

THE END

Dangerous

Morgan Smith

The day my mother took away my sword and daggers was the worst day of my life.

Well, that was what I thought then, anyway.

"It's not that you mean to, I know," she said. "It's just – it's just that no one can tell what you'll do. I know you were only sparring…but there's Caliana down at the healing tent, and Jarrah, last moon, he nearly lost an eye. You're dangerous, Samiana."

Like any chieftain, she had learned to mask her emotions, to present an impassive countenance to the world, but I could sense her pain and sorrow.

She was trying to be kind.

It was true, though, all the same.

And it wasn't that I was any good with a sword. That? That she would have understood. That, she could have coped with. If I'd had the aptitude, she could have trained me into something useful to her.

But I wasn't dangerous with a sword through some kind of talent. I was dangerous because even without the slightest idea of what I was doing (much less, what training was for) I was liable to do things that put anyone within ten feet of me at risk. None of the people I'd injured had been people I was aiming to hit.

I said nothing. I thought if I spoke at all, I would burst into tears, as much in remorse for my sister's broken arm as for my banishment. I just stared at the dusty ground and wished myself anywhere but here.

Once back in the tent I shared with Caliana, I did cry. I buried my face in the cushions and wept.

What was I going to do?

My first attempts to learn the way of the blades had been seen as just a step along a learning path. I was too small, in the beginning, to do much damage.

You'll get better if you practice, my mother said. Pay attention. Try harder.

But this had been, I saw now, just wishful thinking. Bladecraft would be the same as everything else in my life.

If I was set to help secure the herds at dusk, some always got loose, and very often, found injured.

If I carried anything fragile when we stopped to make camp, it invariably got broken.

Once, during the dry season, when we'd been staying at the way-station at Samaal, I'd tried to turn off the cistern tap after filling a bucket for the cooks, and instead, the thing had broken, and most of the water had poured out uselessly on the parched earth below it before anyone could fix it.

I'd messed up everything I'd ever attempted. The harder I tried, the greater the damage seemed – and the outcomes were always the opposite of what I had intended to do. The harder I worked to do a thing right, the more it all went wrong.

When I was small, it was treated as a joke, and put down to a clumsiness that I would surely outgrow.

But here I was, rising sixteen, and as far as I could tell, my life was over. I was good for nothing, and in all honesty, I could see that I was nothing more than a liability – a drag on the well-being of my clan.

It wasn't just my opinion, either.

I'd seen the covert looks, whenever I was assigned some chore. I'd heard the muttering behind my back. I was acutely aware of how many times people crossed their fingers and spat as I passed by.

And I'd listened to the reminiscences of the elders, about how pleasant and easy life had been, years ago.

Before I was born.

My tears were pointless. I couldn't change what I was.

But I could, I realized, change what could be, for the clan. Without me, there was every chance they could recover. I could do it.

If I loved them, I should.

If I loved them, I must.

Out at the edge of the camp, where we'd pegged out the herds and horses alongside the pack animals, there was no one on watch. We'd swung well south of the usual trade routes this year, trying to avoid the storms that were wreaking havoc in the northlands, so the fear of another clan attacking us was far less.

I considered my options.

My own horse was a fine one, befitting the chieftain's youngest daughter.

Did I have the right to take her away from the clan? She had been a gift, on my last name-day but one, yet I hesitated. I had been taught that a chieftain's family owned nothing, in actual fact: that everything we had was a gift of the clan, and in service to its honour and well-being.

So, not Little Pearl. She deserved a better fate than I could provide, anyway. And I could not just take someone else's mount and call it an exchange, because people grew fond of their horses.

A pack pony? They were hardy little beasts, committed to the slow but steady, and we had a lot of them – my mother liked to be sure that the loads were spread evenly enough that the loss of one did not mean that we would overburden any other animal.

I looked down to the end of the row, at the smallest, skinniest pony we had.

She was called Serena. She was a kind of a joke, as pack ponies go, because she was anything but serene. The least little thing spooked her, she had a tendency to bite, and she was small and scrawny, unable to carry much more than a bundle or two of spare rugs or cushions.

Perfect. Serena and I would hardly be missed at all.

§ § §

Months later, I found myself at the very tail end of a merchant train heading south, and much further west than I had ever expected to go.

I hadn't really had a plan, when I left, other than getting as far away from my clan as I could, so that they could flourish once more. Apart from Serena, I had taken next to nothing with me: a spare shirt, a full water-skin, a loaf of stale bread. None of the arm-rings or neck-chains I had been given, feast-day after feast-day, down through the years, because they were like Little Pearl: gifts that honoured the clan. The only thing that was truly mine was my birth-bead, hung on a leather thong around my neck, the gift of my father before he left us. It was the only thing of his that still existed in my life, since he'd walked away before I was even born.

To my surprise, Serena, small as she was, turned out to be able to earn us a tiny living.

Despite her size and skittishness, she was stronger and more stalwart than my mother had ever imagined, and in exchange for food and shelter, along with a small sum of coin if I stayed to the end of the trail, any number of Bilaadii merchants were willing to load her with the miscellaneous small goods they took in trade along their way.

I might be useless, and they thought me incurably lazy, since I tried hard to avoid any camp chore that might have carried even a hint of risk to anyone, but they tolerated me in exchange for not having to buy an extra pack pony that might only be useful for that one lone journey.

This caravan, though – I wished I hadn't signed on. Zahit was a mean one, parsimonious with everything from horse-feed to water, and I was fairly sure he would try to cheat me out of my caravan fee when we got to our destination.

And the route he'd had chosen was hard.

The river we were following angled its way through a landscape devoid of features. Three weeks out from our destination, the coastal city of Huna, the grasslands had given way to a low-lying, foul-smelling malignant swampland, prone to small biting insects and rutted, irregular pathways. There were some occasional boggy humps of mud and dead vegetation that might possibly have been sandbars or islets, and along the river's edge there were withered brown reeds clinging limply to the waterlogged banks.

But there were no trees or bushes to speak of, and the water moved sluggishly along, as if it could barely be bothered.

As the villages got poorer, though, Zahit's prices for even the most petty tools and trinkets rose. Consequently, we seemed to sell very little as we wound along the ribbon of dark water that constituted Bone River, but Zahit's spirits, never visibly high, did not alter at all, which surprised me. He wasn't getting much out of this venture, as far as I could see, but it seemed he was not disappointed.

There were fewer way-stations and fewer villages the further west we went, until one afternoon, we reached a place called Qareen.

It wasn't a village. It wasn't even a way-station. It was just a few ramshackle reed huts crowded together where a spit of land jutted out into the river, and then one larger hut a little farther out, enclosed by piled brush in a sort of intricate fence arrangement.

Oddly, encircling them all, they'd laid some small, smooth

rocks in a deliberate and not unpleasing pattern: three white ones, then a glossy black one, again and again, until the rocks met up at the point where, if it were meant as a barrier, there would have been a gate, Instead, at that place, there were three big black stones, and when we arrived, Zahit stopped us just shy of them, until a man came out and carefully moved the centre one out of the way.

Curious. The stones were very carefully shaped and placed, and apparently important, but it didn't fit the squalor that the rest of the place was home to.

There were only six people living here – two bearded, filthy-looking men, accompanied by three skinny, pinch-faced women, and not a child in sight.

The sixth…well, he looked like a man, but then again, different.

In another time, in another place, one might have called him beautiful. Feature by feature, there was much to admire: the deep-set eyes, the aquiline nose, the long, straight limbs and broad shoulders, the skin as deeply black as a midnight sky…

But those eyes were vacant and dull, the smooth skin ashen and slack, and his whole posture drooped, so that his arms hung limp and purposeless.

There was something indefinably misshapen and wrong about him, as if someone had dug up a corpse and propped it up on sticks.

The younger of the two men shoved at his back, cursing, and he shambled forward to the first of the pack animals and began to fumble at the leather straps of the top-most bundle. Once he had freed them all and set them on the ground, he stood unmoving and silent, until the man beside him shoved him again, towards the second pony in the line, and cursed at him. He started undoing the next set of straps.

Zahit began setting out the wares he'd brought, carelessly,

as if he knew for a certainty that these people were not prepared to buy. It seemed unlikely they had money for glass beads or brass-handled daggers, and still less cash to spend on woven linen cloth. Surprisingly, he did appear to be making some deals, although they were, as far as I could see, largely theoretical, since no money or goods had changed hands as yet.

The unloading was nearly finished. The man pushed his companion towards Serena.

She balked, even before he touched her, lashing out sideways with one hoof, and snapping her jaws at empty air. I stood up.

"It might be best if I…" The man in charge looked at me, then at Zahit, who laughed.

"It's the most work you'll get out of her today," he said.

I moved past the man-thing. He stood motionless, his eyes on the ground.

"Here," I said, gently. I took his arm, and edged him away from Serena, whose ears lay flat against her skull, a sure sign that she was still unsettled and ready to bite anything she did not understand.

His skin felt cold, but that might have only been the dampness and his inadequate clothing.

§ § §

I woke up that night to the sound of someone crying.

More accurately, to the sound of an almost childlike sobbing, to whispered, hissing curses, and the intermittent thwack of a braided reed whip hitting naked flesh.

All around me lay the sleeping forms of my fellow packwrights. Zahit had been given a place inside one of the huts, but the rest of us had been shrugged off as beneath respect or courtesy, and left to make our own encampment on the damp ground, in front of the dwellings.

I sat up, trying to see where the sound was coming from. It wasn't one of the three huts. The noise seemed to come from a little farther away, where this little tongue of land pushed out into the river.

That fourth hut, the one that was fenced off: that was the source.

I should mind my own business, I thought. Everyone and everything had told me that, when I'd asked casually about the shambling man.

A slave. A madman. An idiot, good for nothing, and lucky they didn't just turn him out to die alone, but were willing to feed him and give him a place, in exchange for doing what few chores he was capable of.

I heard a cackle of laughter, and then saw, as the door of the fourth hut opened and a shaft of weak yellow rush-light spilled out, a bent and huddling figure scuttling out past the fencing.

You could say that it must be frustrating, dealing with something like that. The creature didn't understand much. That was obvious.

You could say that it was more than could be expected, and no wonder that their notion of kindness extended no further than not abandoning him to his obvious fate.

I thought of my clan, of my mother, and how, despite the bane I'd been to them all, there had never been a point where anyone had overtly mistreated me, and that they might have been said to have had far more cause.

I got up. It was still nearly full dark, but in the east, there was the faintest thin line of a grey dawn forming, and the moon had already set.

I saw him huddled up by one of the black rocks at the edge of the settlement – just a darkish lump against a darker sky.

He was silent now, but it still tugged at me. I couldn't say quite why, except that it seemed cruel to hurt someone so obviously unable to defend himself.

I mean, what was the point? It wasn't as if he could understand what his misdeeds were, if, indeed, he'd done anything, right or wrong, at all. He was just a cipher, a blank slate. It was like beating a pack pony for not being a horse.

He was shivering.

I put out a hand and touched his shoulder, very gently. His body jerked back in fear, but then he looked up at me and seemed to relax.

"Here, now," I said. "It's all right. I won't hurt you."

This seemed useless, even as I spoke. I might not hurt him, but I couldn't help him either, and maybe I was wrong — maybe he'd done something to deserve that beating. Even the feeble-minded can be malicious, sometimes, in their own way.

I crouched down beside him.

"What's the trouble? Have you done something you shouldn't?"

He was still trembling, but it felt less like fear now.

"Wouldn't – wouldn't drink…"

I was surprised to get words. All I'd heard from him before had been animal-like grunts of exertion, when he'd been unloading the ponies, and those childish whimpers just a few moments ago.

Something tugged at my mind. He could speak, but did not…this made no sense.

"Whyever not? You must be thirsty."

"Don't let them…"

"Let them what?" But there was nothing but the silence that stretched out into the night.

§ § §

We had been in Qareen for two days, and Zahit showed no signs of wishing to leave.

It was odd, because he'd grumbled every day before this about the slowness of the journey, and how we were behind schedule, but now, for no adequately explainable reason, he seemed content to sit in this miserable, flea-infested little settlement and do nothing.

The first morning, there had been a cauldron of boiled grain cooked up by the women and handed around. It was watery and smelled odd – the brackish water, I thought - and gave it a miss after the first mouthful. I had bought some dried figs and mutton strips in one of the little villages we'd stopped at along the way, because of Zahit's habit of shorting us all on our rations, so I didn't exactly go hungry, but I was, on that second morning, wishing hard that we could pack up and move on and get this venture over and done with.

No one else seemed to share my impatience. In fact, like Zahit, they seemed content to loll in the weak sunlight, doing as little as possible, and only the complaining whinnies of the livestock at feeding time roused them.

In the late evening, there was another pot boiling on the fire. One of the women began ladling its contents out, and someone eventually handed me an unglazed pottery cup filled with weak tea. I squatted on the ground, setting it carefully beside me.

When I looked down, I was not surprised to see that it had developed a crack and started to leak.

It might not have been my fault. It was a crude thing, and ill-made.

§ § §

The next morning, no one woke early, and when they did, it took some time before any of them did more than groan, as if they'd been up all night carousing.

No one from the huts appeared until mid-morning, and the woman who emerged had an odd expression on her face when she saw me trying to coax a small fire into being, with the intention of making some porridge.

"I'll do that," she said, bringing out a kettle of that foul river water.

The damp sticks I had collected hissed, then cracked in the little flames I'd achieved, and a spark leapt out into her skirts and caught. In the hasty scramble to put it out before she got burnt, my elbow connected with the pot, and it overturned, spilling the mixture of water and herbs onto the ground.

The woman froze, looking horrified.

The wet grass began to turn a little browner, and the dirt beneath seemed to redden.

A worm poked its end above the muddy earth, and then flopped sideways.

The woman swore, and scuttled back to her hut.

I looked at the receding puddle for a long, long time.

§ § §

I spent the day aware that I was being watched. At first I'd hoped I'd been imagining it, but as the day wore on, and my comrades continued to laze around, only moving when a need for the latrine ditches prompted them, the reality had to be faced.

The significance of the lone hut at the edge of the river was clear now.

These people – and Zahit – were slavers.

They were systematically drugging us into a state of

submission, and at some point, probably in the next day or so, we would find ourselves shackled inside that hut until they were ready to drive us the rest of the way to Huna, to be sold.

A neat scheme. Twenty or so slaves at once, which this small group could not have gotten in any other way, because what could a half-dozen scruffy and ill-nourished beggars do against so many of us in a fight?

But they could overpower me, once the others were sufficiently stupefied and unable to resist.

I needed to get away. Where, exactly, I could go, I had no idea. We were miles from anywhere, although I guessed we were not that far from Huna, because at some point, Zahit had mentioned that this would be our last stop before reaching the city, and that only another four days were needed to reach it.

He might have been lying, of course. Still, I thought I knew the way back to the trail, and once on it, might be able to put enough distance between myself and Qareen to escape capture. If I could slip out in the night, and not be missed until morning, it might work.

So I imitated my fellow packwrights, and lazed about – not that I had been terribly active before, which was, I thought, all that was saving me now. This morning's attempt at the fire might have alerted them, but I guessed that they merely surmised that my doses of whatever concoction they were giving us was just not strong enough, and I took care that both the tea and the noon-day gruel they served out disappeared unobtrusively: I perched on a bare little hump of dirt near the edge of the clearing and dumped the porridge by discreet spoonfuls into a clump of dead grass beside me, and later I sat hunched in my blankets and let the tea dribble onto the damp ground while I pretended to drink.

I tried not to sleep at all, when night fell, but to lie still in my blankets, and indeed, I had thought my fear would keep me awake if nothing else did, but suddenly, without warning, I jerked with a start, because I *had* slept, and deeply, too.

Over top of me loomed the vague figure of the shambling man.

For a moment, I thought he meant to do me some harm, and groped for the little dagger at my belt.

But then, as the last of the sleep-fog left me, I saw he was not staring at me blankly, or with malice, but with a tiny frown, as if he could not understand what I was doing, asleep at such a time.

Well, neither could I. I sat up.

Nothing else moved in the night. It was very quiet.

"Take…"

I had picked up the soft leather saddlebag that doubled as a pillow, and was stuffing my blanket into it.

"Take what?"

"Me…"

I stared. I could see, now that my eyes had adjusted, that his gaze was not as dull as it had been, but also that this was costing him no little effort. There was the shine of sweat on his face, and his breath was gasping.

His eyes were desperate. "Take. Me."

There was something about his voice.

As if he was not asking, but ordering me to do this.

"Why should I?" I hissed, thinking that if we stopped to whisper all this for much longer, someone would surely hear, and come to investigate, and where would I be then?

But it seemed as if his moment had passed. He just stared, blinking, and as blank and mindless as ever.

"What *are* you?" I asked, without much hope.

I thought he wouldn't answer. Couldn't answer, maybe.

But then, long moments later, when I had all but given up and was turning back to fetch Serena, I heard it, like a rustling in the grass, so quiet that it floated on the soft air like a ghost.

"*Sabhar.*"

I froze.

A wizard.

A mage.

How on earth had they done it – enslaved someone like that?

Trickery, obviously, and their own magic, perhaps – there are rumours of how people can buy power, even if they have none of their own. A spell written on parchment, strict instructions on exactly what one must do, and of course, the things only work once. The cost was always enormous, and only the most powerful magic-wielders could make them, but it could be done.

They would have needed him to drink the tea, first, I guessed. How they'd done that without him knowing it was drugged, I couldn't imagine, but once done…I shook my head.

"Come on, then," I hissed. I couldn't stop to think. Time was running short.

I slid the saddlebag onto Serena and started for the entrance-way.

A light shone out suddenly from one of the huts, and I heard a man curse.

I turned. They were all there: Zahit, and the men and women, and they looked terrified.

The Sabhar was standing straighter than he ever had before, his hands raised in a pose of power.

Zahit yelled out, "You *idiot*!"

The Sabhar laughed.

It was the sound of pure evil – malevolent and triumphant. I shuddered.

"Look what you've done!" Zahit was panting with fear and fury. "He's a blood-mage. He'll use you, and then he'll kill us all."

Son of a dog – a blood-mage. No wonder they'd drugged him and bound him. No wonder that they were hysterical with fright now.

"Don't let him go any further." Zahit sounded desperate. "If he gets past the gate-stones… I swear to you – I'll pay you well. I'll cut you in on the profits. Just don't let him past you."

The mage laughed again. "Too late. She's a dead woman walking, Zahit. And all of you will be corpses, too. I'll have my vengeance."

The bastard had tricked me. Played on my sympathies and used me to start breaking the chains of his enchantment.

"Come," he said. "You haven't served your purpose yet, little one. I assure you, I won't kill you until you have."

He pushed me towards the entrance, but he misjudged it – his shove was too hard, and I stumbled and fell, banging my head on one of the smooth white stones, dislodging it.

It rolled a few inches and stopped.

There was a moment of the purest silence. Not a whisper of wind moved among the grasses, and the soft glow of the dwindling central hearth fire died, leaving only cold starlight and the weak light of the waning moon.

The Sabhar stood even straighter. He looked enormous and terrifying, and he raised his arms higher.

I wasn't scared. My anger left no room for fear. I was so furious, I didn't even stop to think. My hand landed on the hilt of my dagger and pulled it free from my belt.

You can throw a dagger. It isn't weighted for the purpose, and it takes a lot of practice and skill, but it can be done.

I rolled to my knees, aimed, and let the weapon go.

§ § §

Anyone who knew me could have predicted the result.

The Sabhar was the only person I could see. His form blocked my view of anyone else.

And yet, there he still stood, unharmed.

Zahit gave a small, stuttering cry, and dropped, the dagger planted squarely in the middle of his chest.

For one long, last moment, that unearthly silence held.

Then, there was a brilliant flash of light and the low roar of thunder.

I dragged myself to my feet and faced the mage. Behind him, the residents of Qareen were kneeling, faces nearly touching the ground, and babbling.

It wasn't their fault. It was all Zahit – he'd tricked them, and conned them, and promised them riches. They wouldn't have ever done it on their own, and they were sorry, oh so sorry, lord, please…

The Sabhar ignored them. He was looking at me and he was smiling.

"Thank you," he said to me, courteously. "I really do appreciate it."

I tensed, waiting for the inevitable.

"Could everyone please calm down?" he asked. "Seriously. I'm not in the mood for this."

§ § §

Tarik was not a blood-mage.

Well, he sort of was, he admitted, but not primarily. He made it sound almost apologetic, as if his acquaintance with dark arts was a kind of accident.

And that wasn't why they'd ensorcelled and enslaved him, anyway. That was apparently at the behest of the Qawiun, who ruled all the clans, at least in the sense that his was the final word in terms of justice, and the only one to whom the clans were willing to take orders from in the event of war.

The Qawiun had decided Tarik was too powerful to be trusted. He'd bought the spells needed, and found the people desperate enough to risk the deed. Pardoned criminals and thieves…people like that — there's very little they won't do, and their prices are never high.

"So you see," Tarik said, "I owe you everything. I just needed to figure out how to get you to do what was needed, because otherwise, Zahit might have noticed that the spells were weakening. He's got just enough training to have pulled this off, and just enough power to feel any real changes. And then you would have gone off to the slave markets, and the chance might never have come again."

I thought about this.

"You knew I'd throw the dagger at you? How could you be sure I would miss?"

He just smiled.

"Is it a curse?" I asked. I'd never met a Sabhar before. I might never again. It might be the only chance I had to find out.

"Not exactly. It's on you. A curse is different. This is something that's part of you, but not you."

I shook my head. "It's been this way all my life. And right now, there's nothing I own that I had from the clan, except for Serena, and we only got her two rain seasons before I left."

"Are you sure? Nothing at all?"

Even as I opened my mouth to deny it again, the thought came to me, cold and dry, like the wind that comes down off the high plains in the north.

It's a terrible thing when two clans fall out, and sometimes, to avoid outright war, the clans make a marriage between chieftain families, in the hopes that shared bloodlines will ease the anger.

That was how I had come to be: my mother had wed a man of the Jahura, to end a feud that stretched back into the misty past.

It hadn't worked. The pair of them warred inside the tents almost from the very first day, not just as a couple, but him against everything about the clan and our customs and ways of being. In the end, my father had walked away, declaring that he would rather live clanless than with us.

I pulled out my birth-bead.

Tarik looked at it for a long time in silence.

"Well," he said, "that *is* interesting."

"What should I do?"

He shrugged. "Throw it in the fire. Or the river – the Bone holds more secrets than yours, and keeps them well enough. There's coin, buried under the sleeping mats in one of the huts. Dig it up, take it, and go on to Huna. Take over the pack-train: they need someone to be in charge."

He was right about that. My comrades had woken up, still disoriented and stumbling about, unable to grasp much about what had happened to them, or to Zahit.

"And you? What will you do?" I felt suddenly bereft, rudderless, without purpose. If I wasn't really a curse, if I had no reason to drift aimless and alone through the world, what was I supposed to do?

"I have some scores to settle." He glanced at his former owners, still silently groveling in the dirt and waiting to see what violence would come to them. "Don't worry. I rarely kill anyone, even when I'm provoked." He paused. "Just go, Sami."

"No."

"What would you stay for?"

The bead. I didn't know much, but I knew this: magic like that had a purpose. And not just a little one directed at a small and insignificant clan.

Something else was at work here. I couldn't, with the best will in the world, figure that out on my own, but I could see that Tarik could. That he would. That the moment I was out of sight, he'd fish it out from the fire or the water, and try to unravel its secrets.

I slid the thong over my neck and let the glass sphere dangle from my fingers.

"Oh," he said. "You aren't easy to deflect, are you? I warn you, it's a long road, and I – the Qawiun was right. I am not the most trustworthy companion."

"I'll take my chances."

He looked at me for a long time in silence.

"Fine," he said. "I'll hire you and the pack train as escort to Huna. After that – well, we'll see. But I say it again: I'm no fit companion for you, Sami. I'm dangerous."

I grinned, and slipped the thong with my birth-bead back over my neck.

I was dangerous, too.

THE END

Muliebral the Bald (or Bold)

Nav Logan

High in the inhospitable wilderness of the northern moorlands, where the shadows of the Pennines run deep, there lies a somewhat rundown wooden hill fortress: Ighmordan. This shabby fortress is the ancient stronghold of the warriors of the Briganti. Far removed from civilisation, these walls have withstood raiding parties of Pects, neighbouring tribes, and even the might of Rome, although Julius Caesar was once heard to say, "Taking the last stronghold of the Briganti could be done, but was it really worth the effort?"

The current ruler of the ancient fort was none other than the infamous bandit-king: Todhmhii Bedwetter, (although he claims that this only happened once, and he had been eight at the time). Todhmhii, and his fearsome band of warriors still clung to the old ways: - plundering, pillaging, and getting off their faces on strong mead and having a sing-along whenever the opportunity arose. Cattle-raiding and sheep-rustling was in their blood, passed down from generation to generation, and they had no intention of giving it up: even if the other Celtic tribes had long ago made their swords into ploughshares. Besides, the rough land around Ighmordan was good for nothing but coarse mountain grass and maybe a poor crop of oats, and the winds that blew across the moor usually flattened the oats before they could be harvested, that is of course, if the Fell ponies didn't gobble them up first.

Todhmhii's (*Tommy*) one regret was that he had no sons to pass his kingdom on to. His wife, Hayleigh, had given him two daughters: Chastity and Muliebral, and they were as different as chalk and cheese. His mother-in-law, Lannau, regularly and publicly scorned him for his inability to produce any male heirs.

"If I told our Hayleigh once, I must have told her a

hundred times," the old hag would mutter to anyone who was daft enough to heed her, "You need to marry a strong virile Iceni man and you'll be blessed with godlike children, not go gallivanting off with a worthless bog-trotting Briganti brigand who can't tell the difference between a ewe in heat and a tavern wench! My grandmother, Queen Boudicca, would turn in her grave at the shame of it. Her last surviving kinswoman marrying a foul-mouthed, crotch-dribbling, goat fondler!"

Sitting by the hearth one winter's evening trying his best to ignore Lannau's deranged prattling, Todhmhii studied his two daughters with a shrewd eye.

His oldest child, Chastity, took after his side of the family. She was broad of shoulder, a little flat-faced, and her head was topped off with a wild mop of curly russet locks. Despite her best efforts, her needlework was a complete failure. As for her cooking, even the pigs wouldn't eat it. Nevertheless, she never gave up trying.

Had she been a boy, she would have made the perfect heir.

Muliebral, on the other hand, took after their mother's side of the family tree. She was tall and slender, with long blonde tresses flowing like a waterfall down her elegant back. She also had the steeliest blue eyes that could look deep into your soul.

Muliebral had lately blossomed into womanhood. They both had in fact, but whereas Chastity had grown heavy of hip and flattish of chest, Muliebral's body had developed curves in all the right places.

Finding a suitable husband for Chastity had proved challenging, despite her kind demeanour. He had hoped that finding a match for Muliebral would be easier, but he hadn't allowed for Muliebral's sharp tongue and feisty temper. She certainly took after the Iceni side of the family. Muliebral was cut from the same cloth as her grandmother, although thankfully, at least Muliebral didn't pick her nose at the dinner table and flick the nasal offerings at the nearest Briganti warrior with a derisive sneer.

Plenty of men had expressed an interest in Muliebral, but Muliebral had declined every suitor. In fact, she had punched two of them in the nose, and stabbed one poor fellow through the hand with a knitting needle when said appendage had become overly familiar.

With no son of his own, Todhmhii needed his daughters wed so that they could breed a punnet of grandchildren from which he could select a suitable heir. After all, he wasn't getting any younger.

Lannau was in the process of a long-winded, and over-exaggerated story of one of the battles she had fought in. "…We raced down the hill towards where the Romans had made camp, shrieking and hollering like a bunch of demented banshees.…"

"Didn't your dresses get tangled up?" asked Chastity.

Todhmhii rolled his eyes heavenward, knowing what was coming next.

"Oh, no child! Most of us were as naked as the day we were born."

"What about Boudicca?" interrupted Muliebral. "Surely the Queen wasn't naked?"

Lannau considered her answer, as if dragging up the memory from the dusty depths of her addled brain. "You are quite right, child, she wasn't. Boudicca, as I recall, was dressed in a skimpy chainmail outfit, that covered her feminine parts, if barely, but left her unencumbered."

"Ram droppings!" muttered Todhmhii, into his mead.

Despite her aging years, there was nothing wrong with Lannau's hearing. "May the sky fall on my head if I tell a word of a lie. I swear it by all the Gods… In fact," she added, "I believe I still have the garment in one of my chests. I'll go and fetch it, if you like."

An image flashed through Todhmhii's brain; one of the wrinkly near-naked Lannau, prancing around in an alluring fashion, dressed in a two-piece chainmail outfit that was both impractical as armour and left little to the imagination.

In fact, Todhmhii concluded, the only benefit of such an outfit being worn on a battlefield, was that it would be very distracting. Perhaps, it was for that very reason that Queen Boudicca had worn it… if indeed she had!

The image of Lannau in such an outfit would haunt Todhmhii's dreams for days to come. More so because, to his horror, he discovered that his loins had become disturbingly aroused by the vision.

"I don't think that will be necessary, Mother!" mollified Queen Hayleigh. "Now girls, I think it's past your bedtime…"

"Awwwww, Mum!" the girls protested in unison.

§ § §

A year passed, and still his daughters remained stubbornly single. In desperation, an idea came to Todhmhii. He broached the topic tentatively over dinner that evening.

"Girls… ya Da ain't getting any younger. Already, I can feel the frosty bite o' winter in my knees. Even a wise king…" He was interrupted by a choking sound from the far end of the table, where his mother-in-law was sitting. He glared over at her.

"Sorry, the soup went down the wrong hole!" she explained, with doe-like innocent eyes, "…you were saying?"

"Yes, right… what the bloody 'ell was I saying?" asked the King.

"Frosty knees, Da," prompted Chastity.

"Aye, that'd be it! Frost in tha knees. Anyhow! Ta cut a

long tale short…"

"Please do, my dinner's is getting cold!"

Todhmhii glared at Lannau, before taking a deep breath and continuing, "It's time I 'ad an heir! Someone to wield my battle-axe when I get too owld to protect thee all."

"We can do that, Da," pointed out Chastity. "You've been teaching us both how to fight since we were nippers."

"Aye, I know that, but it ain't reeight an' proper! Tha' needs a bloke about tha place to do that sorta stuff for thee!"

"Why?" asked Muliebral.

"Why what?" asked Todhmhii.

"Why do we need a fella to do it for us? We can fight as good as any bloke. Ya knows that, so why exactly do we need some big lump to do what we can do a'selves?"

"None of that back-chat from ya now, Muliebral. Show ya Da some respect!" scolded Hayleigh, though she was a bit confused herself, to be honest.

"'Cause I said so! That's why." answered King Todhmhii, reverting to the answer his father had given him, whenever he'd asked any awkward questions, and his father before him going back down the eons since time began…

"That's the most stupid thing I've heard!" argued Muliebral.

"Hush up now!" pleaded Hayleigh.

"I'll take none of thy gump, lass!" warned Todhmhii, "Or thee'll feel tha back o' my 'and, so thee will!"

"Yeah, you and whose army?" challenged Muliebral, rising to her feet with clenched fists.

"My bloody army, that's who's! Now shut ya mouth and sit down!" He knew this was going to happen. It always ends up in an argument. Slamming his fists on the table, he declared, "Come Lughnasa, I'm holding a tournament, and one of ya is going ta be tha main prize! An' if I 'ave ta, I'll chuck in a chest of gold to sweeten tha deal. One way or tuther, one of ya'll be wed afore tha summer is out! I'll declare that whoever wins the games will be ma rightful successor and tha next King o' Eymoorden!"

"And can we compete, Da?" asked Muliebral waspishly.

"Of course, tha' bloody well can't! 'Ow can thee!? Tha' can't marry thee-self, can thee!? The whole point is to get thee wed off, so we can 'ave some grandchilder!"

That sounds splendid, Da!" exclaimed Chastity enthusiastically.

Muliebral rolled her eyes in disgust at her sister and stormed off with a shriek of unfettered rage.

§ § §

Spring came and went, most of it with Muliebral slamming doors, breaking crockery, and glaring threateningly at anyone who came within range of her wrath.

Even the huge war-hounds shied away from her, and they've been known to face down an angry she-bear or a pack of starving wolves without so much as a backward glance.

Finally, Lughnasa came around, and preparations were complete for the tournament.

Challengers had travelled from near and far. Some had even come from mainland Europe. Others had come from the ice-riddled islands of the Norsemen. There were a few Pects from the wild northern Highlands, and even a Gaelic prince.

An area in front of the fort had been cordoned off, and a great crowd had gathered to witness the fighting prowess of the candidates.

Todhmhii sat upon his own throne, with his wife Hayleigh by his side. Next to her sat the ever-dutiful Chastity. An empty stool proclaimed the absence of Todhmhii's youngest daughter.

"Where's Muliebral?" asked Todhmhii.

Hayleigh shrugged her shoulders.

Todhmhii sighed and asked Chastity, "Eh up, Chaz luv!? Where's tha sister?"

Chastity shook her head, "I don't know Da! I ain't seen her in days. Last I knew, she wur rootin' around in one o' Granny's chests, lookin' fur summat!"

"She's probably still sulking, luv. You know how she gets," placated Hayleigh.

"She should bloody well be 'ere!" grumbled Todhmhii. "Taint right, it ain't! I'll be a laughing stock if the winner chooses her an she ain't about! I'll look like a right numpty! What sort of King can't control 'is own daughter?"

"She's right there, in front of you. Are you blind, man?!" sneered Lannau knowingly, pointing at the crowd.

It was then that Hayleigh spotted Muliebral's long blonde mane. The sun broke through the clouds at that moment, and shimmered in her hair, and glittered provocatively off the garment she was wearing. It was as if the Gods themselves were mocking Todhmhii.

"By the heavens!" muttered Hayleigh.

"Wow! I wish I could pull that look off," cooed Chastity enviously.

King Todhmhii was on his feet, however, racing across the field. "Muliebral! Muliebral! Get o'er 'ere this instance!"

"Stop making a scene, Da! You're embarrassing me."

"Embarrassing you! Embarrassing YOU!!! Hast thee seen tha'self, lass!? What about me? What about ya poor mother?! What, by the 'eavens, are you wearing?"

Todhmhii cast a critical eye over the chainmail garment, before whipping off his cloak and smothering her nakedness in it. It was even skimpier than his imagination, and to see his daughter trolloping around in broad daylight, wearing such a thing, put his heart sideways. "You're a princess, for crying out loud! A princess shouldn't be seen in public wi' that on!"

"It was good enough for Queen Boudicca!" argued Muliebral, doing her best to shrug off his cloak.

"Those were different times, Muliebral! Less… civilised times." Anyway, what're you doing out 'ere? Tha' should be up there, with tha' family."

"I'm competing, Da. The notice says, 'All competitors should gather at dawn in the fair green', so here I am."

"You bleedin' well not competing!"

"I am too!"

"No, you ain't. I forbid it!"

Muliebral pulled out a piece of parchment, and started to read, "'Open to all comers'! That's what it says, Da!"

King Todhmhii couldn't read, but he vaguely remembered saying something like that to his scribe. "That's as maybe, but you're my daughter! That makes thee exempt. It wouldn't be fair on t'other competitors, now would it? They'd accuse me of being biased."

"It doesn't say that here…"

"I'm bloody well saying it, ain't I!"

"But that's not fair!"

"Bugger fair! I'm tha King! I make tha rules up as I go along! Now get ye to tha room, and find summat decent to wear, before I put ye across ma knee and spank some sense inta ye! The race will be starting shortly, and I need ye up there, next t' ya sister."

Muliebral considered defying him, for just a moment, but she knew that she wasn't going to win this particular battle.

I could tell you that she accepted defeat graciously, but I'd be lying.

"I hate you!" she hissed through gritted teeth. "Gobshite!" she muttered under her breath, as she stormed away.

King Todhmhii was wise enough to ignore the insult to

his royal personage. He was used to his daughter giving him lip. In fact, to be fair to her, she was showing a modicum of restraint. She hadn't thrown anything at him, for once.

§ § §

A short while later, drums beat, horns blew, and the tournament began.

Some had come in hope of winning the prize, while others sought fame.

Whatever their reasons, over fifty strapping contestants lined up at the starting posts for the first event: which was a gruelling race to the peak of Cross Fell and back.

Such a race would weed out the wheat from the chaff. Then the real tests would begin.

Only the fastest score of warriors would be eligible to compete in the second event.

It was nightfall by the time the twentieth warrior returned from the gruelling race, and dawn before the last stragglers trickled in. Two never returned. They had probably been eaten by wolves.

On Day Two of the tournament, the successful challengers were each handed a short length of rope. They were to capture one of the wild Fell stallions that roam free on the desolate moors.

Only ten of them completed the task before the dusk deadline.

The third and final day of the tournament was given over to combat.

Todhmhii again sat upon his own throne, with his wife Hayleigh by his side.

"Where's Muliebral?" asked Todhmhii.

Hayleigh shrugged her shoulders.

Todhmhii sighed and asked, "What about Chastity?" He could usually rely on her, at least, but on this occasion, she too was absent.

Hayleigh shook her head, "I don't know! The last I seen of Chastity, she was in the infirmary, helping out with the injured. She's always had a healing touch, that one."

"She bloody well aught t'be 'ere! They both should!" grumbled Todhmhii.

"Calm thee'self! Here she comes now!" said Hayleigh.

Chastity hurried over, looking flushed. "Sorry, Da!"

Soon, the contest was down to four:

"Who's the giant of a man, Da?" asked Chastity.

"That's the Dane: Victah the Pimply. They say tha' 'es killed a 'undred men!" explained Todhmhii.

"He's so ugly, people would probably die o' fright. What about the short lad beside him? He's handsome,"

"He's a Gaelic prince: Fionn something-or-other. His Da is King of Termanfeckin; wherever the hell that is."

"A prince, you say!" gushed Chastity.

"That's not saying a lot, luv! They'll make anyone who can grow a beard a king in Ireland. I hear tell tha' there's even a billy goat ruling over the northern part of Connacht."

The third surviving contestant was a Cornish pirate captain by the name of Caden One-eye, which didn't make a lot of sense to Todhmhii as he still had both his eyes.

Of the fourth contestant little was known, apart from the fact that he was a Western Briganti. He kept to himself and said little. He was a skinny-looking strap of a lad dressed in ill-fitting chainmail tunic and woollen threws. He went by the odd name of Mully the Bald, (or was it supposed to be Bold?) His accent was so thick, it was hard to tell, especially as he hadn't removed his full-faced helmet throughout the tournament.

Nevertheless, a lot of the crowd had got behind the lad;

him being a local, and all.

The second to last event was wrestling, and the local lad surprised everyone by beating the Cornish pirate in three straight rounds, whilst the Dane pummelled the Gaelic prince into submission, eventually dislocating the prince's shoulder. After that, Fionn accepted defeat.

And then there were two.

Local love was one thing, but the heavy betting was on the big Dane and his battle axe in the final contest: Close combat with their weapon of choice.

Mully the Bald looked the Dane up and down before selecting a stout oak staff from the rack of weapons offered.

Victah grinned wickedly and hefted his axe as he approached the smaller opponent. On deceptively nimble feet, the big Dane danced within axe swinging range, and swung the mighty weapon around in what should have been a decapitating blow, but the axe cleaved only air.

The scrawny Briganti had stepped inside the swing, ducked under the axe handle and countered with a sharp knee to the Dane's groin.

The crowd 'ooohed' and winced in sympathy. The more squeamish looked away at the crunching sound of the blow upon leather codpiece.

Mully the Bald followed up the knee to the balls with a vicious head butt to the face; a classic move much beloved by all Briganti warriors. The full faced helmet shattered the Dane's nose and made his eyes stream water.

The battle axe slipped from Victah's grasp, but the skinny local hadn't finished yet.

'Kick 'im while 'e's down' was a well-used mantra in all parts of Briganti, 'Afore da buggah can get back up agin!'.

Sure enough, Mully swung the staff for all it was worth. The staff whistled through the air; it struck the big Dane square on the temples with a mighty crack.

Victah the Pimply fell to the ground like a storm-felled beech … and didn't stir. He was out for the count.

The crowd went wild!

Mully the Bald/Bold bowed to the King in victory.

"Ladies and … ahh, the rest of ye rabble, we have a winner!" declared Todhmhii, marching over and raising Mully's arm. "A big cheer please for my successor!"

Again, the crowd went wild.

"Which of my daughters will you choose to marry, lad?" asked Todhmhii, pointing to the royal box. It was then that Todhmhii noticed that not one, but both of his daughters were again absent. "What the f…, Chastity! Muliebral! Where are ye?"

Chastity, looking flushed of face, popped her head out of the marquee that had been erected for the injured contestants. Her mouth dropped open when she saw the crowd looking at her. She flushed even redder and disappeared back into the tent.

"Chastity! Get thee out 'ere right now!" commanded Todhmhii.

Chastity reappeared, and after some hesitation, walked over; adjusting the buttons on her bodice as she approached.

"What, by the 'eavens, were thee doin'?" demanded Todhmhii.

"Administering to the needy, Da," lied Chastity, refusing to meet his stare.

"With thy bodice undone?"

"It's new, Da. They call it snogging. Fionn was just showing me how to do it. He's feeling a lot better already."

"I've never heard of that before! What, by all the Gods, is snogging when it's at 'ome?"

"It's the latest craze in Gaul, Da! You put your tongue inside the other person's mouth, and sort of wiggle it about a bit in a tongue wrestle. It's very invigorating!"

"I'm not sure how that can be called medicine. Did the druids come up with it? ... Anyway, I still don't see why tha' needs ya bodice undone for that?"

"Oh! It doesn't, Da. I was showing Fionn the new chainmail halter top I designed. He took quite a liking to it."

"I bet he did," growled Todhmhii. "I think I'll need to 'ave a word with this Fionn fella. Is he that Gaelic prince ya' bin mooning o'er?"

"Yes, Da! ... We're in love!" declared Chastity. "He's asked for my hand, an' everything."

King Todhmhii was at a loss for words.

Turning back to Mully the Bald, he muttered in a hushed voice, "Look, I'm sorry about all this, but it looks like I only 'ave one daughter available anymore. Is that a'reeight?"

Mully the Bald nodded, muttering something inaudible from under the helmet.

"Right! That's settled then. You'll marry Muliebral, take over ma kingdom when I step down, oh, and I didn't forget about the treasure. Tha' can 'ave sum of dat too. Is tha' a deal?"

King Todhmhii spat on his hand and offered it to the victorious Mully to seal the bargain.

Mully shook it firmly and waved to the cheering crowd.

§ § §

"Speech!" the crowd roared. "Speech!"

"Aye, lad. Let's 'ear a few words then," prompted Todhmhii, knowing how to milk a crowd for all it was worth.

Everyone leaned closer as Mully the Bald started to speak, but it was hard to understand anything he was saying through that helmet.

"Take off the soddin' 'elmet, will ya, lad? They can't understand a word tha sayin'," commanded Todhmhii.

Reluctantly, Mully removed the helmet and for the first time revealed what he looked like.

To Todhmhii, the lad's features looked hauntingly familiar, even through the thick layer of Woad dye that covered most of Mully's head.

Mully wasn't in fact bald as his title had suggested.

Todhmhii could make out tufts of short blonde stubble, cut close to Mully's scalp. In a few places, the cut had beem a bit too close. A few bloody scabs could be spotted, here and there, around the lad's scalp.

Before Mully could speak, however, a shriek of anguish could be heard from the royal box. "Muliebral! Is that you?" wailed Hayleigh. "What in 'eavens have you done to your hair!?"

Todhmhii looked at Mully, and looked again, his mouth agape.

"Hi, Da!" greeted Muliebral.

"No!"

"I won the contest, fair and square, Da! No one could say you had any bias towards me…"

"No!" repeated Todhmhii, unable to find anything more coherent to utter.

"A King is only as good as his word. That's what you taught us. Isn't it, Da?" Muliebral argued calmly. "And a deal is a deal. We shook on it… before all these witnesses."

"No!" repeated Todhmhii.

"Oh, yes we did."

Todhmhii knew when he was beaten, and accepted defeat with at least a modicum of grace.

"I should have known it was ye when ya kneed Victah in 'is balls. Tha' were a cheap blow."

"Effective though, wasn't it? Granny Lannau taught me that one."

Todhmhii smiled sheepishly. "Aye, I bet she did! Tha' 'ead

butt in da face though, were a thing of beauty, mind.”

“*You* taught me that one,” pointed out Muliebral. “I only learned from the best.”

Todhmhii grinned with fatherly pride. “I did, didn’t I.”

Almost as an afterthought, he added, “Don’t think tha’ I’m gonna let ya wear Boudicca’s battle garb though. Tha’ ain’t ever gonna happen!”

“We’ll see,” replied Muliebral with a cheeky grin. “So…Does that mean I can come on the next cattle raid?”

“Howld ya ‘orses, Lass! Let’s not get carried away!”

“But Da, I’ll need to learn everything about the family business if I’m gonna be an effective Queen.”

Todhmhii sighed. “We’ve a sheep rustling planned. I’ll take ye on that, and we’ll see how we go. Is that fair enough?”

“Fair enough.”

§ § §

Lying in bed that night, Todhmhii smiled to himself. All things considered, his tournament had worked out quite well, even if it hadn’t been the way he originally planned.

He’d found a worthy candidate to take over his legacy.

He’d managed to find a husband for at least one of his daughters, with the prospect of grandchildren on the near horizon.

And… the gold he’d offered to sweeten the deal was going to stay within the royal treasury.

Not a bad day’s work, if he said so himself.

He could even claim that the whole thing had been his idea all along; that he’d subtly guided Muliebral into taking on the mantle of leadership, knowing she had the potential in her all along. She just needed a gentle push to guide her along, and he, as a wise father, had coaxed her into defying him.

Of course, this was all an outrageous lie, but he was never going to admit that, and nobody could prove otherwise.

The trick with being a wise King was not to look surprised as events unfolded. Act like it was all part of a cunning plan you were in the process of hatching, even as your world is falling apart around your ears. When everyone else is panicking, look benign. Leadership is all about putting on a brave face, even if you want to run away and hide in a closet.

THE END

PEOPLE TO BLAME (Editor Bios)

Jaq D Hawkins

Jaq D Hawkins has worked as an outsource editor for several small publishers between 2013 - 2016, but after forcing herself to read far too many stories not ready for the editing stage decided to give it up and only edit for selected anthology projects with high standards and at least some authors known to her.

A traditionally published writer since 1999 and one of the founding members of both the Paganarchy Press and Golbin Publishing collectives, Jaq now devotes her time to Indie writing and publishing with an unapologetic commitment to the proper and artistic use of the English language.

Guy Donovan

Guy holds a BFA in animation from The University of the Arts in Philadelphia, Pennsylvania. Before graduation in 1993, he won a nationwide internship from the Academy of Television Arts and Sciences sponsored by Film Roman, the studio responsible for The Simpsons, Garfield and Friends, Bobby's World, and The Tom and Jerry Movie.

After that, Guy spent the next decade working in the industry as a storyboard artist, prop designer, and animator for, among others, Marvel Films, DiC, Hannah-Barbera, Saban Entertainment, Nickelodeon, Warner Brothers Feature Animation, Walt Disney Studios, DreamWorks SKG, and Meatball Animation (Sony).

Guy's notable credits include Spider-Man: The Animated Series, The Real Adventures of Jonny Quest, Sabrina: The Animated Series, Quest for Camelot, The Iron Giant, Osmosis Jones, and Eight Crazy Nights.

Guy chooses to ignore the "expert" opinions about Indie authors doing their own book covers and does all his own. Additionally, the book you now hold in your hands (either e-book or paperback) is his work, though he freely admits that Nils Visser chose the base image.

A more detailed filmography (though certainly not "complete") for Guy can be found at:

https://www.imdb.com/name/nm0232988/…

Nils Visser

Apart from writing books himself, Nils Visser has been involved in editing books by other authors as well. Most of this work has been conducted on behalf of Invisible Voices of Brighton & Hove, a community group in Brighton that aims to spread awareness about homelessness. One of these activities is to help homeless or former homeless artists display their talents by publishing their work. These include poetry collections by Craig Neesam, Ro Bodley, Jovannah Bär, and Julie Deason, as well as the collective efforts of the Cascade Creative Recovery writing group. IV publications also include two non-fiction books and a fictional treatise of homelessness as seen through the eyes of a child called *On Brighton Streets*.

His first attempt at co-ordinating an anthology was a few years ago with the first Dreamtime Fantasy Tales collection *Dreamtime Dragons*. When that was done, he swore an oath never to attempt such madness again. The book in your hands, be it paper or digital, allows you to question the strength of his resolve.

www.nilsnissevisser.co.uk

Morgan Smith

Morgan Smith turned to editing other authors' work after she saw what were potentially great stories being released into the wilds much too young. Also, she has massive student loans to pay off.

Hillary Anderson

I had the pleasure of being asked to help edit this anthology after some involvement with the last. I am not a professional editor but hope I was helpful to the team. My involvement is due to the fact the authors kindly donate their royalties from this series to charity. Both the first book – Dreamtime Dragons (recommended as well) – as Dreamtime Damsels & Fatal Femmes make donations to cover the medical needs and costs of Specs, a long-stay resident as Abington Ferret Refuge in Northampton, UK. I have some involvement with this refuge and this support for an under-appreciated animal is truly valuable.

http://abingtonferretrefuge.com/

AUTHOR BIOS

A.M. Young

A. M. Young fuels her addiction to books and board games by working as a proposal writer in Northern Virginia. She writes fantasy of all kinds, but mythpunk and elfpunk might be her favorites. Her hobbies include bookbinding, hiking, and playing D&D on the weekends with her husband and friends.

Guy Donovan

Guy once spent a decade working as an artist in the animation industry beneath the smogberry trees of Los Angeles. In the wake of nearly all that work's outsourcing in the name of corporate profits, he got out of the biz before they could throw him out of it and got a "real" job.

Driven nearly bonkers by a mind-numbing lack of creativity in his new…endeavor, he turned to writing as a release. Since then, Guy has authored the four-book "Dragon's Treasure Series," and quite a few short stories for different multi-author anthologies, including this one. Along the way, he has even managed to sell a few of those, though his selfishly hungry family insists he keep the paycheck job.

Guy and his aforementioned family live in Northeast North Dakota, where they enjoy a crime rate nearly as low as the winter temperatures.

You can catch up with Guy (he's old now, and much slower than he once was, after all) at:

https://www.amazon.com/Guy-Donovan/e/B00EO3VRD8

And:

https://www.facebook.com/The-Dragons-Treasure-Series-1728791295537712

Nimue Brown

A creature of The Shire, Nimue Brown can sometimes be persuaded out into the wider world to attend events, but only if there is a reasonable chance of second breakfast along the way. It is entirely possible that she is an eldritch hobbit – if on the tall side. Most of her adult life has involved trying to figure out how to get people to pay her for reading books and making stuff up.

Nimue writes and now also colours for the graphic novel series Hopeless Maine, and its various tentacular offshoots. Aside from the short story in this collection, there is also a Hopeless Maine role play game, assorted music and performance material, and a community site where people who want to play with the island, do so. Illustrated prose novels are also likely to be a thing.

When not involved with uncanny island life, Nimue tends to be steeped in coffee so as to enable her compulsive blogging habits. She's a steampunk, folky, book reviewer. She's an activist with The Woodland Trust (part of Special Branch, in fact!) and is heavily involved with her local Transition Towns movement. She has womble inclinations and likes turning other people's rubbish into useable things – which also goes well with the steampunk.

Nimue writes poetry, magazine articles, newsletters, mumming plays, short stories, flash fiction, songs, odd little cartoons about drama llamas, non-fiction books about Paganism, and speculative novels. Some of this is because she has a low boredom threshold, and some of it is because she is far too easily persuaded...

Hopeless Maine videos
https://www.youtube.com/playlist?list=PLd-6bmI3UuPAWJrYIDrlMvpb0XuSR6jmM

The Hopeless Maine blog -
https://hopelessvendetta.wordpress.com

Nimue on Patreon (where there is even more of this silliness)
https://www.patreon.com/NimueB

Penny Blake

Penny Blake comes from a storytelling background and writes Steampunk and Mythpunk inspired by her Rromani and Celtic heritage.

www.blakeandwight.com

@PennyBlake1827 twitter

@BlakeandWight fb

Jaq D Hawkins

Jaq D Hawkins is a published writer with 10 books in publication in the Mind, Body, Spirit genre published by Capall Bann Publishing, as well as four Fantasy novels in print and E-book; *The Wake of the Dragon*, *Dance of the Goblins*, *Demoniac Dance*, *Power of the Dance*, and *Chase for Choronzon* published by Golbin Publishing. A combined edition of the *Goblin Trilogy* is also available.

Information on all titles can be found through her website at www.jaqdhawkins.com

Samples from various projects occasionally appear on her blog at https://goblinsandsteampunk.wordpress.com/

Amazon page http://www.amazon.com/Jaq-D.-Hawkins/e/B0034P4BFI

Paul Michael

Paul Michael has been described as "a shining example of the best kind of man" by a gentleman hoping to borrow money from him. After many years residing in England he relocated to the Mediterranean for the weather. In particular, he is hoping there will be less of it. He is the lead, and indeed only, writer for The Benthic Times wherein one can find more stories involving the resourceful Miss Henderson and her employers, the paranormal detectives Sir John and Marie Jennings.

Link for Benthic Times is https://thebenthictimes.com/

Leslie Conzatti

Leslie Conzatti, author of "Red, The Wolf", is an avid reader and prolific writer who lives in Washington State. Since publishing her first book— *Princess of Undersea*, a fantasy re-telling of "The Little Mermaid"— back in 2016, she has published short stories in several anthologies, including *Cracks in The Tapestry, Forest of The Fearless,* and Dreamtime Fantasy Authors' first story collection, *Dreamtime Dragons*. Leslie works full-time as an elementary school staff assistant, and spends her free time adding to all the full-length novels she hopes to eventually publish, as well as producing even more short stories for future anthology opportunities. Current project updates, old ideas, new motivation, and dozens of indie book reviews can be found on Leslie's blog, "The Upstream Writer."

www.upstreamwriter.blogspot.com

www.facebook.com/leslieconzattiwriter

Mary R Woldering

Mary R. Woldering is an author, artisan, art historian, madwoman, visionary and devoted wife to Dr. Jackie F. Woldering, mother of Ruth and Thom and grandmother of four. She lives in Euclid, Ohio. She has always written something and likely always will. There are novels, stories, poetry, theses and essays. She has published 4 novels in a five novel series Children of Stone, and 3 spinoff short stories from the same universe of gods, demigods and mortals.

www.amazon.com/Mary-R-Woldering/e/B00OND7QMU

Thomas Woldering

Thomas is an engineer by profession with experience across multiple fields including computer engineering, process/quality improvement, and project engineering. When he's not writing technical procedures and flowcharting processes, he writes fiction and follows many hobbies like sewing, leatherwork, board and computer games, and even home renovation. He has been a life-long fan of Science Fiction and Fantasy. He started writing longer stories in high school, beginning with fan fiction for the various book series and shows which he followed. Since then, he has written several novel length fanfiction stories, albeit unpublished, and edited several novels for his Mother, Mary Woldering. Mobius will be his first story to be officially published. He is a loving husband to his wife Romelyne, and they are raising a growing family. They currently have one daughter, Seraphima.

Benjamin Towe

Benjamin Towe is a vintage (epic) fantasy writer, dedicated Whovian, devious Dungeon Master, and lover of all things Magick and make believe. Ben is a graduate of Mt. Airy (NC) High School, Davidson College, and the University of Virginia School of Medicine. After serving five years in the US Army Medical Corps, Dr. Towe has practiced family medicine in Augusta, Georgia, since 1981. The Old Dungeon Master "Doctor T" loves reading and writing science fiction and fantasy novels. Thirttene Friends, Dawn of Magick, Lost Spellweaver, First Wandmaker, Wandmaker's Burden, Emerald Islands, Mender's Tomb, Deathquest to Parallan, Orb of Chalar, Death of Magick, Chalice of Mystery, and Unwonted Spellweavers, the twelve novels of the Donothor and Elfdreams series are Doctor

T's Rx for fantasy. Escape to an Elfdream! If he's not lost in Middle Earth, Donothor, Parallan, Sagain, or the Wyrde Woods, you can find Ben at…

Facebook: www.facebook.com/elfdreams

Twitter: @bftowe

benjamintowe.com

https://www.amazon.com/Benjamin-Towe/e/B002PN9FAG

www.authorhouse.com/en/search?query=benjamin+towe

Nils Visser

Nils Nisse Visser was born in Rotterdam in 1970. He has lived in The Netherlands, Thailand, Nepal, Oklahoma (USA), Tanzania, the United Kingdom, Egypt, & France. He currently resides in Brighton, Sussex, although he likes to claim he moved into his imagination full-time after having been told he spends too much time there once too often. He still hasn't paid his Poll Tax and hopes to become a pirate when he grows up.

After five years of writing non-fiction for magazines around the world, Visser self-published his debut novel (*Escape from Neverland*) in 2014. Ten novels and novellas later, as well as over a dozen short stories published in international anthologies, and there is no end in sight yet. Visser's great-grandfather's cousin Piet Visser wrote twenty-one books, a number that obviously needs to be equalled or surpassed. Somewhat socially awkward, Visser doesn't understand the purpose of idle chit-chat, but can be triggered into speaking about books, archery, pirates, smugglers, steampunk, animal rescues, homelessness issues, or his love of Sussex.

www.nilsnissevisser.co.uk

Johan Klein Haneveld

Johan Klein Haneveld (1976) spends almost all his time writing. He is the editor for the Dutch Veterinary Journal and uses almost every other moment to work on SF and fantasy novels. Up to this point he has thirteen books published, among which two collections of short stories. He regularly appears in Dutch SF magazines and writes reviews and essays for the magazine 'Fantastische Vertellingen'. Next year will see the publication of his first horror collection and a short dystopian novel. He lives with his wife in the beautiful city of Delft, where he maintains his four fresh water aquariums and a growing collection of carnivorous plants …

Greg Alldredge

Greg Alldredge grew up reading all the excellent Science Fiction and Fantasy of the past decades. He hopes to add his voice, in a small way, to the giants of the genres. He wants to write stories he himself would want to read and hopes to be successful as a storyteller first.

He is currently living out of a suitcase, with his wife Connie and no pets. They travel too much. Please enjoy the journey.

Marc vun Kannon

Ghostkiller. In order to save a soul, he must doom a world.

http://authorguy.wordpress.com

https://tinyurl.com/amzn-Ghostkiller

Morgan Smith

Morgan Smith is a former goatherd, a textiles geek, and occasionally an archaeologist. She is also the author of several fantasy novels including "The Shades of Winter", "Casting in Stone", and "A Spell in the Country", a romantic fantasy called "The Mourning Rose", and a memoir about growing up hippie in the 60s. Her life is held together by caffeine, cigarettes, and cheap granola bars, and she will drop everything to go anywhere, on the flimsiest of pretexts.

Nav Logan

Many years ago, when I was just a small boy gazing in wonder at his first chest hair, I decided that I was going to become a tramp. I was going to drop out and go to Strathclyde. Why Strathclyde? God only knows, but every man must have a goal in life. Being an engineer or a pilot didn't cut it for me. My soul was filled with wanderlust and the need for adventure.

So, after leaving home, I dropped out. I even went to Strathclyde, passing through it in a sleepy haze while being rocked gently to slumber in the passenger seat of an unknown truck.

Since then, I have done many things and seen many places, always following my instincts and trusting in my destiny. I am self-taught in many things; a jack of all trades and a master at none, but I've always got by. A strong self-belief has brought me through many adversities. I try to be the best I can be and often fail, but I continue, nevertheless.

I've been writing since I was that small boy, mainly poems and an occasional short story. Maerlin's Storm was first written over a decade ago. It wasn't something I planned to do. I didn't wake up and say, I'm going to be an author. Far from it. Like many things in my life, it all started with a dream. The next morning, I wrote a poem. Later, it became a story, and this small seed became my beanstalk. People read it and enjoyed it, but then life became busy again. For many years the story sat, collecting dust. It would have stayed on the shelf, forgotten, but fate had other plans.

I now have 5 published novels. Three are part of the Storm-Bringer Saga, an Epic Fantasy series. I also published a collection of drabbles and poems: Little Words ... Full of Big Worlds, a collection of short stories and drabbles: Bananas In My Shorts, and a collaboration short story: Happy Halloween.

Facebook Page: www.facebook.com/StormbringerSaga

If you enjoyed this book, and we sure hope you have, why not give our first one a try? It can be found in all of the usual places.